JOHANNA

A Novel of the van Gogh Family

CLAIRE COOPERSTEIN

A LISA DREW BOOK

SCRIBNER
New York   London   Toronto   Sydney   Toyko   Singapore

SCRIBNER
1230 Avenue of the Americas
New York, NY 10020

SCRIBNER and design are trademarks of Simon & Schuster Inc.
An excerpt from this novel first appeared in *Pig Iron No. 17* in April 1991

Designed by Jennifer Dossin

Manufactured in the United States of America

1 3 5 7 9 10 8 6 4 2

LIBRARY OF CONGRESS CATALOGING-IN-PUBLICATION DATA
Cooperstein, Claire.
Johanna: a novel of the van Gogh family/Claire Cooperstein.
p.   cm.
"A Lisa Drew book."
1. Gogh-Bonger, Johanna van, 1862–1925—Fiction.
2. Painters—Netherlands—Family relationships—Fiction.
3. Women—Netherlands—Fiction. I. Title.
PS3553.06324J64   1995
813'.54—dc20   94-35517   CIP
ISBN 0-684-80234-1

For all the women whose accomplishments

have been forgotten

CONTENTS

MY SINCERE THANKS

Imagine a writer who has become obsessed with the story of an unusual Dutch woman who lived a century ago, a writer who doesn't speak a word of Dutch, and knows not one single person in the Netherlands. How does such a writer research such a story? With the generous assistance of a great many people. My thanks to:

Alie Wiegersma Smaalders, a retired librarian, now living and writing in one of the San Juan islands northwest of Seattle. I met her at a Centrum writer's conference when *Johanna* was less than a few thousand words long. We've kept in touch ever since. Lucky for me, Alie's career as a librarian began in the Netherlands, then continued in the United States. Being a writer herself, she knew what details I lacked in order to bring Johanna to life. Alie answered my many questions about Dutch customs, sent me an out-of-print 1905 Dutch travel book, and described the furnishings of her grandmother's villa in Bussum and her own family's canal house in Amsterdam. It took me five years to simultaneously research and write *Johanna*. Without Alie Smaalders it would have been ten.

The Chapel Hill Dutch Club, a group of Dutch expatriots who meet monthly to socialize and practice their mother tongue. When I explained my project, they made me a honorary member, invited me every December to their St. Nicholas celebration (complete with Sinterklaas) and to their pot-luck rijsttafel feasts in the Spring. They patiently answered my inumerable questions, and tried (mostly in vain) to correct my pronunciation of Dutch words. My thanks especially to the Dutch Club's organizer, Piet Tax, a retired professor of the University of North Carolina, and his wife, Maria, the group's gracious hostess.

I owe a great deal to Barbara Rodbell-Ledermann, who grew up in Amsterdam, came to the United States after World War II, and lucky for me, moved to Chapel Hill several years ago. A mutual friend introduced us and Barbara offered to do translations for me. I almost ignored a newspaper article I received in 1990. After reading Barbara's translation I completely rewrote chapter 4.

To Dr. and Mrs. H. R. Parker, Jr., of Greensboro, North Carolina, my thanks for their assistance with medical research. We met at a writer's conference in the Blue Ridge mountains. If Dick and Brenda hadn't told me about their own treasured nineteenth-century book by Dr. Osler, it would never have occurred to me to see if our university medical library had anything similar. It did! *Consumption in General Practice* provided the missing details I needed for chapter 8.

Katherine (Kerry) Nelson took time from her own Amsterdam sightseeing to go the Zorgvlied cemetery and double check who was buried beside Johanna. The year before, I tried to do it myself. My taxi had pulled up to the cemetery's padlocked gates two minutes after closing time. After Kerry provided me with photographic evidence, I could complete chapter 9.

I am fortunate to live in a university town filled with libraries: The University of North Carolina's graduate library, art library, and medical library. Each for a time became my second home. But I confess the research staff at the Chapel Hill public library became my second family. A special *thank you* to Susan McClure, now head of research facilities at the town's new public library.

While every member of the research staff is outstanding, Susan has a special affinity for authors. I'm glad I had her assistance before she got promoted.

I am especially grateful to Carolyn M. Bloomer, a cultural anthropologist now teaching at the Ringling School of Art and Design. She was finishing her doctoral dissertation in Chapel Hill while I was working on *Johanna*. An omnivore of knowledge, she generously shared her eclectic library with me. Who else could supply a friend with turn-of-the-century *Ladies' Home Journals*, as well as yellowing *Merck Medical Manuals*?

My thanks to my father, the late Gilbert Stadeker, who took me to see Vincent van Gogh's work at the Chicago Art Institute. A gigantic traveling exhibition with every gallery a color symphony—an experience I never forgot.

And to my late husband, Samuel Cooperstein, who always urged me to try the impossible, to be all that I could be.

Claire Stadeker Cooperstein

PROLOGUE

"Concealing facts that might distress the family—"

WERELDBIBLIOTHEEK
Postbus 3089, Amsterdam

9 July 1913
J. van Gogh-Bonger
Jan Luykenstraat 44, Amsterdam

Dear Mrs. van Gogh-Bonger:

We are sending you via messenger the publisher's proofs of *The Letters of Vincent van Gogh to His Brother,* and would greatly appreciate your making certain there are no typographical errors. All of us at the Wereldbibliotheek are delighted with this project. Vincent van Gogh's letters are indeed a rare record of the aspirations of an unusual artist.

Arranging these 651 mostly undated letters according to time and place, then copying them over, must have been an incredibly time-consuming undertaking. You are to be complimented on your devotion to your brother-in-law's memory.

We anticipate two volumes for the 1914 publication of 458 letters in Dutch, with the balance (the letters in French from Arles, St.-Rémy, and Auvers) to be published in a third volume next year. All of us are aware of your professional reputation as a translator, but after much discussion, it was decided that, since every educated Dutchman can read French, the letters in the third volume would remain in the language in which your brother-in-law wrote them.

We feel that a prefacing Memoir by you would greatly enhance this literary project—detailed biographical information about the van Gogh family and the two brothers whose unusual correspondence is being published. This would give you the opportunity to eliminate facts, known only to intimates, which might distress you or your family.

> Your servant,
> J. C. Winterink, Director
> Publishing Division: Wereldbibliotheek

—.—.—

Rough draft of a reply written on the back of the preceding letter—but never sent

Oh yes, my dear Mr. Winterink, those letters were indeed an incredibly time-consuming undertaking. For over twenty years all my spare time was devoted to this project that now delights the directors of the Wereldbibliotheek. When I speak of spare time, Mr. Winterink, I speak of time left over after caring for my son, running a boardinghouse to support us, supervising the local *femme de ménage* and the laundress, shopping for and cooking breakfast and dinner daily for seven to ten people, and in addition, carrying on a voluminous correspondence concerning the exhibition of Vincent's work, and subsequently arranging for the crating and shipping of his paintings and drawings to various museums and galleries. At his own insistence, all of this devotion to the Vincent legend did not cease during my second husband's terminal illness, nor did it even pause for his death.

How I do appreciate being given the opportunity to eliminate facts, known only to intimates, which might prove distressing to me or my family. There is, of course, no way one could hide the fact that Vincent committed suicide. Were you aware he shot himself, not in the head or heart, but in the abdomen, thus insuring a lingering death? After being notified, Theo had plenty of time to make the journey to Auvers and spend 24 hours with his brother—comforting him, holding his hand, watching him die.

Were you also aware that this ordeal destroyed Theo's sanity? It's common knowledge that Theo spent the next six months in various *maisons de santé,* including a final two months in The Utrecht Medical Institute for the Insane. I recently discovered that The Institute's Director had been most circumspect about the cause of death, discreetly concealing facts that might distress the family. And if I write your requested biographical Memoir, I suppose I shall do the same.

Sometimes I think I too must be mad. I seem to have devoted my life to Vincent's letters, Vincent's art. The brother who ruined my life has become my life.

Johanna van Gogh-Bonger: 10 July 1913

1

"In another life I must have been a harlot—"

24 December 1888
Andries' apartment: Paris
This will be one Christmas I shall never forget! At five, Theo, Andries, and I will be taking the Evening Express to Amsterdam. And on Christmas Day, Father will announce the engagement of "Johanna Gesina Bonger to Theodoor van Gogh" at a family dinner being given in our honor. My favorite brother's best friend—a fairy-tale betrothal!

Later: It's after four—they're late. Andries was to hire a fiacre, pick up Theo and his luggage at the gallery, then stop here for me. There's an open fiacre coming up the hill now. But only Andries in it—waving a letter at me, shouting, "Hurry! No time to explain—we'll miss the Express. You can read Theo's letter on the train."

— · — ·

TELEGRAPH FRANCAIS
TO THEO VAN GOGH GOUPIL'S GALLERY 18 BOULEVARD MONTMARTRE
PARIS STOP FROM HOSPITAL HOTEL DIEU ARLES STOP VINCENT COMATOSE
AFTER MUTILATING SELF POLICE INTERVENED AFTER COMPLAINT FROM
MISS VIRGINIE'S MAISON DE TOLERANCE STOP IMPERATIVE YOU COME AT
ONCE STOP PAUL GAUGUIN 24 DECEMBER 1888

— · — ·

GOUPIL'S FINE ART GALLERY
18 Boulevard Montmartre: *Theo van Gogh,* Mgr.

Christmas Eve
Dearest Jo,
Just as I was about to close the gallery to join you for the holiday, the enclosed telegram arrived. I have no alternative but to take the next train to Arles, and see for myself. Your brother and I both agree that the two of you should take the Evening Express to Amsterdam as arranged. Your parents will

be expecting you. Even though I cannot be present, I hope your father will announce our betrothal tomorrow as planned. It may be that Gauguin has exaggerated the gravity of Vincent's condition, in which case I may be able to join you and your family in Amsterdam in a day or two. Didn't you say the engagement festivities would last until New Year?

If this proves an impossibility, assure your father that I consider us irrevocably engaged, and shall take care of the registration of our intentions at the Town Hall on my next business trip to Amsterdam. My darling, you are still my betrothed, my beloved, my future wife. Nothing can or will ever change that. Always your *Theo*

— · — ·

THE PERSONAL DIARY OF JOHANNA BONGER

(En route to Amsterdam)
24 December

Gauguin's telegram sounds so strange. (Naturally, one can never be explicit in something as public as a telegram.) But what did he mean by "mutilating self"? Whatever did Vincent do? And what happened at "Miss Virginie's *maison de tolérance*"? I'm sure I read somewhere that this is the French term for house of ill repute. Did Vincent mutilate a prostitute? And then himself? If Father finds out he'll immediately withdraw his consent to our marriage!

Andries is trying to calm me, urging me to write Theo while we're on the train. He says if we mail it from the station tonight, it should reach Arles tomorrow. He's asked the porter to bring some tea and stationery.

— · — ·

THE NETHERLANDS EXPRESS
Fastest Route Between Paris and Amsterdam

24 December
Theo, my dearest,

Though I have yet to meet Vincent, I can't help sharing your present distress. To receive a telegram like that out of the blue! The last you told me was that you were pleased because Vincent seemed so happy since Gauguin had joined him. What in heaven's name could have happened?

It would be wonderful if you could join us in Amsterdam in a few days. I only wish that you and Dries had not arbitrarily decided that it would be unwise for me to accompany you to Arles. I feel left out of an important part of your life. My darling, your family is my family now, and your worries are mine. Please! Let me know *immediately* what you find when you arrive in Arles. Always, *Jo*

— · — · —

THE PERSONAL DIARY OF JOHANNA BONGER

25 December

Just yesterday I see that I wrote, "This will be one Christmas I shall never forget." Indeed it will! The tension of waiting to hear from Theo is almost unbearable. Like reading a horror story, afraid to turn the page and see what has happened. Theo described Vincent to me as being brilliant but erratic and totally unconventional. I won't really mind if he is quite mad too, but Father will!

I'm not exactly an ordinary person myself. Under no condition would I ever submit to a marriage arranged the old-fashioned way. Theo is the only man I ever wanted to marry. It seemed a miracle that he wanted me too. If Father withdraws his consent, will Theo wait three years until I'm thirty?

I know it is very un-Christian, but right now I hate, *hate* Vincent van Gogh!

— · — · —

HÔTEL-DIEU
Public Hospital, Arles

Christmas Day 1888
My dearest Jo,

When Dr. Rey escorted me to Vincent's bedside yesterday, my poor brother looked so pale and lifeless I could scarcely believe I had not come too late. I slept on a cot beside Vincent in the men's ward last night. His condition is so grave I am afraid to leave him unattended.

Dr. Rey tells me that Vincent lost an enormous quantity of blood. He had cut his ear, and in the process an artery was punctured. As near as can be re-constructed, all this occurred the night before last.

Shortly after injuring himself, he went out to see a lady of his acquaintance, presented her with the piece of ear, then returned home. When they arrived the next morning to investigate, the police followed a trail of blood to the bedroom where Vincent lay in a coma. Gauguin was nowhere to be found! Had he only returned to the Yellow House that night, Gauguin could have sent for medical help.

Vincent's condition is now so precarious Dr. Rey can make no prognosis. I may return to Paris when the crisis is past, but Amsterdam is too distant for comfort, should the situation worsen quickly—as well it might. Dear Jo, this is not the joyous Christmas you and I were anticipating, is it? Please say you understand. Love, *Theo*

— · — · —

JOHANNA BONGER
Herengracht 204, Amsterdam

27 December 1888
Dear Theo,

My darling, of course I understand! I even see the wisdom of your deciding I not accompany you to Arles. I could hardly have joined you in your overnight vigil in the men's ward, could I? How dreadful it must have been for you, seeing your beloved brother so pale, almost lifeless. Dearest, your love and your devotion to your brother only make me love you more.

You are not to be concerned about anything except Vincent. You and I will have a lifetime of Christmases together. We can surely spare this one apart. Always your *Jo*

27 December

Dries and I have been discussing how much Father should be told. We ended with this version of the ear incident: "Vincent had been drinking ale in a brothel when he stumbled, dropped his drink, fell and cut both his ear and an artery on the broken glass. He almost bled to death, but there's a good chance he'll recover."

Naturally I can't discuss brothels with Father—even though Holland's have been government-regulated for years. My brother will take Father aside for a man-to-man talk. Later we can mention that they think Vincent had a "fit," similar to the ones Uncle Dirk used to have. The aunts are always whispering about "bad blood" in everyone's family except ours. *That* should keep them quiet.

No word from Theo since Christmas. Mail must be delayed by the holidays.

— · — · —

THEODOOR VAN GOGH
8 Cité Pigalle, Paris

28 December: Almost midnight
My dear understanding Jo,

Your reply to my Christmas letter was the best gift you could have given me. Bless you! Dr. Rey assured me that there is nothing to be done but wait, so I boarded the train to Paris today, with Dr. Rey's assurance that he will keep me informed of any change. I am content to leave Vincent in his charge. He is not an expert in mental conditions, but he does favor the modern, enlightened approach which believes in relieving, not adding, to the patient's suffering (as they do in such places as Bedlam). "I, too, have a brother," he told me, "and understand your concern."

Did not realize how exhausted I was. Goodnight, sweet Jo. Will have to continue this letter tomorrow.

29 December: Early morning

The train ride to Paris was almost unendurable. Gauguin, who never once came to see Vincent in the hospital, insisted on accompanying me. He spent the entire time telling me how much I would benefit if I bought more of his paintings to exhibit. Doesn't he realize that the only reason I had bought some of his work was that Vincent begged me to, said Gauguin needed to clear off his debts in Pont-Aven before he could join Vincent in Arles? The man is impossible!

It's good to be in Paris again, but not without my Jo. *Theo*

THE PERSONAL DIARY OF JOHANNA BONGER

New Year's Eve 1888

Finally, the last gala in this week of engagement festivities. For me, these parties were nightmares. I felt like a clown in the children's theater at the Dam—a painted smile on my face—everyone asking, "Where's the lucky groom-to-be?"

All week my dear Father managed to simultaneously smile and look grim, while telling the guests that "we expect Theo to join us in a day or two." Once I received Theo's letter describing Vincent's condition, I knew there was no way he could come, but Father refused to believe it.

My sweet Mother is being sweetly solicitous, as though I were left waiting at the church. My sisters follow her lead, while the aunts are whispering about "bad blood"—"This never happens with a betrothal carefully arranged the old-fashioned way." Bad blood, indeed! The van Goghs settled in Holland in the sixteenth century, distinguishing themselves as gold drawers, art dealers, magistrates, clergy, even a vice admiral in the navy. I am grateful that Theo's mother and sister did *not* to come from Leiden as planned. This would not have been a happy way to meet my future in-laws.

2 January

The mail is delayed because of the holidays. I am sick with worry about what is happening in France. Theo must be so lonely—waiting for word from

Arles. Andries is returning to Paris next week. I'll ask if I can return with him, stay with him again in his apartment. I feel as though Theo will need my comfort and support now, more than ever. I want to be there for him.

—·—·—

THEODOOR VAN GOGH
8 Cité Pigalle, Paris

New Year's Day
My dear patient Jo—
Good news! Vincent appears to be making a remarkable recovery. Dr. Rey is encouraging him to walk daily in the hospital gardens. If all goes well, he estimates that Vincent should be able to leave the hospital in a week or two. Till now I didn't realize how much I was worrying. The relief I feel is inexpressible. I think we can now safely begin talking to your parents about wedding plans. It cannot be too soon for me. Even this seven-day separation has been unbearable. My love, always, *Theo*

—·—·—

THE PERSONAL DIARY OF JOHANNA BONGER

3 January
I can't believe Theo actually wrote it—"wedding plans." We will have a church wedding, of course, following the legal ceremony at the Town Hall. And the traditional reception for family and friends the day before. Everyone will want to come by and meet Theo. The aunts will surely stop whispering about "bad blood" once they meet the handsome groom.

I remember, when Andries first introduced me to Theo, how impressed I was by his aristocratic profile, his pale complexion, his blond hair, like the head of a saint on a medieval coin. His voice is so soft, yet he has a quiet authority about him. And a wonderful, sardonic sense of humor. Of course, that's only a part of it. Even to her diary, a well-bred young lady does not describe in detail the feel of his encircling arms, the touch of his hand caressing.

ANTON BONGER
Insurance: Marine and General
Herengracht 204, Amsterdam

9 January 1889
Dear Theo:

We were all pleased to learn that Vincent's condition took a sudden turn for the better on New Year's Eve and that he was able to leave the hospital entirely recovered just one week later. One wonders if it was absolutely necessary for you to rush to Arles leaving your betrothed alone during the announcement of her engagement. Johanna now speaks of returning to Paris with her brother in order to be with you. Both Mother and I feel that it would be most unwise, under the circumstances.

We are naturally quite concerned about our dear daughter, and cannot help wondering about your devotion. Your place was clearly beside Johanna during the holiday betrothal festivities. Surely there was some friend or family member you could have called upon to go to Arles in your stead. Will you abandon Johanna anytime Vincent imagines he is ill?

I cannot help questioning the wisdom of giving you permission to marry my daughter. Because of these new doubts, Mother and I feel it our duty to insist on an engagement of several months, instead of the anticipated few weeks. I'm sure you understand our position. As ever, *A. C. Bonger*

— · — · —

JOHANNA BONGER
Herengracht 204, Amsterdam

10 January
My dearest Theo,

Father and I are barely speaking. He showed me the letter he was sending you regarding delaying our marriage. I had told him of Vincent's desperate condition. I wept when I read, "I slept on a cot beside Vincent in the men's ward—his condition is so grave I was afraid to leave him unattended." And Father expected you to leave Vincent just to attend parties in Amsterdam!

If you sent money for a train ticket, I could come to Paris, and we could be married immediately. In France, a young lady of twenty-seven does not need her father's consent. You must be as furious with Father as I am. Dearest, let me know quickly what you think of my plan. Forever your *Jo*

— · — · —

THEODOOR VAN GOGH

8 Cité Pigalle, Paris

11 January 1889

My dear sweet impetuous Jo,

I was not angered by Mr. Bonger's concerns about our marriage. Like any good Dutch father, he is trying to protect his daughter. Because we have spoken of it often, you understand fully the special relationship that exists between Vincent and myself. Lacking that knowledge, your father cannot be expected to.

My dearest Jo, he did not forbid our marriage, merely requested we postpone it. As far as I'm concerned, my darling, you are worth waiting for. Under no circumstances would I allow you to break with your family. Would you want our children to grow up without grandparents? To spend every St. Nicholas without Sinterklaas? The closeness of a Dutch family is a special thing—something to be cherished, as I cherish you. All my love, *Theo*

— · — · —

THE PERSONAL DIARY OF JOHANNA BONGER

15 January: Amsterdam

Andries returned to Paris this morning without me. When I was five, Father took me to my first marionette show, and I wondered how the marionettes felt—being pulled hither and yon by strings, no will of their own. That's how I feel now as I wait for Father to decide in his infinite wisdom that Theo has been sufficiently punished and we can be allowed to marry. The worst part of it is that I am forced to *live* with my puppet master. I know full well that if I sulk too much, Father will never relent. So I force a smile.

20 January

What does Father want of me? I will *never* fault Theo for taking the southbound local to Arles, instead of the northbound express to Amsterdam. Yes, it surely was embarrassing attending engagement parties without the groom-to-be. If *only* Vincent had decided to cut off his ear the week before, there would have been time to postpone the betrothal festivities, and all would have been well. How *very* inconsiderate of him to select Christmas Eve for his hospitalization! And what *could* Vincent have been thinking of when he recovered just a week after New Year's?

— · —

JOHANNA BONGER
Herengracht 204, Amsterdam

2 February 1889
Dear Theo,

I simply could not bring myself to write, once Andries returned to Paris. I'm certain you're quite right about not wanting me to break with my family, but if you included train fare in your next letter, I'd be at your side faster than you could say Paris Express!

Winter in Amsterdam: The sun has gone into hiding. I'm not at all certain it will *ever* reappear. The temperature varies from chilly to freezing. This house is like a morgue. Every day after breakfast Mother limps upstairs to her room to nurse her rheumatism, while Father retires to his office downstairs, to check the canal traffic, and Anna goes to the Conservatory, where she is taking music lessons. I do a little dusting, tidy up the kitchen, keep fires going in the *kachels,* and sometimes curl up with my needlework in the window seat. After lunch, Father will go to the Dam to check the incoming cargo ships. When he returns he'll once again complain bitterly, "That ridiculous huge new railway station blocks the view of the harbor."

I'm not used to this life of leisure. I've taught school since I was twenty-two, English language and literature. (Yet I still don't have a guilder to my name. Father says he's saving it for my dowry. The law says he doesn't have to do even that!)

Just discovered a frown line between my eyes. That won't do! Whatever will you say if I turn into a hag during our separation? Sunday I'm going ice-skating with Anna. I have yet to see anyone ice-skate while frowning.

Always your *Jo*

— · — · —

GOUPIL'S FINE ART GALLERY
18 Boulevard Montmartre: *Theo van Gogh,* Mgr.

7 February
Dearest Jo,

No amount of frown lines could turn my beloved into a hag! Your father is being the typical Dutch parent. If we're patient, I'm absolutely certain he'll relent.

I know how difficult patience can be. Today, for example, I had to politely listen to another tirade about the Impressionists—"those madmen you insist on exhibiting in the gallery's mezzanine!" I assured Adolphe Goupil that the new modern art brought many people to the gallery out of curiosity, and was even more provocative than a Bouguereau nude in the street-floor window. After Goupil reviewed last month's profits, I once again was able to prevail.

I don't want to raise false hopes, but I've been deliberately arranging the gallery's exhibitions so no major one is scheduled for the month of April. In a few weeks, I'll respectfully ask your father if he would be willing to consider an April wedding date. I've written him every now and then, reporting on Vincent's recovery—which, incidentally, has been surprisingly rapid. Dearest, I can imagine how difficult this waiting is for you. It is for me too. I am in-complete without my Jo!

But as I wrote a month ago, my Johanna is worth waiting for.

All my love, *Theo*

ANTON BONGER
Insurance: Marine and General
Herengracht 204, Amsterdam

28 February 1889
Dear Andries:

Mother and I are hoping you can be of assistance to us in making a decision concerning your dear sister. Since you were present, you are undoubtedly fully aware of the embarrassment caused poor Johanna because her betrothed was nowhere to be seen last Christmas when their engagement was formally announced. Mother is still making excuses to the entire family as well as her intimate friends.

Theodoor's inexcusable conduct forced us to rethink our approval of the marriage, and I regretfully informed him that we felt it necessary to insist on an extended engagement. Theodoor surprised me by saying he understood our concerns and accepted the extension of their engagement with dignity and grace.

Mother and I have been impressed by his honesty and respectfulness and are now inclined to be lenient. He is asking us to consider an April wedding, since his gallery has no major exhibitions scheduled for that month. Are we being too hasty in giving our approval? I know Theodoor is a good friend, but I'm sure you care too deeply for your dear sister's welfare to let that friendship color your advice. Let us hear from you as soon as possible. *Father*

—·—·—

TELEGRAPH FRANCAIS

3 MARCH 1889 FROM ANDRIES BONGER
TO ANTON BONGER HERENGRACHT 204 AMSTERDAM STOP RE APPROVAL
OF APRIL DATE FOR WEDDING STOP SEE NO NEED FOR DELAY STOP URGE
YOU TO BEGIN PLANNING AT ONCE

ANTON BONGER
Insurance Marine and General
Herengracht 204, Amsterdam

5 March 1889
Dear Theo:

Mother and I are inclined to be lenient and respond affirmatively to your request for an April wedding. There is only one thing that makes us hesitate—your brother's state of health. We all know that bad blood tends to run in families. We cannot help but wonder if inebriation was the sole cause of Vincent's unfortunate accident?

Mother, of course, is somewhat conservative, but I, being more worldly, can understand a young man's need for recreation (provided of course, the *maison de tolérance* is regulated by the authorities). But there was some mention of the possibility of a "fit." Has this ever happened before? Can you assure us that our dear Johanna will not need to worry about the children she will bear? You do understand that it is our duty as her parents to ask these questions. As ever, *A. C. Bonger*

— · — · —

THEODOOR VAN GOGH
8 Cité Pigalle, Paris

6 March
Dear Jo,

I had difficulty answering the enclosed letter from your father. Although Vincent has always been totally unconventional, this is the first incident of this kind.

If Vincent had recently seen a bullfight (they're popular in the South of France) there seems to be a certain insane logic in what he did: After the matador has shown himself skillful in the placing of the banderillas, in the play with the red cape, and finally in the thrust of the sword, the crowd, full of enthusiasm, cries, "The ear!" This means that the matador has earned the highest reward, the ear of the bull he has just been fighting. The matador parades triumphantly with the bull's ear around the arena to the applause and hurrahs of the crowd, then presents it to the lady of his choice. When he cut off his own ear and presented it to Ann-Marie, did Vincent see himself as both the bull and the bullfighter?

Of course, I have not shared these details with your father, but I could honestly tell him this was the first time something like this occurred, and according to the doctor, could be the last. Do you think this will satisfy him? Your impatient *Theo*

———·—·———

THE PERSONAL DIARY OF JOHANNA BONGER

10 March

The date has been set. Theo's mother and sister came up from Leiden for the day. I couldn't help loving Mother van Gogh the moment I saw her—she has the sweetest face! After much consultation the two families agreed on April 17.

I'm glad Theo refused to elope with me. He was right about the specialness of Dutch family ties. I realize now that having lived away from home so long, I'd find it difficult living permanently with my parents. Difficult? Father can be exasperating, and Mother—she never disagrees, simply *Yes, Anton's* him to death. Thank heavens Theo would never expect me to be that kind of wife.

So much to do before April 17! I have decided against a traditional Dutch wedding dress. I need something I can wear to art openings in Paris. The dressmaker suggested tailored mauve alpaca, a high neck, long sleeves, with only a hint of the new bustle fashion in the back, just a touch of appliqué on the fitted bodice.

We won't have time for a wedding trip, but will have a week all to ourselves in the Paris apartment. Theo is having his apartment redecorated, the curtains and drapes laundered and rehung, "so that everything will be clean and fresh for my Jo." He writes that he has assured Juliette, his *femme de ménage,* that her services will still be required, provided she pleases me, wants to know if I want to hire a cook.

15 March

Dearest husband-to-be,

I'm sure your *femme de ménage* knows more about housecleaning than I do, and will please me just fine. As for a cook, no thank you—I've been looking forward to cooking for my husband. However, he must be willing to accept an occasional piece of black toast. Mother trained my older sister in the art of cooking a complete meal—Anna and I were taught only to "help out in the kitchen," to make individual Dutch dishes. To tell you the truth, I've yet to cook an entire meal. Will you mind if the meat is done before the potatoes, or the tarts before the soup?

Oh Theo—I'm so happy I cannot bear to think of anyone else being sad. I'm writing Vincent a loving letter, inviting him to visit us in Paris.

Always your *Jo*

— · — · —

JOHANNA BONGER
Herengracht 204, Amsterdam

18 March 1889

Dear Vincent,

I know Theo has informed you of our wedding plans. We're both so disappointed that your recent unfortunate accident prevents your attending the ceremony.

Theo has told me so much about you. I do hope you'll look upon me not as just as a sister-in-law but as your very own little sister who loves you as much as her husband does. As soon as your recovery is complete, you simply must visit us in Paris. The guest room in our apartment will always have your name on it. Sincerely, *Johanna*

20 March
Dear Theo:

Received a sweet letter from your Johanna telling me of your wedding plans. I thoroughly approve. Marriage is almost a necessity in view of your position in society and in commerce. With a wife you will not need to dine out constantly, and by getting married you will set Mother's mind at rest and make her happy. From me, dear brother, I know you would not want banal congratulations and assurances that you are about to be transported straight into paradise. (If she is one of those very proper Dutch maidens, you may still need to visit one of the better Montmartre bordellos for real recreation now and then.) The important thing is that your marriage not be delayed because of any trivial difficulties I may be having. *Vincent*

— · — · —

THEO VAN GOGH
8 Cité Pigalle, Paris

25 March
Dearest Jo,

When you become the wife of Theo van Gogh, you will soon discover that his brother, whom he loves dearly, lives in a continual state of crisis. Over the years I have learned to distinguish a major crisis from a minor one, for if I permitted myself a constant state of anxiety, I should soon be a candidate for an asylum myself. When we set the date for our wedding, I thought all was well.

All was indeed well with Vincent, but unfortunately not with his neighbors, who are now afraid of him, even petitioned to have him locked up. The hospital recommends lodging in another section of town, where the neighbors will be unaware of the episode of the ear. Dr. Rey wrote me a personal note saying his mother owns a small house on the outskirts of Arles that she might consider renting. She's away on holiday now, but he promised to explore the possibility with her when she returns.

Meanwhile I have been deluged with alternate ideas from Vincent. He wanted to enlist in the French Foreign Legion . . . to join our brother Cor in South Africa . . . to voluntarily commit himself to an asylum. I have come to dread each ring of the postman. I must patiently review each of his ideas, pointing out the areas of undesirability. I fear if I do not respond, the next letter would be postmarked AFRICA. Dearest Jo, just the thought of you makes it all bearable. Ever your *Theo*

— · — · —

JOHANNA BONGER
Herengracht 204, Amsterdam

28 March 1889
Dear husband-to-be,

You must surely have the patience of a saint, responding to Vincent's wild ideas with such reasoned calm. South Africa, indeed! What amazes me is the realization that you, not Vincent, are the younger brother. It surely seems the other way around. Vincent is like a child crying for the moon—you, the wise parent who distracts him with a white balloon. My darling, I hope we have a very large family. You will make the most wonderful father. Just eighteen more days! Love, *Jo*

— · — · —

HÔTEL-DIEU
Public Hospital, Arles

5 April
Dear Theo,

Wonderful news! Dr. Rey's mother has agreed to rent me a small apartment with running water in a house she owns on the outskirts of Arles. My favorite painting spots, the orchards and the river with its drawbridge, are just a short distance away. She is asking a mere eight francs a month, which is so reasonable I'll be able to ask another painter, perhaps even Gauguin, to visit or to join me—and as my guest!

I should be moving the middle of April, after the completion of some minor repairs. I've already hired a charwoman to clean up after the workmen, and a cart to move my furniture from the Yellow House. No mail delivery that far out. My address will be Postbus 59. *Vincent*

— · — · —

THE PERSONAL DIARY OF JOHANNA BONGER

10 April 1889: Amsterdam

What a relief that Vincent's problems have been resolved before our wedding day. Worrying about them would have dimmed our happiness. It may be selfish—but the only thing I want Theo to worry about on the seventeenth of April is *me,* Johanna, his bride.

What will our wedding night be like? Theo may not realize it, but his fiancée is a very experienced young lady—at least as far as books can supply experience. When I was studying in England, I was amazed to discover that the very proper English had lists of books their daughters were not allowed to read. And since most of these books were French novels, enforcing the ban was no problem. For the Dutch, French is almost a second language. Reading French novels is something most Dutch girls don't talk about—we just *do* it. The rental bookstores are full of them. I'm not sure Theo would approve—he tends to want to put me on a pedestal. What would he say if he knew I had read both *Madame Bovary* and *Nana?*

What will living in Paris be like? I don't think I'll be lonely. Theo says Goupil's is just a short walk from the apartment. I expect he'll be home every day for lunch. (I wonder—will he want to "do it" in the afternoon, after lunch? Or before dinner, after an Opening Day reception, when he's had a little too much wine?)

15 April

Theo arrived today—after all these months he seems like a stranger. I felt actually shy when he kissed me at the station. Tomorrow the two of us must endure the pre-wedding reception. We'll be standing all day and

most of the night receiving congratulations. The next day, two ceremonies.
Afterwards, a wedding dinner. Later—the Evening Express to Paris, and
then . . .

16 April—Evening

Father has just left after giving "his girl" a lecture on household management and budgeting. This morning he presented Theo with a check—the
money I'd saved while teaching. Theo seemed embarrassed, whispered to me
that we'd cash the check in Paris, and he'd turn it over to me in francs. I'm
glad he had sense enough to whisper. I don't think he realizes that in Holland
once a woman marries, everything she owns belongs to her husband. Father
would never have understood.

Still later: Mother has just left after giving her daughter the expected
"pre-nuptial talk." I am to obey my husband, and satisfy his "needs." (No
problem.) I am to realize that a man's "needs" are different from a woman's. (I
doubt that.) I am supposed to be very shy on our wedding night. (Maybe for
the first few minutes.) I have in my trousseau the most demure nightdress—
embroidered white dimity with a matching ruffled nightcap. What intrigues
me most are the tiny pearl buttons fastening the front.

Amsterdam: 17 April—Late afternoon

After two ceremonies, a wedding feast, innumerable toasts, I am now a
married woman—Madame (as they say in French) Johanna van Gogh-
Bonger. Dries and Theo just took my trunk downstairs. Wish they'd used the
roof pulley, the stairs are steep!

It would never do to have the groom fall down and break something on
his wedding night.

Paris: 18 April—Morning

After all that preparation, there was no "wedding night"! There had been
no porters to be found at the Gare de Lyon—we left my trunk with the white
nightdress in the baggage shed. It was after midnight when our rental carriage pulled up in front of Theo's apartment. I was exhausted, climbed into

bed in my chemise, and was fast asleep before Theo finished opening the shutters and turning down the lamps.

I woke to the rustle of chestnut trees, the smell of lilacs, and Theo's kiss on my cheek. After breakfast I borrowed one of Theo's smoking jackets, waltzed around the room waving the sleeves like windmills—they were only a foot too long. We were laughing so hard I fell on the bed breathless . . . and soon discovered I'm no prim Victorian. (I'm absolutely shameless.) Theo says that if the Egyptian belief in resurrection is true, in another life I must have been a harlot—or at the very least someone's expensive mistress. We both dozed off, woke to discover my trunk outside the front door. Neither of us had heard the porter knocking.

When I showed Theo the white nightdress, he reminded me of my vow to obey, then gave precise orders about the tiny pearl buttons fastening the front.

2

"Oh, Mother—he was so my own, own brother!"

HÔTEL-DIEU
Public Hospital, Arles

18 April 1889
Dear Monsieur van Gogh:

I regret very much the need to send you disturbing news so soon after your wedding day. Vincent was scheduled to move into my mother's apartment yesterday. The cart he'd hired to haul his furniture had just arrived when he quite suddenly insisted he lacked the courage to move and start a new studio. No amount of reassurance could sway him. He insists he does not feel able to live unsupervised, says the only solution for him is to voluntarily enter an asylum.

There is such an institution in nearby St.-Rémy, which has a reputation for treating its residents well. The director is sending you a prospectus.

Dr. Félix Rey

— · — · —

THE PERSONAL DIARY OF JOHANNA BONGER

20 April: Paris

I can't understand it. Ever since yesterday when he received a letter from Arles, Theo's been acting strangely. I asked if he'd heard from Vincent. He muttered, "No." Whoever the letter was from Theo is not about to share it with me. This is no way to begin a marriage.

22 April

I'm miserable. Every night, we're so close, yet each day Theo continues to keep me locked out of his thoughts. This can't go on, but I don't know what to do—

23 April

My husband is a foolish man! Today he finally broke down and showed me the letter from Arles—said he had been afraid that Father would annul our marriage, force me to leave him. I assured him I was his forever. Whether

41

Father likes it or not, our marriage has been happily consummated over and over again! And Theo had responded as honestly as he could to Father's query about Vincent's mental condition. When one thinks about it, recognizing his need for supervision is probably the sanest thing Vincent has ever done. Theo is writing Vincent today, but he whispered that, just to be safe, he'd like to consummate our marriage one more time.

—·—·—

THEODOOR VAN GOGH
8 Cité Pigalle, Paris

24 April
Dear Vincent:

Dr. Rey wrote me of your decision not to move into the apartment offered you, though he feels quite certain you are now sufficiently recovered to leave the hospital and live unsupervised. I was therefore surprised and distressed to hear of your desire to voluntarily enter an asylum.

I hope you are not considering this drastic move in a spirit of self-sacrifice. Think it through carefully. You have other alternatives. You could join the artists' colony in Pont-Aven. Gauguin's presence there might make things a bit strained at first; however, I hear he is hoping to leave for the tropics shortly. Or you could come to Paris. If the city proves stressful as it did in the past, there are small towns on the outskirts that lend themselves to landscape painting and a tranquil life.

Dear Vincent, only you can decide what is best for you. If you insist on going to St.-Rémy, I'll support your plan. However, I do urge you to consider all alternatives before coming to a final decision. Your loving brother, *Theo*

Afterthought: If you leave Arles, be sure to remove your paintings from the Yellow House and ship them to me. From what I have seen, they are among your best!

30 April

Much excitement! The crates with Vincent's paintings from the Yellow House have just been delivered from the goods train. Theo is so relieved—everything arrived safe, without any damage.

I have never seen such exhilarating colors! It's as though I'd been walking around looking at everything through a gray veil, and with a stroke of his paintbrush, Vincent removed it. The drawbridge, the bedroom in the Yellow House, and the chair with pipe and tobacco pouch are Theo's favorites. But I am entranced by the four orchards in bloom. Theo says he will hang one in our bedroom.

How could Vincent be unhappy with all those color-symphonies inside him, just waiting to be heard?

— . — . —

THEODOOR VAN GOGH
8 Cité Pigalle, Paris

9 May 1889
Dear Mother and Wilhelmina,

Today is such a sad day for us. Even as I write, Vincent is being admitted into the asylum at St.-Rémy. Vincent may have a few problems, but he does not belong in such a place. I tried, but there was no dissuading him. Mother, if only you could see the recent paintings he sent from Arles. They are magnificent! He has finally found his oeuvre. I am insisting the doctors permit him to continue to paint at St.-Rémy and am paying for a separate room he can use as a studio. Once a monastery, the buildings are described in the prospectus as "picturesque" and "surrounded by gardens." Perhaps this will inspire him. I know it saddens you that Vincent almost never writes. I'll try to encourage him to do so. Jo sends you her love, as do I. *Theo*

Date: 9 May 1889. *Patient:* Vincent van Gogh, age 36. (Escorted by Dr. Félix Rey.)

Previous hospitalization: Hôtel-Dieu, Public Hospital, Arles: From 24 Dec. 1888.

Family history: Reported incidence of epileptic-type illness in mother's family.

Police record: Arles, 24 Dec. 1888. Mutilated self by cutting off lobe of ear.

Diagnosis: Patient suffers from sporadic attacks of acute mania with hallucinations of sight and hearing. Treated 1881 in Belgium for syphilis. No present symptoms. Some history excessive use of alcohol, especially absinthe. Poor nutrition and tendency to overwork when living unsupervised. During intake interview appeared rational and calm. Patient is a painter—possibility of toxic reaction to poisons in paints, especially white lead and chrome yellow, should be considered.

Treatment: Prescribing our warm bath hydrotherapy twice a week, opiates only when necessary. Encourage abstinence from tobacco and alcohol.

Prognosis: Before definitive prognosis is possible, patient should be observed for a full month. (Send bills to brother in Paris. Add 25% for requested private quarters.)

Dr. Théophile Peyron, Director

—·—·—

THEODOOR VAN GOGH
8 Cité Pigalle, Paris

17 May
Dear Mother,

Quoting your own favorite phrase, "I'm sending you just a little word" to let you know that all is well with your two eldest sons. Vincent has written that he is adjusting to life in St.-Rémy, finds the attendants very kind—the other patients a little frightening. I'm glad I arranged for a private room instead of the ward, where the frequent screaming would have distressed him. I'm now happy that we let Vincent decide for himself what would be best for him. A few months of rest and tranquility at St.-Rémy may well find him sufficiently recovered to resume an unsupervised life.

As for your second son, dear Mother, if you'll look at the date you'll realize that Jo and I completed the first month of our marriage. Despite some distress from all that standing, the wedding gave me a great deal of pleasure, principally because the three women I love the most—my mother, my favorite sister, and my wife—got along so well.

Financially, this past year has been a good one for me, and there will be no problem with my continuing the monthly check I've been sending since Father died. Tell Wilhelmina that Jo is redecorating our guest room and practicing her cooking, so that both of you will be able to visit us shortly. I tease her about her cooking, but the truth is she's becoming quite adept at it. (Don't tell her I said so.) *Theo*

—·—·—

JOHANNA VAN GOGH-BONGER
8 Cité Pigalle, Paris

23 May
Dear Mother and Anna,

My new stationery just arrived, so now I have no excuse for not writing—it's about time! Tomorrow Theo and I will have been married all of five weeks. It seems as though it happened long, long ago—as though we'd always been together. However, I guess I don't look like a married lady yet. When I went to pay the baker, the good man could not understand that I myself was Madame van Gogh, and kept calling me "mademoiselle." (Theo threatens to call me "his girl" like father does, unless I manage to look more matronly.)

He's been so patient with my culinary inexperience. Twice I burned the rice, and once let the soup boil away! But I'm learning. Last night we had our first dinner guests—Theo's artist friends, Pissarro and Bernard, and of course Andries. I was so pleased with myself—nothing burnt, and everything served hot or cold as required. Theo says he expects I'll be transformed into a cook worthy of any Parisian gourmet before our six-month anniversary.

Paris in the spring is delightful. Montmartre may not be an aristocratic quarter, but in May it's like a floral bouquet. Across the street, chestnut trees blossoming in front of a painter's studio; behind our apartment, an arbor with lilac bushes in full bloom—how I love the fragrance at night! I keep telling Theo I'm sure the scent is an aphrodisiac. (He says he doubts I need one.) He teases me unmercifully about everything—even *that*. (Happiness is being teased by Theo.) Love, *Johanna*

—·—·—

THE PERSONAL DIARY OF JOHANNA BONGER

26 May 1889

I have been feeling very lazy lately. After Theo leaves for the gallery in the morning, I go back to bed for a catnap, don't get up until an hour before lunch. Then I rush around—get dressed, make the bed, empty the chamber pots, wash the breakfast dishes, make lunch. And I'm ashamed to confess I often take another catnap before dinner! My whole body seems to have slowed down. Is this "spring fever"?

27 May

I had the most curious dream last night. Sunday afternoon we went to the Louvre, and I was particularly drawn to a painting of cherubs, said to be done by a student of Raphael. I dreamt the cherubim were flying over my bed—the sound of their laughter merging with the whoosh of their little wings. They looked so soft and plump, with dimpled fingers that reached out to me. I yearned to hold just one of them, to lavish kisses on that angelic face. The longing was so intense that when I awoke I was certain I could still hear faraway laughter and the faint whoosh of wings.

28 May

Just realized I did not have a visit from the redhead the first of May. This happened once before when I went to England. I was so seasick during the

Channel crossing—my visitor was delayed almost three weeks. But this is *four*. I don't see how I could possibly become pregnant so quickly. I'll wait a while before saying anything to Theo. How will he feel about having a baby? It will change our life.

2 June

I didn't have to say anything! My observant husband asked me today. He seemed delighted at the prospect of becoming a father. If it's a boy, we're going to name the baby Vincent Willem. I feel guilty being so happy while Vincent is locked up at St.-Rémy. (I wonder how he'll feel about it.) To be absolutely sure, we intend to wait another month before telling anyone.

— · — · —

JOHANNA VAN GOGH-BONGER
8 Cité Pigalle, Paris

5 July

Dear Vincent,

Theo and I have the most wonderful news—in early February we expect a baby. We are hoping for a little boy so we can name it after you, if you will consent to be its godfather. There is now much excitement among the grandmothers-to-be in Amsterdam and Leiden. Both are planning to come down for the confinement, and Wilhelmina as well. I have already expressed my concerns to the doctor, wondering how I can assure our baby the best of health. He has given me a nourishing diet to follow that includes some vegetables, such as spinach and broccoli, that I could do without. For the past month I've had such a queasy stomach I could eat hardly anything, let alone spinach and broccoli! But now I am feeling fine, and am prepared to make any sacrifice for your namesake. Theo sends his love, as do I. *Johanna*

St.-Paul-de-Mausole,
An Asylum in St.-Rémy

8 July 1889
Dear Monsieur van Gogh,

Regret to inform you that after two months of calm, Vincent unexpectedly turned manic—attempted to poison self by ingesting paints. Patient had hallucinations, plus nightmares during sleep. Emetic prescribed to bring up pigments, bromide to nullify disturbing dreams. (*Cost will be added to monthly bill.*) Forced to padlock studio to enforce injunction against painting.

Dr. Théophile Peyron, Director

—·—·—

THE PERSONAL DIARY OF JOHANNA BONGER

10 July

This time Theo shared the bad news with me immediately. My poor husband! He had convinced himself that Vincent's problems were merely transient ones. This morning he seemed resigned to the fact that these terrible "attacks" might happen at any time. We talked about how fortunate it was that this one occurred in a place where he could be immediately prevented from injuring himself. Theo says he will write Dr. Peyron and thank him.

23 July

Good news from St.-Rémy—Vincent recovered from his attack in two weeks; however, Dr. Peyron is keeping the studio padlocked until August, says he thinks Vincent has acquired a toxic addiction to chrome yellow and lead white.

19 August

Paris in August has been unbearable—like living inside a baker's oven. I'd look up at the three windmills on top of the Montmartre hill, and become positively homesick for one of those windy, rainy days in Holland.

Although it's my coolest summer ensemble, I didn't dare wear the white voile skirt and blouse. We had almost no rain this month. Every horse and carriage that clattered over the cobblestones sent up a cloud of dust. In Amsterdam, every Dutch housewife would have rushed outside with mop and water to wash down the street, the house bricks, even the trunks of the chestnut trees. But of course, back home every other street is a canal filled with water. Next year, Theo has promised that the baby and I will spend both July and August in Holland. (I can't bear Paris in summer, but I'm not sure I could bear to be away from Theo that long.)

31 August

I'm beginning to "show" just a little now. How I pitied the woman from the studio across the street. She looked almost ready for her confinement, and I'd watch her waddle up the hill every morning with breakfast rolls and croissants bouncing in her market basket. She evidently doesn't have a husband as considerate as Theo.

(Maybe she doesn't have a husband at all! Theo is always teasing, telling me how innocent I am.)

— · — · —

THEODOOR VAN GOGH
8 Cité Pigalle, Paris

20 September 1889
Dear Mother,

We'll be seeing Mr. Bonger when he comes to Paris on a business trip this month, and are looking forward to your visit next month. If you'll check the date, you'll realize that you will be here in time to celebrate our six-month anniversary. Despite Jo's early morning sickness, and worrying about Vincent, it has been an unbelievably happy six months.

I will confess that I did have some misgivings about how Jo would adjust to living in Paris. While I am not, like Vincent, *completely* unconventional, as you know, my life here is very much involved with the avant-garde—not only in the new art but also in new ideas in general. I worried that Jo might find both hard to understand, even perhaps distasteful. I needn't have. She has an intelligent, inquiring mind—new things delight her. And oh, Mother, I cannot tell you how much she delights me! I never dared dream of such happiness. We seem to be of one mind. Every day I bless Andries for introducing us.

My love to Wilhelmina, and to you— *Theo*

—··—··—

THE PERSONAL DIARY OF JOHANNA BONGER

26 September

I told Theo I hoped he wouldn't want me to withdraw from *all* social contacts now that I'm beginning to "show." I won't be so brazen as to go to the opera or the Salon, but I've so enjoyed having Theo's friends drop by for dinner—especially since my cooking and my French have improved vastly. What is so terrible about a pregnant woman that she should hide, as though something shameful had happened to her? The baby has just answered with a kick!

28 September

Paris in autumn is exhilarating! I simply refuse to become a recluse because of my "condition." Theo suggested I purchase one of the new "bustle" fashions and wear it backwards—but I came up with a less outrageous solution. Today I removed some of my savings from the Limoges cookie jar, and went shopping for shawls. Bought two: a voluminous brown silk, and for cooler weather, a midnight-blue wool. Modeled both for Theo before dinner. After dinner, discovered my withdrawal from the cookie jar had been replaced. Hope Theo doesn't spoil the baby the way he does me.

I'll be showing off my cooking to Father tomorrow night. He's staying with Andries. We asked Andries to casually mention Vincent's transfer to St.-Rémy. Andries reports that Father didn't seems surprised!

ANTON BONGER
Insurance: Marine and General
Herengracht 204, Amsterdam

13 October 1889
My dear Andries:

I very much appreciated the hospitality of your guest room when business necessitated my being in Paris last week. (The people with whom one must associate makes staying in even the best hotel quite unpleasant.) And I'm especially happy that I did not have to stay with Theo and Johanna.

You know how reluctant I am to interfere in the lives of my children, but had I been your sister's house guest, I fear I could not have been able to contain my displeasure with her conduct. It is perfectly acceptable for an "expecting" young woman to invite close relatives to dine at her home. But including her husband's clients, such as Bernard and Pissarro, is inexcusable! The silk shawl your sister wore barely disguised her condition. I am very disappointed in Theodoor. Your sister has always tended to take liberties with what is considered acceptable conduct, and requires stern guidance. As she is no longer in my charge, is it too much to expect her husband to point out the error of her ways?

I have not mentioned Johanna's brazen lack of modesty to Mother. You know her health is delicate—we try not to burden her with unpleasantness.

Father

Afterthought: What was all the fuss about the crate of paintings that was delivered after dinner? Bernard, Pissarro, Theo, even you, acted as though this was a collection worthy of the Rijksmuseum.

One does not need to be an art critic to recognize the difference between a masterpiece and a mess. Those wildly undulating cypress trees, and wheat fields could only have been painted in one place—by a madman in an asylum!

THEO VAN GOGH
8 Cité Pigalle, Paris

10 November
Dear Vincent,

Your *Starry Night over the Rhone* and *The Irises* created much comment in this year's Independents' Exhibit. Then last week I received a note from Albert Aurier, the art critic for *Le Mercure de France*. He had been very impressed with the Independents' Exhibit and asked if he could come to the apartment to see more of your work. Jo, who is now quite proud of her culinary accomplishments, immediately invited him for lunch.

And now for the important news. Octave Maus was in Paris last week and asked if you would like to exhibit in Les Vingt's Annual in Brussels. This is quite an honor. Les Vingt was organized for the same reason as the Independents, as an alternative to the official Salon. Each year, their exhibit includes work by the Belgian members as well as that of a selected group of invited foreigners. So very prestigious is this event, it is not uncommon for the avant-garde painters of Paris to solicit invitations.

Jo sends her congratulations, as do I . . . *Theo*

Afterthought: Dr. Peyron reports you have had no recurrence of your problem since he lifted his ban on painting last August. We pray it's a permanent cure.

———

THE PERSONAL DIARY OF JOHANNA VAN GOGH-BONGER

21 December

Theo noticed I had only a handful of pages left in my diary, so when we had our own private St. Nicholas celebration on December 5, Sinterklaas presented me with this new one. "Considering your condition," Theo teased, "it's high time your diary revealed that it is being written by a married lady with a proper hyphenated name."

I would so much have enjoyed being with the family this holiday season—but it was quite impossible. I look like a huge hot-air balloon, ready at any moment to float away to "hurrahs!" and champagne. I don't walk, I waddle. I can produce my own attached bookshelf when reading. I eat prodigious amounts of strange foods—and I feel like I've been pregnant forever! Fortunately, Dr. Blanc says his first estimate was too distant. Now he says my confinement will be the end of January.

24 December

Both grandmothers-to-be keep asking why I'm having a medical doctor instead of the traditional midwife. Theo and I want a modern doctor who believes in the virtues of boiling water and antiseptics to prevent childbed fever. Despite all our precautions, I confess I'm more than a little frightened—and for all his joking, I think Theo is too. Thank heavens all has been well with Vincent since last August. I fear that one worry at a time is all that Theo can handle. Must stop now—the postman rang.

— · — · —

ST.-PAUL-DE-MAUSOLE,
An Asylum in St.-Rémy

23 December 1889
Dear Monsieur van Gogh,

It is with great regret that I must report that after two months of calm, your brother had an attack yesterday, almost exactly on the anniversary of his first. Patient became manic—attempted to poison himself by ingesting his paints as well as swallowing kerosene from the lamps. Fortunately, an emetic was administered in time. Last night patient had hallucinations, plus nightmares. Bromide administered to nullify disturbing dreams. (Cost of medications will be added to bill.)

Studio once again padlocked to enforce injunction against painting. I regret having to send bad news during what should be a joyous holiday season. Let us hope that this time his attack will be short-lived.

Dr. Théophile Peyron, Director

Christmas Eve 1889

I am not going to let him do it! I am not going to let Vincent ruin another Christmas for us. A year ago I remember writing, "You and I will have a lifetime of Christmases together. We can surely spare this one apart." A lifetime of Christmases worrying that Vincent might relapse, have yet another attack? I'm putting a stop to it.

This Christmas Eve is going to be wonderful, just as we planned it. We've stocked up on candles, borrowed candelabra and candlesticks from all our friends, invited them to join us for a candlelit supper. We've stocked up on centimes and chocolates. When the neighborhood children come caroling, we're prepared to reward them with showers of silver and sweets. It will be a memorable Christmas Eve, and no one will worry about Vincent. Because I just hid Dr. Peyron's letter under my savings in the Limoges cookie jar. The day after Christmas will be time enough to give it to Theo.

(After all, the mail is often delayed during the holidays. It's snowing— our mailman could have slipped, twisted his ankle, and been unable to finish his route.)

Johanna, aren't you ashamed of yourself? This time they reached Vincent with an emetic in time. Think what it is like for poor Theo, worrying about the next time, and the next. Think what it is like for Vincent, finally beginning to find recognition after those long hard years of practice and study, being accepted by the Independents as one of them, being described by Aurier as "the only painter I know who perceives the coloration of things with such intensity," and then the final coup—being invited by Les Vingt to exhibit with them in their prestigious Annual in Brussels. All these triumphs cut short by yet another attack. The worst of it is, no one knows how long each will last— a day, a week, months?

Yes, I'm ashamed of myself. But the letter from Dr. Peyron is *not* coming out of the cookie jar until December 26.

30 December

Theo is all smiles—a letter from Dr. Peyron saying Vincent woke up yesterday morning with no memory whatever of his weeklong manic episode. Theo immediately wrote asking which paintings Vincent wanted sent to Brussels. I cannot help wondering, where will we three be next Christmas and what lies in store for us? The baby just gave a kick. Please excuse me, little one, I should have said "we four."

— · — · —

THEODOOR VAN GOGH
8 Cité Pigalle, Paris

New Year's Eve 1889
To: THE ANTON BONGER FAMILY, Amsterdam
From: THE THEO VAN GOGH FAMILY, Paris

Dear All—

This group letter is Jo's idea—I think it's her way of letting you know how much she misses being with all of you to greet the New Year. I suspect Jo is actually looking forward to her confinement, when she'll be petted and spoiled by two mothers, after turning all culinary tasks over to the wondrously efficient Wilhelmina. I never dreamt having a baby could be such a complicated affair. This one will come into the world amidst a throng of admiring relatives. Just remember who the Papa is—he insists on being the first to count baby's fingers and toes.

I can hardly believe that before this coming year ends I shall be a Papa! To all the Bongers, Happy New Year. And thank you for my precious Jo. *Theo*

Dear All—

If Theo sounds a little tipsy, it's because we've been toasting the New Year in with a bottle of Chardonnay. Theo has been doing an excellent job of spoiling me himself. He gets up early, and before going to the gallery, brings me breakfast in bed. He has our *femme de ménage* come every single day—I'm not allowed to do a thing!

Happy New Year to everyone—and how happy I will be once this baby finds his way into the world! Love to you all— *Johanna*

—.—.—

THE PERSONAL DIARY OF JOHANNA VAN GOGH-BONGER

New Year's Eve 1889

My tipsy husband lies snoring on the sofa. For the past several hours snow has been falling in veils of white that almost obliterate the streetlamps. I'm so homesick for Holland! More than anything in the world, I long to go skating—the Seine will do if I cannot find a canal. But Theo said that if I dared step outside he'd put a gypsy hex on me so I couldn't move, and with snow falling on my present rotund shape, in five minutes one would not be able to distinguish Jo from the snowman the neighborhood children made this afternoon. (Will I *ever* be able to get into my corselet again?)

17 January 1890

I'm so bored I could scream! The weather and the apartment's stairs keep me indoors. Juliette comes every day—there's nothing for me to do except read. Theo brings me countless bland books from the rental library (but NO romantic French novels). I've just finished embroidering a dozen infant gowns with matching bonnets and half a dozen flannel blankets. Next, from Mother van Gogh's gift box, are two dozen infant swaddling cloths that require hemming. As the gray days creep by, I sleep a lot, daydream a lot, and pray more than a little. I can't forget all the horror stories I've heard—seemingly healthy women dying of childbed fever.

29 January

This afternoon my water broke. No pain. Juliette sent a messenger to the gallery to get Theo—Theo sent Juliette to get Dr. Blanc. Dr. Blanc suggested we get telegrams sent to the grandmothers-to-be. Theo rushed around, bringing me more pillows than I needed, and endless cups of chamomile tea.

30 January: Six in the evening

This is what is meant by confinement. I'm confined to my bed—unless I need to use the chamber pot. After washing his hands (Doctor Blanc's standing orders), Theo brings me a tray (tea and toast), then leaves to eat dinner with the family. A buzz of conversation mixed with laughter—it sounds like they're having a wonderful time. I feel like a leper. The pains are not unbearable yet, they just never completely stop—keep returning over and over again.I'll never be able to sleep tonight. Why is this baby such a slowpoke? And why am I crying?

31 January: Three in the morning

That baby! One minute he was part of me—and several unbelievably agonizing minutes later there were two of us. When Doctor Blanc laid him in my arms, all pink and moist, he looked straight at me with startled, wide-open blue eyes and the most comical questioning frown.

I was certain he was about to ask, "Just *who* are YOU?"

—·—·—

THEODOOR VAN GOGH
8 Cité Pigalle, Paris

1 February
Dear Vincent,

A brief note to let you know your namesake arrived last night and is crying lustily. A beautiful boy—his lungs are exceedingly healthy, and if my count is correct, he has the required number of fingers and toes.

My poor little wife suffered a great deal because the waters came too soon. They say that often with the first child, labor can last a long time. This labor seem to go on forever! We had an excellent doctor with extraordinary patience. Anyone else would have used forceps. Jo is well; no fever yet. *Theo*

St.-Paul-de-Mausole
3 February
Dear Theo,

I was happy to know that finally the waiting is over, and that all is well with your wife and child. There is a general custom, which I think most sensible, of sending mother and child for a long stay in the country immediately after the confinement. St.-Rémy, for example, is known for its healthy climate. I think you should seriously consider this.

Let me know if you want me to make arrangements. *Vincent*

— · — · —

St.-Paul-de-Mausole
4 February
Dear Theo,

You say you are going to name the baby after me. I should much prefer you name it after our sainted father. I have always regretted that he and I never quite made up our quarrel before he passed on. But you, who were his favorite, could honor him now by naming your son after him.

Incidentally, did you know that in the Hebrew faith, one always names a child after someone who has *passed on?* The Hebrews believe that if you name a child after someone still living, it is the same as telling him, "I wish you were dead."

How pleased Mother must be with her new grandchild! I know you have made her very happy. Tell Mother I'll write soon. *Vincent*

— · — · —

St.-Paul-de-Mausole,
An Asylum in St.-Rémy

7 February 1890
Dear Monsieur van Gogh,

Regret to inform you of another sudden attack. This time our attendant noticed it coming, restrained patient before he could injure self. The next day patient appeared normal, had no memory of incident. Am reexamining my previous diagnosis concerning addiction to painting. This time will wait only twenty-four hours before permitting patient to paint again.

For patient's protection, will require that attendant be present whenever patient paints. (Cost of attendant will be added to bill.) *Théophile Peyron*

— · — · —

THE PERSONAL DIARY OF JOHANNA VAN GOGH-BONGER

12 February

I never dreamt such a tiny baby could be so demanding! Fortunately I have plenty of milk, because this little one does nothing but suckle and sleep every couple of hours day and night, night and day. I feel rested, because I can nap when the baby does, but poor Theo! The circles under his eyes worried me. Once Wilhelmina left, I insisted he sleep in the guest room, where the baby couldn't disturb him.

At first, Theo was afraid to hold him. I had to assure him the baby wouldn't break. But now I think he is secretly looking forward to everyone going home so he can have his son all to himself. Wilhelmina and Mother van Gogh stayed until three days ago, when Doctor Blanc said I was allowed to get out of bed for a few hours each day. My mother will stay until the end of the month. My strength is returning slowly but surely. And no sign of childbed fever! Have to stop now—the little one just gave his warning whimper that precedes his "I'm starving!" wail.

— · — · —

JOHANNA VAN GOGH-BONGER
8 Cité Pigalle, Paris

20 February
Dear Vincent,

Your namesake, now three weeks old, is doing very well. It's amazing how a tiny baby can become one's whole world as though nothing else mattered. We're so pleased to hear you sold a painting at Les Vingt's. Theo has casually mentioned it to half of Paris. (But you should hear him making all sorts of foolish baby talk whenever he holds his son.) Theo is now totally involved in arranging an extensive presentation of Monet's work at Goupil's. (While I am totally involved in whether my little one burps or spits up.) The rest of the Impressionists are still considered "wild men," and despite Theo's best efforts, rarely sell. (Despite my best efforts, your namesake rarely sleeps more than four hours at a stretch.)

Theo tells me you feel that you need to get away from the depressing atmosphere of St.-Rémy. And I have been telling Theo I'm sure the sight of your namesake would dispel any and all depression! We all look forward to seeing you very soon. Must stop—the baby is calling. Time for his lunch with . . . *Jo.*

— · — · —

THEODOOR VAN GOGH
8 Cité Pigalle, Paris

24 February 1890
Dear Mother and Wilhelmina,

The good news is that Jo and the baby are fine. The bad news is that Vincent had another attack two days ago. Dr. Peyron reports this appears to be one of his worst.

The week before, Vincent had written that he wanted to leave St.-Rémy, that living with all those madmen was beginning to depress him. Dear Jo suggested finding a rooming house in Paris, and having him take his meals with us—but she's never met Vincent. Much as I love my brother, you both know that when he shared my apartment in Paris, I spent the most miserable two years of my life—his incredible untidiness, the incessant arguing!

A city is no place for Vincent. His best work has been done in the calm of the countryside, but he does need medical supervision. Pissarro knows a semi-retired doctor in Auvers who specializes in treating artists. I intend to consult him as soon as Vincent's present attack has passed. Jo sends her love— *Theo*

St.-Paul-de-Mausole,
An Asylum in St.-Rémy

Patient: Vincent van Gogh, (age 37)

15 May 1890. For the past month, patient has appeared completely recovered from a severe attack which commenced last winter. Today patient formally requested a release from his voluntary commitment to go live in the North of France. His brother has written requesting that patient be accompanied by an attendant at least as far as Tarascon. *Note: Add cost of attendant and luggage transit to final bill.*

— · — · —

The Personal Diary of Johanna van Gogh-Bonger

16 May

What will it be like with Vincent living just an hour away by train? He'll no longer be a brother-in-law I occasionally write to. He'll be staying with us for a few days before going to Auvers. Meeting him for the first time will seem strange. Suppose he doesn't like me? How terrible that would be for Theo!

I shall simply have to win Vincent over, be as nice to him as I can.

17 May

9 A.M..—I don't think Theo slept a wink last night. Yesterday evening we received a telegram from Tarascon saying that Vincent was boarding the night train, would arrive at ten this morning. Theo had begged him to arrange to be accompanied during the entire journey (suppose he has an attack while on the train), but Vincent refused. The baby must have sensed our tension. The little one has been sleeping through the night since the middle of March—but not last night. He kept waking every few hours. Finally, at seven, I got up, prepared breakfast, fed my husband, then my son. Theo has just left for the park at the bottom of the hill where the fiacres for hire line up. Now it's my turn to worry. I wonder if Vincent will like me. I pass the time by lining up all of Vincent's self-portraits, trying to imagine what he'll look like.

Here's one he painted while he was in Paris, looking unexpectedly fashionable—beard trimmed to a point under a homburg hat. Here's a disturbing one painted in St.-Rémy—an emaciated man, head shaved, green eyes blazing with fury. And one from Arles done after the ear incident—a pipe in his mouth, a bandage under his winter cap. The portraits are no help. They're all so different!

10 A.M.—If it has not been delayed, the train from Tarascon should just now be arriving. From the Gare de Lyon to the Cité Pigalle is a long distance. It will take quite a while. Does Vincent like flowers? To pass the time I fill vases with lilacs.

11 A.M.—At last! An open fiacre is turning into the Cité. I throw open the shutters, lean out to see Theo and Vincent waving at me. Vincent surprises me. I had expected a wan invalid. Here is a broad-shouldered man, looking ruddy and healthy. My first thought—"He looks stronger than Theo." My second—"What amazing red hair!" My third—"What an untidy beard. If he's not careful, he'll set fire to it with that pipe."

Later—The two brothers have been admiring Vincent's namesake, sleeping in his cradle. (I wish Vincent wouldn't smoke near the baby—but hesitate to say anything.) "Do not cover him with too much lace, little sister," Vincent tells me. (Lace? It's only Mother van Gogh's crocheted coverlet.)

18 May
We wake to find Vincent has been up before us, has pulled all his pictures out from under the beds and the sofas and has spread them over the floor throughout the apartment, so he can study them. (As usual, there is a trail of ashes from his pipe.) Juliette arrives to clean, is dismayed. I tell her to take the day off.

Evening: The doorbell has been constantly jangling. My brother has stopped by to see Vincent, as have Pissarro, Bernard, Aurier, Sisley, even Père Tanguy. They sound like a hive of bees. Theo worries that all this company may be too much for Vincent. Tomorrow they plan a quiet day, seeing an exhibit of Japanese prints, and buying art supplies.

19 May

We rise to find Vincent gone. Every morning he goes out to buy olives which he insists we also eat, claiming they have all sorts of health-producing qualities. He now is impatient to get settled in Auvers. Finally it is agreed they will not wait for Dr. Gachet's Paris clinic tomorrow. Today he will take the noon train to Auvers and go directly to Dr. Gachet's home, which Pissarro said is a short walk from the station.

I can't tell if Vincent likes me. He is so energetic, I feel overwhelmed!

— · — · —

DR. PAUL GACHET
Specialist in Nervous Disorders
16 Rue de Vessenots, Auvers-sur-Oise

2 June 1890
Report to Theo van Gogh
Re: Vincent van Gogh

When I examined your brother immediately after his arrival, I could find no cause for restricting his activities, except to encourage him to abstain from alcohol. As I wrote you, I regret being unable to offer him accommodations. Although I'm now a widower, my home is already shared with my son and daughter.

Vincent felt the inn I recommended was too fancy, found himself an inexpensive small café by the river that has a few rooms for rent above the restaurant. The food is excellent, the rooms are somewhat small, but there are other artists boarding there, and he seems quite content. He immediately discovered scenes he wanted to paint—thatched-roof cottages, winding lanes, a very picturesque old stone church. My only worry is the source of his indefatigable energy.

Vincent is anxious to see you and your family again. I should be pleased to offer the hospitality of my house and garden, which is particularly suited to an outdoor picnic. Would next Sunday, June the eighth, be convenient? If you took the morning train there would be time for lunch, and a leisurely visit with your brother before returning to Paris.

Let me know if this is agreeable. *Dr. Paul-Ferdinand Gachet*

—··—

THE PERSONAL DIARY OF JOHANNA VAN GOGH-BONGER

8 June

Just returned from our day in the country with Vincent. He met our train, proudly bearing a gift for his namesake—a bird's nest! A four-year-old boy would have loved it, but our four-month-old baby tried to eat it. After our picnic. Vincent thought the baby should be introduced to all the animals in Dr. Gachet's barnyard—chickens, turkeys, even goats and sheep. Vincent held his namesake close to each animal, mimicking the noise each makes: "The turkey goes gobble, gobble; the sheep baa, baa; and the cock COCK-A-DOODLE-DOO!" (This last in a loud voice.) The little one was startled, turned red, began crying hysterically. Vincent thought it was so funny! Theo was terribly upset—he can't bear hearing his son cry. (Neither can I.) I finally took the baby inside the house, soothed him, nursed him, and rocked him to sleep.

Vincent means well, but he appears to know very little about infants. The baby's chin is still scratched from the bird's nest.

9 June

Still trying to sort out my impressions of Vincent. Contrary to my expectations, this is no invalid. Being with Vincent is like living with heat lighting. To me, the difference between the two brothers is amazing. They are like two sides of a coin. I'm probably prejudiced, but it seems to me that Theo is gentle and tender and very sensitive to the moods of others, while Vincent is dynamic, opinionated, and can often be completely oblivious to those around him. (Perhaps this is what permitted him to survive among those poor souls at St.-Rémy.) The paintings he did between attacks at St.-Rémy are amazing. Theo is so pleased—he finally feels vindicated for his faith in Vincent's talent, for all those years of guidance and support.

12 June
    I'm worried about Theo—he looks so tired lately. Goupil's is constantly harassing him about his exhibiting the Impressionists, even if only in the up-stairs mezzanine. Theo says they would like to see the entire gallery devoted solely to scaled-down lithographs of the wall-size Salon prize winners, and limit originals to sentimental genre paintings in the approved brown-soup-of-Europe technique. Yesterday Theo stormed into the house saying, "After ten years, they act like I know nothing about the art business!" and talked about going into business for himself. So far it's only talk.

—⋅—⋅—

JOHANNA VAN GOGH-BONGER
8 Cité Pigalle, Paris

20 June 1890
Dear Mother van Gogh,
    We are beside ourselves with worry, I have not been well—a touch of dyspepsia, nausea, and general malaise. We've had an unusually hot June. Ordinarily a few days' bed rest and Mrs. Smullin's All-Purpose Tonic would be all I would need to recover. But now my milk is failing and the baby has been crying incessantly. We do not know if he too is ill or is merely hungry. He suckles constantly but never appears satisfied.
    I cannot ask my own mother for advice because she has been insisting I get a wet nurse. This is something Theo and I want to avoid at all costs. In my family, it is considered déclassé to nurse one's own infant. Theo says you nursed all your own babies. Is there any advice you can give me about how to increase lactation? Should we start supplementing with cow's milk? Theo feels we should consult Dr. Blanc. If he were a woman, I'd feel more comfort-

able discussing my problem—but of course, there are no women doctors, only midwives. Must stop—the little one is screaming again. It drives poor Theo to distraction. And me too! *Johanna*

— · — · —

RIVERSIDE CAFÉ & INN
Market Street, Auvers-sur-Oise

21 June
Dear Theo,

I was greatly disturbed to learn that my namesake was ill. Consulted Dr. Gachet, and he assured me the baby was probably just teething. As I have mentioned before, I am convinced that the city is the *wrong* place for any baby. Here in Auvers, all the children, and their mothers as well, are healthy and happy, *without exception.* That is why I am now *insisting* that Jo and the little one come to Auvers for at least a month to recuperate in the fresh country air. Dr. Gachet has a large house with plenty of room. Or, if preferred, mother and child could stay at the Café with me. It is not at all expensive. On the other hand, if they are too ill to travel right now, I feel it my duty to join all of you in Paris, where I can be of help in your time of travail. I will come this Sunday, when Theo will be free to meet the Express. *Vincent*

— · — · —

THEODOOR VAN GOGH
8 Cité Pigalle, Paris

24 June 1890
My dear brother,

Not that we don't appreciate your willingness to come and share our troubles, but with two patients in the house, the fewer visitors the better. Jo is almost recovered, except we fear her milk has not returned sufficiently. The baby cries constantly, day and night—you would find it unbearable. And there's nothing you or anyone can do. I hope you understand that there is no question of Jo and the baby traveling anywhere just now.

Doctor Blanc is coming tomorrow. I fear we should have consulted him sooner. We tried supplementing with cow's milk, and it appears to have made things worse. Vincent, if we were to lose this child I could not bear it! Jo and I do want you to come visit, but not just now—later. *Theo*

—·—·—

JOHANNA VAN GOGH-BONGER
8 Cité Pigalle, Paris

25 June
Dear Mother van Gogh and Wil,

We almost lost our baby—and all because of my own foolish modesty, because I was shy about discussing lactation with a male doctor. It was Theo who finally insisted on sending for Doctor Blanc.

And not a moment too soon. He just left. It seems my own "touch of malaise" was a severe case of summer flu, which often interferes with lactation. I was on the road to recovery, but my milk was scant, and the little one almost starved. Doctor Blanc says, however, that the biggest mistake we made was attempting to supplement with cow's milk, which due to the hot weather was undoubtedly contaminated. The baby's recent screaming was not only due to hunger but also to pain from severe colic and cramping. I never ever want to hear him cry like that again!

Doctor Blanc considered hiring a wet nurse, but even with careful screening, said the risk of syphilis was too great. (There is a point in the disease process when a woman's nipples become infected.) Instead he has arranged for the nearby Flaubert Farms, whose sanitation he trusts, to bring a lactating ass to our rear garden door every morning. He showed us how to hold the baby so he can suckle directly from the animal, how to collect milk into sterile bottles to be given later in the day, how to wash and sterilize the bottles and nipples in boiling water after each use. I am to nurse the baby every evening, and as my milk returns, gradually discontinue milk from the ass.

Today the baby already had two bottles from the ass, in addition to a direct feeding. He is sleeping now, a dribble of milk at the corner of his mouth. He makes little mewing noises of pain, but seems too exhausted to cry. Doctor Blanc assured us that the colic will diminish. Theo wants to add a few words and I want to sleep. Love, *Jo*

Dear Mother,

My poor Jo is absolutely exhausted. For a while I was terrified that I might lose both my wife and my child. But Doctor Blanc assures us that within a week we should see an improvement. Despite our upbringing, I have never been deeply religious. But lately I found myself stopping to pray in the church at the bottom of the hill. Even though it is Catholic, not Dutch Reformed, I believe He heard me.

Theo

— · — · —

RIVERSIDE CAFÉ & INN
Market Street, Auvers-sur-Oise

2 July 1890
Dear Theo,

I was happy to learn that my namesake is out of danger. According to Dr. Gachet, there are plenty of asses here in Auvers, so there is really no need to remain in Paris. What concerns me is that the child is less than six months old, and already Jo's milk is drying up. And you, Theo, seem exhausted.

That is why I am recommending you seriously consider *not* vacationing in Holland this summer as planned. The journey is always very expensive, and visiting both families is fatiguing. Instead, I feel what you all require is one month of absolute rest in the country—in Auvers. I insist on it! I know Jo says she finds the summer heat in France unbearable, but if she is to continue to be your wife, she will simply have to learn to adjust to it.

Mother, of course, will be disappointed at not seeing her grandchild this summer, but we must all make sacrifices. As soon as your two patients have recovered, I want to visit you and discuss it.

Vincent

THEODOOR VAN GOGH
8 Cité Pigalle, Paris

5 July 1890

Dear Vincent,

Good news—Jo is fully recovered, and her milk is gradually returning. The ass's milk agrees with our little one, his crying has lessened, and today he smiled at me! Doctor Blanc is pleased, said yesterday's consultation was the final one.

We both appreciated your concern for our health and your suggestions for a month of rest. This month, I have business in Holland, so when I go, I'll be able to take Jo and the baby to Amsterdam and leave them with her family. I'll be joining her the first of August, when my own vacation is scheduled.

There is now no need for you to delay visiting us. We do need to have a family discussion with you. I am seriously considering leaving Goupil's and becoming my own art dealer. In the beginning it will perhaps mean a little belt tightening, but nothing we can't manage. If we all keep our health and good spirits, I'm sure the new venture will be successful. Would you like to come on the first train next Sunday? I'm enclosing fifty francs. Jo sends her love, as do I. *Theo*

— · — · —

THE PERSONAL DIARY OF JOHANNA VAN GOGH-BONGER

14 July

I've had my fill of "family discussions"! It's not like Theo to be so insensitive. He upset Vincent terribly. A three-day visit in our apartment, one day together in Auvers, and this Sunday in Paris: five days—that's the sum total of the time I've spent with Vincent. Yet even I could see that Theo's "supposings" were making his brother extremely apprehensive.

"Suppose Theo resigned from Goupil's and became his own art dealer." Could we all manage financially? "Suppose the baby, or Vincent, or I, or even Theo became ill." Could we manage the extra expense? Should we move into a smaller, less expensive apartment? But if Theo were selling paintings in his home, wouldn't we need a larger, more expensive apartment? In the end the whole idea was put aside. But I must speak to Theo about reassuring Vincent that we will always continue his support. Our "family discussion" seemed to cause Vincent a great deal of anxiety.

— · — · —

JOHANNA VAN GOGH-BONGER
8 Cité Pigalle, Paris

15 July 1890
Dear Mother van Gogh and Wilhelmina,
    We leave this afternoon for Holland. My brother is taking his vacation now so he can visit our family with me. I shall spend two weeks in Amsterdam, then join Theo for our visit with you in Leiden.
    Wait until you see your grandson! To look at him, you'd never know the little one had been ill. At six months, he's a charmer, with no discrimination whatsoever—he smiles and flirts with any and everyone. And he is now positively fat! My milk continues to be abundant. (Theo keeps threatening to hire me out as a wet nurse.) You'll see for yourself in August!
                                                        Love to you both, *Johanna*

— · — · —

JO VAN GOGH-BONGER
C/o Anton Bonger, Herengracht 204, Amsterdam
23 July
Dearest Theo,
    Mother gasped and Father went "Hurrumph!" when they discovered I did not have a wet nurse, am still nursing the baby myself. Because my brother is always around, I've escaped the unpleasantness of comments and arguments.
    I don't miss the Paris heat—but how I miss you! I'm counting the days till you come for me, and we're together again on the southbound train to Leiden. Can we hold hands like real honeymooners? Counting the days—
                                                        Your impatient *Jo*.

GOUPIL'S FINE ART GALLERY
18 Boulevard Montmartre: *Theo van Gogh*, Mgr.

25 July

Dearest Jo—

Ignore the stationery—this is a love letter, not a business letter. Didn't want to wait till I got home to write. My darling, your husband is also counting the days. Just four more and I will again board the Netherlands Express to rendezvous with my milk-filled wife and dimpled child.

I sent Vincent an extra fifty francs this month, and followed your suggestion about reassuring him of our continuing support. However, I just received a somewhat incomprehensible letter from him that worries me—but is probably no cause for concern, for in the same letter Vincent requested I send him more paints, even listed the specific colors. How I wish he could someday be as happy as I am.

Just four more days! Ah, Leiden! How glad I am Mother moved last year to such a romantic medieval town. After all the tension, all the worry of this past month, how I will revel in our long-overdue "honeymoon." Darling Jo, you'll know how much I've missed you when I take you in my arms.

Your impatient *Theo*

— · — · —

TELEGRAPH FRANCAIS

TO JOHANNA VAN GOGH-BONGER HERENGRACHT 204 AMSTERDAM STOP UNABLE TO JOIN YOU AS PLANNED STOP RECEIVED WORD FROM GACHET THAT VINCENT WOUNDED HIMSELF WITH A PISTOL STOP LITTLE HOPE FOR RECOVERY STOP REMAIN IN AMSTERDAM STOP DO NOT COME TO AUVERS STOP LETTER FOLLOWS SIGNED THEO 27 JULY 1890

RIVERSIDE CAFÉ & INN
Market Street, Auvers-sur-Oise

28 July
Dear Johanna and Andries,

At Vincent's bedside. Arrived to find Vincent somewhat better than I expected. When he saw me he said, "Please, no tears; I did it for the good of everyone." My God! What did he mean by that? Did he feel like he was a burden, fear another attack?

Dr. Gachet says that when he told him it looked like he might not die, Vincent calmly replied, "Then I shall simply have to do it all over again." My poor brother! He has had so very little happiness.

As nearly as we can tell, the gun was borrowed several days ago from the inn's proprietor for the purpose of scaring away crows. Vincent left the inn as usual with his paints, easel and canvas strapped to his back. He thinks he fainted after he shot himself in a barnyard by the river. The bullet apparently entered below the left rib, missing the heart. This next sounds incredible, but seems true. Upon reviving, Vincent walked the mile and a half back to the inn, then collapsed as he tried to go up the stairs to his room.

Naturally Gachet wanted to notify me immediately, but Vincent refused to give him my home address. (It was Sunday, and the gallery was closed.) I think Vincent wanted to spare me, was hoping it would all be over by the time I arrived.

Later: Under no circumstances do I want you or Dries to come to Auvers. Until you hear otherwise, you and the baby are to remain in Amsterdam with your parents. There is nothing you can do here. I myself feel so helpless. At times his pain seems to be excruciating. I just hold his hand, and when he weeps, weep with him. For the first time in years, we have talked intimately, as brothers should.

He told me he feels so alone. I promised to never leave his side. *Theo*

ÉMILE BERNARD
Montmartre, Paris

30 July 1890
Paul Gauguin: Waterford Inn, Pont-Aven

Dear Paul:

Eight of Vincent's artist friends came from Paris for the funeral. I know you would have joined us if you could. (The July heat made immediate burial necessary.) Theo said he was glad that there was not time enough for his family to come from Holland. "Vincent may be gone, but not his art," he said. "Only his fellow artists can know how to mourn him."

We tried to do what we could to make it truly an artists' funeral. On the walls of the room where Vincent lay, we nailed all his last canvases (they are magnificent), forming something like a halo around him. On the coffin, a simple white drapery and masses of yellow flowers—the sunflowers he loved, and yellow daisies, yellow dahlias. On the floor in front of the coffin, we placed his easel, his palette and brushes.

Because of the circumstances, the local priest refused a hearse, but Dr. Gachet procured one from the neighboring town. At the cemetery, Theo broke down, sobbing uncontrollably. On the train to Paris, he talked almost hysterically about the retrospective exhibitions he was planning for Vincent, and the Society of Artists he would organize in Vincent's name.

Theo needs all the support his friends can offer. Write him soon.

Émile

THEO VAN GOGH
8 Cité Pigalle, Paris

30 July 1890

Mrs. van Gogh-Carbentus
Postbus 817, Leiden

Mother dear,

We laid your son to rest today on a hill overlooking the wheat fields that he had recently painted. How glad I was to be able to be with him at the end. At one o'clock on the morning of the 29th, he said in Dutch, "I wish I could go home now"—and his wish was fulfilled. Vincent finally found the peace he could not find on earth.

There are no words that can express the grief I feel. It is the kind of grief that lasts and lasts, that I know will be with me as long as I live. My only comfort is knowing that he himself has found the rest he longed for, and that his art will live on.

Oh, Mother—he was so my own, own brother! *Theo*

3

"Rats are too good for him—vipers would be better!"

5 August 1890
Dear Mother van Gogh,

Something is very wrong. The last I heard from Theo was a telegram telling me of Vincent's passing and another instructing me NOT to come to the funeral. It was as if I were no longer part of his life. I kept telling myself perhaps he felt a funeral was no place for an infant. But my God, our child bears Vincent's name! And you said he did the same to you. I wrote asking Theo if he still wanted to visit you in Leiden. No reply. I wrote asking when he wanted me to return to Paris. No reply. Finally, my brother wired him saying we would be returning today. Still no reply. I keep telling Andries I know something is wrong. Dries keeps trying to make light of it. However, he assures me that when we arrive, he will stay with the baby and me till we're safely settled in the apartment. You must be as worried as I am. Will keep you informed and write tonight from Paris. *Jo*

— · — · —

Johanna van Gogh-Bonger
8 Cité Pigalle, Paris

Dear Mother van Gogh,

I don't know if I can find words to describe the condition of our apartment. The first thing we noticed when we opened the front door was the odor, intensified by the August heat. There were half-full absinthe bottles on every table, moldy cheese and bread in the kitchen, swarms of flies everywhere. The chamber pots hadn't been emptied in days. We found Theo asleep in the guest room—unconscious might be more accurate. He looked as if he had neither changed his clothes nor bathed in a week, and was so pale both Dries and I let out a sigh of relief when he stirred.

Sent a messenger to get Juliette. She arrived in an hour, but made me promise "not to leave her alone with Monsieur van Gogh." It seems he screamed and cursed, telling her to get out when she came to clean last Friday. Sent Dries out with a shopping list for food, while Juliette and I tried to make order out of the chaos. The apartment soon smelled only of brown soap and carbolic. Theo remained asleep. My brother, bless him, returned not only with the provisions on the list but also with our supper—antipasto and ravioli from the Italian café on the corner.

Dries had just gone to sleep on the living-room couch. I had just finished nursing and changing the baby. I was in my chemise, brushing my hair at the dressing table, when Theo stumbled into the bedroom. He sank down, put his head on my lap, and began to sob. I took him in my arms, soothed him as if he were a child. Poor Theo! It may take time, but I'm sure everything is going to be all right. Love, *Jo*

— · — · —

THE PERSONAL DIARY OF JOHANNA VAN GOGH-BONGER

17 August 1890

How to describe these past two weeks? For the first three days Theo did not utter a word, refused to even look at the letters of condolence which arrived daily, wouldn't even stay in the room when friends called to pay their respects. He ate almost nothing, sat staring into space all day. I could hear him weeping almost every night.

Dries suggested Theo's condition may have been the result of absinthe poisoning. When consulted, Dr. Gachet said he was not certain whether the profound melancholia was caused or simply triggered by bad absinthe. Gachet had brought with him the paintings by Vincent left in Auvers. One look, and Theo was a changed person! My poor husband, who had been listless and mute, suddenly had a great deal to say about arranging posthumous exhibitions of Vincent's work, and organizing a Society of Artists to honor him. Gachet said we should encourage him, keep him busy.

All week, Theo has been *extremely* busy writing letters and sending off telegrams. It worries me that he has so far been getting negative replies. I'm beginning to dread the cheery "*Vite! Télégraph Français*" used by the delivery boys when they knock.

13 AUGUST 1890 FROM THEO VAN GOGH TO PAUL DURAND-RUEL
URGENTLY REQUIRE SPACE IN PARIS GALLERY FOR POSTHUMOUS EXHIBIT
OF VINCENTS PAINTINGS AND DRAWINGS STOP ANY REASONABLE
ARRANGEMENT CONSIDERED

14 August. To: Albert Aurier: Art Editor, *Le Mercure de France*
I am in the process of organizing an exhibition of Vincent's work to be held at
Durand-Ruël. There I should like to distribute a catalogue with a short biography to be written by you. I also have in mind a later full biography, for
which I could furnish the material, which would be all the more authentic as
I have in my possession a nearly consecutive correspondence with him from
'73 onward. Contact me immediately. *Theo van Gogh*

15 AUGUST FROM PAUL DURAND-RUEL TO THEO VAN GOGH
REGRET IT IS IMPOSSIBLE TO ACCEDE TO YOUR REQUEST FOR SPACE IN
PARIS GALLERY

16 August. To: Mme. Agostina Segatori, Le Tambourin Café, Montmartre
This is to inform you that the Society of Artists first envisioned by my
brother, Vincent, is now a reality. Their first project will be a retrospective exhibition of Vincent van Gogh's paintings and drawings in Le Tambourin Café,
where he exhibited three years ago. Advise immediately dates available.
Theo van Gogh, Director

16 AUGUST FROM EDITOR MERCURE DE FRANCE TO THEO VAN GOGH
ALBERT AURIER AWAY ON ASSIGNMENT STOP IS NOT EXPECTED BACK
UNTIL OCTOBER

17 August. To Theo van Gogh. from Mme. Segatori Le Tambourin Café
You may be unaware that Vincent and I had a disagreement following his last
exhibit. Regret your present request for exhibition space cannot be arranged.
Suggest you contact gallery owned by Paul Durand-Ruël.

17 AUGUST TO PAUL GAUGUIN
WATERFORD INN PONT-AVEN BRITTANY
DEPARTURE TO TROPICS ASSURED STOP MONEY FOLLOWS STOP
THEO VAN GOGH DIRECTOR

18 August (By messenger) To Andries Bonger, 22 Place de la Concord, Apt. 3
Received telegram from Johanna saying she and baby will arrive today on
Netherlands Express. Wired her not to come, as I am busy arranging exhibitions for Vincent. If she missed my wire, will you meet her train, and send
her BACK? *Theo*

— · — · —

THE PERSONAL DIARY OF JOHANNA VAN GOGH-BONGER

18 August
    Andries is very angry with me. He came to warn me that the baby and I
are in danger—from Theo of all people! Poor grieving Theo. Dries showed
me a ridiculous note Theo had sent him today. Evidently my poor husband
had just found the wireless we sent him on the fifth, saying we'd be arriving
on that afternoon's Netherlands Express. He must have put it in his pocket
without opening it, just now discovered it. He's a little confused—but that
doesn't make him deranged. Haven't we all had the experience of suddenly
wondering what day it is?
    Andries just left, slamming the door behind him, saying he'll find a gendarme. He's convinced Theo is a dangerous madman—Theo, who just last
night put his arms around me and wept, begging me not to leave him, because he was afraid of the dark!

— · — · —

POLICE REPORT: 18 August 1890
District: MONTMARTRE. City: PARIS
    At approximately six in the evening was accosted by a gentleman who
identified himself as Andries Bonger, insurance agent. He informed me he
had reason to believe that his brother-in-law, one Theo van Gogh, was no

longer in command of his senses and posed a danger to his wife and child residing on the second floor of the apartment across the street. "Just as I was assuring Monsieur Bonger that I would keep watch for any sign of violence, we heard screams emanating from the van Gogh residence. The subject of our conversation had evidently walked quietly up the hill and slipped into the apartment while we were talking. We were forced to break down the front door to gain entrance.

The wife and her infant son had taken refuge in the bedroom, locking the door inside. Van Gogh was kicking the door in a rage, screaming, "Go back to Amsterdam! How many times must I tell you to leave—Vincent doesn't want you! Go back, BACK!" This screaming was accompanied by animal-like grunts and growls. Behind the bedroom door, we could hear the wife weeping, the baby crying. When Monsieur van Gogh had been overpowered, a conveyance was summoned from The Asylum for the Deranged. Madame van Gogh then unlocked the bedroom door.

Her arms were bruised, as was the baby's cheek. She declined to be seen by a physician.

— · — · —

THE PERSONAL DIARY OF JOHANNA VAN GOGH-BONGER

18 August
That was not my husband who was dragged down the stairs this evening, manacled and screaming, but some poor unfortunate poisoned by tainted absinthe. That was not my husband who attacked the baby and me, but a demented stranger, tortured by grief. I suppose I should be weeping. I have no tears left. I feel empty, as though someone had scooped out everything inside and left only this aching shell. I suppose I should be grateful to my brother for saving my life. What life? (This heat! No sleep tonight.)

21 August
Was it only three days ago that Theo was sent to The Asylum for the Deranged? I went there today. No visitors are allowed, but I did talk to the attendant at the front desk. He tells me Theo's manic stage is passing.

I think I myself would have gone mad if this had taken place before the French Revolution. Then the Asylum's inmates were kept chained in filthy dungeons. With its barred windows, the Asylum still looks like a prison. But its restraints are padded, the attendants seem to be kind.

22 August

The rent will be due in nine days. Without Theo's earnings, I will soon be destitute. Until the baby is weaned, I cannot even return to teaching. I hope I will not have to accept help from Father. I know it will be accompanied by much advice. (It's so hot—impossible to think clearly. Or to sleep.)

25 August

It is a steaming August evening. Not a breeze, but there is the smell of rain. The baby has just finished nursing and is lost in the deep sleep of the completely satisfied. A dribble of milk has trickled out of one corner of his mouth, and a tear still quivers on his cheek. There is a faint bruise on the other cheek, an echo of Theo's attack. My own arms are still black and blue. Andries stops by almost every day. Yet I still feel so alone. A tentative tapping on the roof—cooling rain at last! Perhaps now I can sleep.

26 August

A letter from the Asylum telling me that Theo is now sufficiently recovered to be transferred to a sanatorium or rest home. Although he is no longer violent, the staff feels his condition is unstable, and will release him "only to a *maison de santé* either here or in your native Holland." They will arrange transport with a medical escort.

It will have to be someplace in Holland—I can't afford to remain in Paris for very long. There's a place just outside Utrecht called The Haven. I'll ask Father to look into it for me. For the first time in days, I feel hopeful.

29 August 1890

Dear Johanna:

As per your request, I am enclosing a brochure from The Haven. I was impressed with the place. Dr. Jan van de Meer, the director, is a professor at Utrecht University. He *personally* showed me around. The Haven is strictly a *private* institution, accepting only the nonviolent mentally deranged.

Originally a hospital for consumptives in a peaceful parklike setting, were it not for the barred windows, the attractive stone buildings would appear to be like any ordinary rest home. The clientele is *all upper-class*. No expense is spared to make the residents feel at home.

Except for the bars on the windows and the padlocked French doors, each ward's common room is like a large, tastefully furnished drawing room. Each resident has his own private sleeping chamber, somewhat small—but pleasant. For the safety of the inmates, no bed chamber has a door. Instead, there is a locked door at each end of the sleeping corridor.

Visiting hours are every Saturday from two to five. Residents may walk in the gardens with their visitors. Treatment is modern, humane, and enlightened. The fees reflect the quality of the care.

Did you say that Theo's Uncle Cent had offered to pay for a private institution as long as necessary? How very gracious of him.

(Of course, that branch of the van Gogh family was always exceptionally prosperous, and they may feel some responsibility because they still have a part interest in Goupil's.)

Dr. van de Meer reports they do have a vacancy at the present time, but it *cannot* be held indefinitely. He suggests you promptly reserve it by sending in the first month's fee and instructing the Paris Asylum to arrange transfer of the patient and his records. I'm enclosing a cheque to cover the deposit and your current expenses.

I took the liberty of asking our firm's Paris representative to make inquiries at Theo's bank. He had a small account, but they say it cannot be accessed unless he is certified as incurably insane.

I had also contacted Goupil's to see if Theo had any commissions still owed to him. They claim not. Mother and Anna send their love and sympathy, as do I. *Father*

— ·· —

GOUPIL'S FINE ART GALLERIES
Paris　London　Brussels　The Hague　New York

3 September 1890
Dear Monsieur Joyant:

It is with great pleasure that we welcome you to the staff of the international House of Goupil. As manager of our showroom in Montmartre, considered the most prestigious of our five galleries, you will be selling lithographic reproductions of paintings by the most accomplished of the Salon prize winners (Bouguereau and Gérôme, for example) plus original oil paintings by popular genre painters such as Rosa Bonheur, famous for her charming portrayals of cows.

Fortunately for us, our former manager, Theo van Gogh, resigned due to ill health. We neither expect nor desire that he return to our employ. A madman of sorts like his brother, the painter, he accumulated appalling things by modern artists which have brought the firm discredit. He had turned the mezzanine of this reputable art establishment into a gallery for "moderns," few of whom had been trained at the Academy or admitted to the Salon Annuals.

You will find a certain number of pictures by a landscape painter, Claude Monet, who we understand is beginning to sell a little in America. (One can seldom account for the taste of our clients in a country like America.) All the rest are horrors. Much to our dismay, a recent inventory revealed the following: several Degas, paintings by Pissarro, Redon, Toulouse-Lautrec, Gauguin, and Seurat. Get rid of them as best you can.

Luckily, paintings by Theo van Gogh's brother, Vincent, were taken only on consignment. Selling those smears of paint would have been impossible at any price.

Looking forward to a long and rewarding association— *Adolphe Goupil*

—.—.—

JOHANNA VAN GOGH-BONGER
8 Cité Pigalle, Paris

4 September
Dearest Theo,

The attendant at the front desk promised to see you got this letter, but he couldn't promise you'd read it. How I hope you do! When the staff at the Asylum said you were well enough to be transferred to a place of our choosing, I tried to find a place where you could find rest and find yourself again. I had heard good things about The Haven in Utrecht. Father investigated for me, and was impressed with the parklike grounds, the pleasant decor, the caring staff. (But if it is not to your liking, let me know.)

The Asylum is providing two attendants to accompany you on the train tomorrow. Darling, don't be upset—they say you will need to wear shackles. But it's only for the journey. The atmosphere of The Haven is homelike, not at all like the Asylum.

I'll be returning to Holland in about a month. Saturdays are visiting days, so save every Saturday in October for your— *Johanna*

—.—.—

THE PERSONAL DIARY OF JOHANNA VAN GOGH-BONGER

6 September

Today a letter from Dr. Jan van de Meer, director of The Haven, informing me that Theo arrived safely on the fifth. After just one day, the good doctor solemnly announces that the diagnosis is profound melancholia and there is little hope for a quick recovery. Why in less than twenty-four hours has he come to that conclusion?

It appears Theo neither speaks nor responds to their attempts to communicate. "His physician read him an article about Vincent that had appeared in yesterday's *Amsterdammer,* and only at the sound of his brother's name did Theo show a flicker of attention." I don't expect his grief to ever totally dissipate, just become less overwhelming. It will take time and patience. I hope I haven't made a mistake selecting The Haven. Dr. van de Meer sounds impatient, even insensitive.

I must write Theo often, so he doesn't feel abandoned.

— · — · —

JOHANNA VAN GOGH-BONGER
8 Cité Pigalle, Paris

6 September
Theodoor van Gogh: C/o The Haven, Utrecht

My beloved husband,

What am I doing still in France, while you are miles away in Holland? Though visiting you was forbidden, and though I cried myself to sleep every one of the sixteen nights you were in that dreadful Asylum, at least we were both in Paris. I could put the baby in his carriage and walk the two miles to the park across the street from the Asylum, peer up and try to guess which barred window was yours. The baby—with a little help from his mother—would wave, first to the right, then to the left, hoping you would see us and be cheered, if only for a moment.

I shall not remain in Paris long. My darling, I long to be near you, if not with you. I must stay here at least until the plans for a Vincent retrospective are finalized. You'll be pleased to know that Bernard has offered to do everything he can to make it happen. Once that is taken care of, I can return to Holland, where I'll be able to visit you every single Saturday.

All my love, always . . . Jo

WATERFORD INN
Pont-Aven, Brittany

2 September 1890
Dear Émile,

Your letter telling me about Vincent's funeral was delayed, and I felt it was too late to write a letter of sympathy. I'm not good at that sort of thing anyhow. In desperation I now write you seeking information. Two weeks ago I received a telegram from Theo saying: "DEPARTURE TO TROPICS ASSURED STOP MONEY FOLLOWS." Overjoyed, I booked passage on the next available ship. I was somewhat surprised at Theo's sudden generosity, but simply presumed he had someone interested in the paintings I'd left at Goupil's. What has been happening to Theo? Not a franc, not a word, has been forthcoming. A wire I sent to Goupil's last week was returned marked "Undeliverable." The *Marguerita* sails next weekend, and I don't even know whether I'll be on it! Please telegraph immediately and let me know what happened. This waiting is unnerving. Counting on your discretion— *Gauguin*

WATERFORD INN
Pont-Aven, Brittany

11 September
Dear Émile,

Thanks for letting me know of Theo's collapse. Just heard from Pissarro that you are now busy trying to organize a posthumous exhibition of Vincent's work. What a blunder! You know how I like Vincent's art. And I've always considered him one of my dearest friends. But he's gone now, and we have to think of ourselves.

Considering the stupidity of the public, it's hardly the moment to recall Vincent and his madness at a time when his brother is in the same condition! Many people say that our painting is mad. Such an exhibit will do all the Independents harm without doing Vincent any good. Well, if you insist, I suppose I can't stop you. Just remember I warned you—such an exhibition will set modern art back many years. It's IDIOTIC. *Paul Gauguin*

ÉMILE BERNARD
Montmartre, Paris

13 September 1890
Dear Johanna,

I wish I had good news for you. With the possible exception of Gauguin, all the Independents were enthusiastic about arranging a posthumous exhibition of Vincent's work, but an appropriate space does not seem to be available. I have spent almost a month on the project, with no success. Finally, Signac, who is in the process of arranging the 1891 exhibition of the Independents, suggested we reserve a corner of the gallery for a "Memorial to Vincent van Gogh."

As I'm sure you are aware, the annual Independent exhibitions are financed by the group, with costs such as gallery rent, invitations, and the catalogue being divided among the exhibitors. Because Theo has done so much for all of us, the group is going to subsidize the costs of the Vincent Memorial.

We were all so glad to hear that Theo had improved sufficiently to be transferred to Holland. Give him my best when you write. *Émile*

—·—·—

THE PERSONAL DIARY OF JOHANNA VAN GOGH-BONGER

13 September

Now that a posthumous exhibit of Vincent's work appears unlikely, there's nothing to keep me in Paris. I shall wait till the end of September before giving our landlord notice, just to make certain that a quick recovery is truly an impossibility. (Sometimes miracles do happen!)

Father is right—I cannot afford this apartment. But before I can move, there is this mountain of paintings, drawings, and papers to sort through. Theo has his own collection acquired from the Impressionists he has been encouraging. Then there are the paintings by Vincent, not only hanging on every wall but hiding all over the apartment. And the drawings—hundreds of them! I cannot leave until everything is catalogued and stored somewhere. Right now it seems like an almost impossible task, but one that *must* be done.

When Theo recovers, his own collection and Vincent's paintings will be the first things he'll ask about. I've asked Juliette to come every day to help. Today we're counting paintings. I'm keeping a tally: "Six Vincents behind the sofa, three Impressionists under the bed," etc.

Later: Juliette just came in to tell me she has found more of Vincent's paintings in the linen closet; says that so far she has counted over 200. I never dreamt there were so many! I can't take them with me . . . Oh, Theo! whatever shall I do with them?

14 September

The post just arrived, and with it a letter from Mother van Gogh. "I just want to send you a little word," she begins as usual. She has enclosed a letter Theo had written to her immediately following Vincent's funeral.

That dear, remarkable woman! How could she have known that I have been feeling so guilty about not being there to comfort Theo when it happened? Over and over again, I keep asking myself, "What would have happened if I'd ignored Theo's request and returned immediately to Paris?" "What would have happened it he hadn't spent those five days alone in the apartment? If he hadn't drunk all that absinthe?" So many what-ifs! I cannot bear this waiting and wondering, this not seeing Theo.

Perhaps I should move to Utrecht, find a boardinghouse near The Haven. The sight of his son might lift Theo's spirits. I'll mention it to Father when I write tonight.

ANTON BONGER
Insurance: Marine and General
Herengracht 204, Amsterdam

16 September 1890
My dearest Johanna,

Mother and I have been discussing the plans you outlined in your letter of the 14th. It is understandable that the *tragic* events of the past month have made it difficult for our usually levelheaded daughter to think *clearly*. Much as it is against my nature to interfere with unrequested advice, in this case *I have no choice*—my dear daughter's welfare is at stake.

We can appreciate our girl's natural desire to move to Utrecht to be near Theo, but are absolutely certain it would be *most* unwise. I have taken the liberty of contacting Dr. van de Meer, and he assured me that at present Theo's melancholia is so *profound* that a visit from you and the baby would be *unlikely to help*. In addition, there is a real possibility of *total regression* to his previous excitable state, which could easily result in physical peril for you both! The doctors at The Haven have, in fact, been contemplating limiting all visitation while they try therapeutic hypnosis.

Johanna dear, you must trust the doctor's judgment. For the sake of the child, you must be *patient not foolhardy*, must follow your mind not your heart. What Mother and I propose is that you consider *closing* the apartment in Paris—*store* the furniture, *dispose of Vincent's paintings* for whatever you can get; if necessary, destroy them and return to Amsterdam. Mother and I rattle around in this four-story canal house that once held five children. Now only your sister Anna remains. You could have the top floor entirely to yourself, and would be welcome as long as you wish. Mother is already happily planning on redecorating it, turning it into a cozy apartment for our dear Johanna and her little one. This appears to us to be the only *sensible* thing to do.

I'm enclosing a cheque. Let me know if train fare and furniture storage require more. Until your arrival, we'll continue the weekly stipend agreed upon when Theo's illness left you without income. Of course, while you stay with us, there'll be *no* expenses for you to worry about. It will be our *joy* to provide our dear Johanna and our grandson with *everything* their hearts desire. After all you've been through, it's time you let your family shelter and care for you. Mother and Anna join me in urging you to come home. *Father*

—·—·—

ANDRIES BONGER
22 Place de la Concord, Paris

18 September 1890
Father—

I have just returned from visiting Johanna, and am greatly disturbed. My dear sister, who has borne her trials of the last month with dignity and forbearance, was totally distraught. The cause of her tears was your letter of 16 September. I assured her she may have misunderstood.

Your letter appears to insist that Johanna immediately close the apartment, put Theo's furniture in storage, sell all his paintings, and come live with you and Mother. From one point of view, this is an excellent plan. But there are two things implicit in it that make it very distressing for Johanna. One is the assumption that her husband will never recover. We don't know that—though most certainly he is very ill. The other is that Theo's collection of paintings, mostly done by his brother, are worthless, and also that his judgment as an art dealer is of no consequence.

Living in Paris as I do, where the new Impressionist painting is beginning to be appreciated, I can assure you that as an art dealer Johanna's husband was greatly respected. Also there is a good possibility that your evaluation of Theo's collection is quite without merit. However, debating these things would be a waste of our time, because for Johanna, Theo's art collection is as important a part of him as her child. She is emotionally incapable of following your advice to "get rid of the paintings for whatever you can get or if necessary, destroy them."

I agree with you that it would be most unwise for Johanna to move to Utrecht to be near Theo. Utrecht is only a short journey by train from Amsterdam. After we had talked it over, Johanna admitted she was not being sensible. I have assured Johanna of my financial support if she requires it, have offered to share my apartment with her—though I will confess the thought of a small baby in my Paris bachelor quarters is somewhat disconcerting. I truly think that the best place for Johanna *would* be with you, but this is a decision she must make for herself. Meanwhile, I am going to pay for the crating of Vincent's paintings, and think I can arrange with the paint dealer Tanguy to store them in his back room, as he has in the past. So that is where things stand now. By time we finished our talk, Johanna had recovered her composure. My love to Mother— *Andries*

— · — · —

JOHANNA VAN GOGH-BONGER
8 Cité Pigalle, Paris

1 October 1890
Dearest Mother van Gogh,

Almost two weeks have passed since I received your letter. First, I do want to tell you how helpful it was to see Theo's letter. That letter helped me understand, and accept, what happened upon my return.

I must keep reminding myself that the Theo who was my beloved husband for almost a year and a half was not the grief-stricken stranger who met me on my return to Paris. I could not survive if I did not believe that his breakdown is only temporary, a manifestation of grief that may never totally disappear but will in time become bearable. Since I cannot afford to keep the Paris apartment, I've accepted my parents' generous offer to live with them in Amsterdam. You'll be pleased to know that Theo's collection is being stored here in Paris at Père Tanguy's art supply store. Tanguy's tiny shop has become a meeting place for the Impressionists, a combination club and art gallery. (He always has one or two paintings in the shop's window.)

This morning the forty crates and ten portfolios that Andries ordered for me were delivered. I looked at them stacked all over the parlor and the dining room, and almost wept. Simply looking at the crates exhausted me. (Juliette and I had just finished packing all the china and silver.) And then the most wonderful thing happened! All the artists Theo had befriended and exhibited in his gallery's mezzanine came trooping up the stairs to help. It was Camille Pissarro's idea—he had posted this notice at Père Tanguy's:

> NOTICE: The packing and cataloguing of Theo's collection will be a monumental task for Johanna. If we all lend a hand, it could be done in a day, and would be an appropriate farewell gift to the wife of a friend and art dealer to whom we are all so deeply indebted.
> MEET AT THEO'S APARTMENT at 9 A.M. on OCTOBER FIRST

From under the beds and chests, from behind every sofa and settee, from the shelves and floor of every closet, the paintings emerged. It was so heartening to me to hear their exclamations of approval, their admiring comments. I was not allowed to do a single thing except list the contents of each crate and portfolio, and rock the baby. These were men who appreciated paintings, knew how to properly handle them.

I'm a little uneasy about the move to Amsterdam. Do write—your letters are always a comfort. Fondly, *Johanna*

— · — · —

THE PERSONAL DIARY OF JOHANNA VAN GOGH-BONGER

2 October

The crates were picked up yesterday. How empty the apartment seems! Just came across a draft of a letter which puzzles me—Theo asking Aurier to write a biography of Vincent, "which would be all the more authentic because I have in my possession a nearly consecutive correspondence with him from '73 onward."

After sharing its contents with me. Theo would slip any letter from Vincent into the top drawer of the drop-leaf desk. When I told Juliette to empty the drawers last week, she brought me piles of pen-and-ink sketches and a few pencil drawings, but I don't recall any letters—certainly not seventeen years of letters! Could it be that the drop-leaf was down and Juliette missed that top drawer? I must look . . .

Yes, I was right—hundreds and hundreds of letters from Vincent! They must be important if Theo saved them. And to think I almost left them as a feast for the mice in Andries's basement. There must be over 600 letters here. There's a small carpetbag I was saving for last-minute odds and ends. It should just hold them all.

3 October 1890

My last night in this apartment. Tomorrow, Andries, the baby, and I will be taking the Netherlands Express to Amsterdam. I sit here writing, feeling a little sad. There is something melancholy about an empty apartment, with moonlight streaming through curtainless windows. (I have a lot to learn about housekeeping. It's evident that Juliette never washed the panes behind the drapes—there is a film of dust on every pane beside the molding; those in the center sparkle.)

I'm surrounded by memories—the packed trunks waiting for tomorrow's journey, the carpetbag filled with Vincent's letters, the storage boxes marked CHINA and STERLING, all look like tombstones in a moonlit cemetery, while the furniture, shrouded with bleached linen dust covers, seem like ghosts.

At first, Father suggested disposing of Theo's art collection. How he managed I'll never know, but Andries changed Father's attitude completely. Paris or Amsterdam—anywhere we may decide to live after Theo recovers, his collection is waiting in Tanguy's storeroom, crated and catalogued, ready for shipment. As for our furniture—Andries is moving it, dust covers and all, to the basement of his apartment, where it can be safely stored until needed.

Like stubborn memories that linger on, Vincent's paintings have left their nails and dusty shadows behind. (Must remember to tell Juliette to remove the nails when she gives the apartment a final cleaning tomorrow.) Over the mantelpiece in the dining room, the rectangle where *The Potato Eaters* always hung. In the bedroom, the shadows of the three *Orchards in Bloom,* my favorites from those he sent us from Arles. In the nursery, the ghost of Vincent's *Almond Blossoms,* painted specially for his namesake. I'm taking it with us, so the little one can have that familiar patch of blue to soothe him. For myself, I am bringing one of the smaller sunflowers studies—a glorious chorus of yellows to cheer me.

I just realized that in an apartment with no curtains and carpet, every little sound becomes a trumpet call. In the next room I can hear the baby whimpering in his sleep, and in this one a cricket chirping in the empty fireplace. Outside, the wind in the chestnut leaves sounds like taffeta petticoats hurrying by. How strange it will seem tomorrow—a full circling as I bring my child to the home I knew as a child.

— · — · —

ANTON BONGER
Insurance: Marine and General
Herengracht 204, Amsterdam

2 October 1890
My dearest Johanna,

I hope this reaches you before you leave Paris, but I wanted you to know the time and thought your dear mother has expended into turning our top-floor apartment into a *cozy nest* for you and the baby. For the past week, our roof pulley has been busy hauling up furnishings.

Mother has borrowed a crib from our neighbor, Mrs. Knopf—the same one she borrowed last summer. She's also interviewed the sister of Mrs. Knopf's latest wet nurse, a healthy, clean country girl whom you may want to consider employing. (Mother and I cannot imagine that you still want to nurse the baby yourself!) You are not to worry about the minor cost. After all she's been through, our dear Johanna deserves some *free time* for relaxation and a few social pleasures. Amsterdam may not be Paris, but we do have our musicales and other cultural events. I have been looking forward to my daughter joining the discussions at the meetings of my Literary Society.

I had business in The Hague a fortnight ago, and thinking our girl might miss the art that always surrounded her in Paris, stopped by Goupil's branch in Holland. At Goupil's the *manager himself* waited on me, and explained that the newest things for children's rooms were inexpensive reproductions of genre paintings, a new type of art that *tells a story* or *illustrates a moral*, such as *Cocoa's Last Ration* and *Abandoned Innocence*.

I purchased four of them—one for every wall in the nursery. For your room, I bought a reproduction of one of Rosa Bonheur's charming pastorals, which I was assured are all the rage in Paris. Mother thought you should have your own bedroom. Should you decide to hire a wet nurse, she could sleep in the nursery—unless you prefer she come to the house four times a day for nursing?

We want you to feel this is your *very own* private apartment, to feel free to rearrange the pictures and furniture as you wish.

And do understand that the decision about a wet nurse is *entirely* yours to make. You may decide it's time to wean little Vincent. Eight months is not too young. The milk in Amsterdam is the *best* in Europe, so fresh even that so-called scientist Monsieur Pasteur wouldn't want to *boil* it. Mother, Anna, and I anticipate your homecoming with joy . . . *Father.*

— · — · —

THE HAVEN
A Hospital for the Nonviolent Insane
Utrecht, The Netherlands

2 October 1890
Dear Madame van Gogh-Bonger:

We regret to inform you that your husband's physicians feel it is not in his best interest to receive any communications from his family at the present time. We are therefore returning (unopened) your letters of the sixth, tenth, fifteenth, and twentieth.

As yet, his melancholia shows no sign of abating. However, we are hoping to achieve some progress shortly. One of our staff, Dr. R. J. Lavier, studied with Charcot in his famous clinic at Salpêtrière, and has designed a treatment plan for your husband that includes hypnotism.

While this treatment is underway, the patient cannot be permitted to receive any letters or visitors, and we must respectfully request your cooperation. Rest assured you will be immediately informed of any change in your husband's status.

Your servant, *Dr. Jan van de Meer,* Director

3 October

I had always considered myself a gentle, ladylike, nonviolent person, but I am so angry with Dr. Jan van de Meer, I find myself imagining the most savage revenge for what he has done. I picture him chained to the wall in the deepest, darkest dungeon of The Asylum for the Deranged. I wouldn't whip him—that would be too banal. What I would do is bring a cage full of starving rats into the dungeon and turn them loose.

His letter is a masterpiece. It isn't Dr. Jan van de Meer who has decided that my poor husband is to be denied "any communications from his family at the present time"—oh no! It is my "husband's physicians," a nameless, faceless group of heartless men, who know what's in the "best interests" of everybody. Then he "respectfully requests my cooperation." If I dare object, the implication is that I will be interfering with their "treatment plan."

Rats are too good for him—vipers would be better!

4

"I sometimes feel very angry with Theo for deserting me—"

THE NETHERLANDS EXPRESS
Fastest Route Between Paris and Amsterdam

4 October 1890

Dear Mother van Gogh,

(The porter has just brought some tea and stationery, and opened the little table.) Today is my birthday, but it's not a happy one. One-way journeys are always sad. Until Theo can accompany me, instead of Andries, I don't expect to return to Paris. But I have other reasons for being unhappy. Just before we left this morning I received a very upsetting letter from Utrecht.

After initially indicating that Theo's melancholia was incurable, The Haven is about to embark on a treatment plan that includes hypnosis. Ordinarily I'd be pleased that they had decided to try *something,* but the doctors have decided that all contacts, all letters and visits from the patient's family, cannot be permitted while he is undergoing treatment. I'm already sounding like Dr. Jan van de Meer, referring to Theo as "the patient"—it makes him seem less than human!

Vincent's Dr. Théophile Peyron used to do the same thing: "Regret to report the patient had another attack this morning. For the patient's protection, I shall have to padlock his studio." I suspect doctors do this to distance themselves from the poor souls they're supposed to be helping, to prove that the doctors themselves are quite sane.

Oh, Mother van Gogh, do write, and often. It looks like I'm going to need a lot of your "little words" to cheer me.

My love to you and Wilhelmina— *Johanna*

— · — · —

JOHANNA VAN GOGH-BONGER
C/o Anton Bonger, Herengracht 204, Amsterdam

7 October

Dear Andries,

We had no chance to talk alone before you returned to Paris, no chance for me to thank you for helping me cope. Father had hinted that he didn't think much of Vincent's art, but I never expected the tongue-lashing I received when I went to hang the *Sunflowers* and the *Almond Blossoms*. What would I have done without Andries, the diplomat? Andries—first solemnly agreeing that "Vincent's *Sunflowers* did not belong on the same wall with Rosa Bonheur's *Cows at Eventide.*" And then rummaging in the storage attic to find an easel for the *Sunflowers*. Father has "suggested" that I remove it whenever his friends come up to see my "cozy nest." I agreed. In return, he let me leave the *Almond Blossoms* above the baby's crib.

I just realized that I owe you another "thank you." My diplomatic brother led me to believe Father had paid for crating Theo's collection so it could be stored at Tanguy's. I now realize that Father never changed his belief that Vincent's paintings weren't worth saving. You paid for the crating, didn't you?

I know that getting along with Father is going to be difficult. With the baby to care for, I have no choice but to accept his invitation to live here, and if we are to live in harmony, I know I must learn to keep my opinions to myself—especially opinions about modern art!

I'm just realizing that Theo has taught me much about art—no, let me rather say, *he has taught me much about life.* When he recovers, I am hoping we can resume our life in France. How I loved it! Do write and tell me what's going on in Paris, so I won't feel so alone. The Salon should be opening soon. Tell me if the old men of the Academy are still having it all their way.

And please be sure to check the Independents' Exhibit—see that Vincent's work is well lit in their Memorial Corner. Once the ban on letters is lifted, Theo will want to hear about it. Your grateful sister, *Johanna*

— · — ·

ANDRIES BONGER
22 Place de la Concord, Paris

9 October 1890
Dear little sister who feels so alone,

Yes indeed, Johanna, the old men of the Academy are still having it all their own way. Went with Pissarro and Bernard to see this year's government-sponsored Salon—circus would be a better word for it. Pissarro says that more than 9,000 paintings were submitted. Close to 5,000 were accepted, hung as usual, frame to frame, from eye level to ceiling in the Academy's gigantic hall. Pictures in poor locations might be next to invisible, but at least they have the Salon stamp on the back. And for the bourgeoisie, this academic stamp of approval is their guarantee of "art." (Theo never submitted any of Vincent's paintings to the Salon jury because rejected pictures are returned indelibly stamped with "R" for *refusé,* rendering them almost unsalable.)

This year, as usual, gigantic historical paintings and illustrations of classic mythology were assured prize winners. And, as usual, history painting of a debased sort, scenes of brutality and terror purporting to illustrate episodes from Roman and Moorish history, were Salon sensations. Scenes of lust and debauchery are acceptable to the jurors as long as they take place in a long-ago, decadent era, and the nude body is sublime, as long as it's in a classical setting. There was one very fine picture by Raffaelli; Zorn had a picture of girls bathing at the beach; there was a *Birth of Christ* triptych by Uhde. Otherwise, we saw little of interest.

One hopeful new trend. Still lifes, animal pictures, and landscapes without historical significance are no longer being rejected as being "just studies." The Academy appears to have promptly imposed its own rules on the new art. Animals are invariably idealized—no painted dog has fleas, no cow has flies (especially Rosa Bonheur's). As for the techniques of painting, slick, highly polished paint surfaces remain the most desirable. The award-winning artist can paint every button on a soldier's tunic with "amazing" accuracy.

Perhaps this will help you understand Father's distaste for Vincent's paintings, or for any modern art. He's never seen anything like it, keeps comparing them in his mind's eye with the Dutch masters in The Hague and the black-and-white lithographs of Salon winners at Goupil's. Be tactful. I have faith in your fortitude. *Andries*

Afterthought: Vincent's Memorial Corner at the Independents' Annual glowed like a jewel! Did Dr. van de Meer say how long the ban on letters and visits might last?

11 October
Today, a letter from Andries that made me so homesick for my old life. A week ago I achieved the mature age of twenty-eight, yet Father still calls me "his girl" and expects me to say "Yes, dear Papa" every time he makes one of his little "suggestions."

I've watched with amazement when Mother and Anna flatter and cajole Father into doing what they want, but I find that kind of feminine trickery distasteful and cannot bring myself to do it. So when Father starts making fun of Vincent's *Sunflowers* or any modern art, I simply sit silently with clenched teeth, afraid to say anything for fear of contradicting him in a completely disrespectful manner.

I keep wanting to gossip with Anna, to giggle about "Papa's girls" like we used to—she always seems busy. I keep wanting to write Theo. Just realized they told me not to *send* him any letters, but they didn't say I couldn't *write* them!

—·—·—

JOHANNA VAN GOGH-BONGER
C/o Anton Bonger, Herengracht 204, Amsterdam

11 October 1890
My dearest husband,

I have decided to write you whenever I choose. I just won't *mail* anything until your treatment is completed. Talking to you this way is the only thing that can make our separation bearable.

How you would chuckle if you saw the "cozy" apartment that Mother has decorated for me. It's so very grand. So much velvet and plush, such an extravaganza of gold fringe and lace—and *the bric-a-brac!* Your son started crawling two months ago and getting into all sorts of mischief. Heaven help me when he starts walking—and climbing! I'm afraid all the charming figurines Mother bought for the curio shelves will need to be put away. I'll be grateful for the heavy drapes when it's chilly and gray, but right now, whenever there's a sunny day, I open them wide. Then our fourth-floor "apartment" fills with sunshine, well worth the climb.

At night, there's a gas lamp outside that competes with the moon. Sometimes, if the baby is asleep, I don't light the table lamp, but sit in the moonlight thinking of you, and missing you terribly. I can't wait till your doctors say I can visit.

Meanwhile, I'll write again soon. And again and again. What a packet you'll receive when the ban is lifted! Your impatient *Jo*

— · — · —

JOHANNA VAN GOGH-BONGER
C/o Anton Bonger, Herengracht 204, Amsterdam

17 October
Dearest Mother van Gogh,

Thanks for your encouraging letter. It cheered me during a difficult time. Before I arrived, Father and Mother had accepted invitations for me to teas and musicales. When I had to decline because I'm still nursing the baby, they were angry and disappointed. Father is furious because I refuse to consider a wet nurse—or weaning the baby to a bottle. But after almost losing our little one last summer, I simply cannot take the risk. (To be perfectly candid, I'm not unhappy about missing their teas and musicales. I much prefer a good book.)

My one consolation is the little one. He has an infectious laugh, seems completely unaware of the unhappiness and tension that surround him. Your grandson looks a little like Theo, the same reddish-blond hair and delicate features, except that while Theo is slender, all that mother's milk has made the little one quite plump. We'll try to visit you in Leiden—perhaps for St. Nicholas.

Give my love to Wilhelmina, and keep a big hug for yourself— *Johanna*

18 October

Almost two weeks since I moved to Amsterdam. Mother comes upstairs to play with the baby almost every morning, but for days on end, Father barely speaks to me. I've been trying to join the family downstairs for supper each evening, but if the little one is already asleep in his crib, I don't like waking him or leaving him. Father mutters about my becoming a recluse, but Anna, bless her, brings me up a tray.

The days may be lonely, but not the nights. The first evening alone in my "cozy nest," I opened the carpetbag, took out Vincent's letters. It was not Vincent I was seeking, but Theo—every word, every detail concerning Theo. Evening after evening I pore over the letters, searching for glimpses of my husband as he used to be, my only consolation after all the miserable days.

They say that in cases like his, there is often a sudden improvement after six months. Theo may not be home for St. Nicholas, but perhaps by January? Always the optimist, I'm counting the days.

ANTON BONGER
Insurance: Marine and General
Herengracht 204, Amsterdam

19 October 1890

Dear Andries,

We are all truly worried about Johanna, afraid she is becoming a recluse. She sits in her room every evening, looking over stacks of old letters she brought from Paris. Much as I dislike asking you to interfere, I feel you may be the only one who can help your sister come to her senses. (I did try to contact Theo, but the doctors at The Haven report he is still totally unresponsive.) Johanna has been behaving in an absolutely irrational manner ever since her arrival. We have done all we can to help our girl forget her worries, but she resists our every effort to cheer her.

Both Mother and Anna have been hurt and heartbroken because Johanna has forced them to abandon all their plans for introducing her to our friends. She was a maiden the last time she lived at home. Now naturally we want her to take her place in Amsterdam society as the charming young woman she has become.

Mother had accepted invitations to a round of teas and musicales, and I had hoped Johanna would join us at the next meeting of my Literary Society. But your sister has insisted on embarrassing the family by declining all invitations because she "must take care of her baby, be available for nursing as needed."

I have offered to hire a wet nurse: We have even suggested *allaitement* (mixing bottle feeding and nursing). Amsterdam is famous for its fresh milk, delivered daily directly from the dairy farms in the country. But Johanna is full of inane excuses. She prattles on about Pasteur discovering that animal milk contains diseases; about some French physician's claim that wet nurses could infect infants with syphilis (of all things!), using this nonsense as an excuse for selfishly refusing to consider anything but her own wishes. You'd think Mother had not managed to raise five healthy children using wet nurses and cow's milk.

After all Mother has done to make Johanna feel at home here, she does nothing whatever to show her gratitude. I hope you can convince your sister that Theo would not want to see Mother's life made miserable over some ridiculous whim concerning child rearing.

Try your best—we're counting on you. *Father*

— · — · —

The Personal Diary of Johanna van Gogh-Bonger

23 October

Today Father sent Anna up to have a "sisterly chat" with me. I know she doesn't dare tell him how she now feels, but she left in tears after I explained the "horrors" of wet nursing.

When I was studying in England, the newspapers and medical journals were full of letters from physicians deploring the trading of one baby's life for another. The immorality of it is sickening. A wet nurse's own child usually dies within a short time. Live-in wet nurses send their own children to "baby farms" where they seldom survive more than a few months. The mortality rate for these bottle-fed babies is horrendous. With Louis Pasteur's discoveries, we now know why.

___.___.___

JOHANNA VAN GOGH BONGER
C/o Anton Bonger, Herengracht 204, Amsterdam

30 October 1890
Theo, my darling—

I like to imagine bringing all these unmailed letters to you the first time I'm allowed to visit, and laughing and crying over them together.

Father keeps saying I am becoming a recluse. He's right. I spend my evenings going over Vincent's letters. You said you were hoping to publish them. If only you had kept them in order—most have no dates. Over six hundred of them! It will take months (perhaps years) to arrange them in chronological sequence. And they'll all need to be neatly copied. I'll never be able to do it alone.

Oh, Theo—if you knew how much I need you, how much I miss you, you'd leave that silent place you've gone to. I know it's a cool gray place where there are no memories, no pain. But, Theo, today your son pulled himself up by clinging to the edge of the sofa, and stood there unafraid. For all of a minute.

You've escaped from pain. But oh, my dearest one, you're missing so much joy. Your son's laughter is something special. Don't stay away too long.

Always your *Jo*

___.___.___

THE PERSONAL DIARY OF JOHANNA VAN GOGH-BONGER

7 November

I'm trembling so much I can barely write. Today I received a letter from Dr. van de Meer informing me he has encouraging news. When their attendant was serving fruit juice this morning, Theo looked at him and said quite firmly and clearly, "Back—go back to Amsterdam. How many times must I tell you to leave?"

Dr. van de Meer reports that since these are the first coherent words Theo has uttered since he arrived at The Haven two months ago, they feel quite encouraged. Encouraged! Didn't The Asylum for the Deranged give The Haven *any* details of Theo's breakdown?

The last time I heard those words, Theo was screaming them in a fury at the baby and me while he kicked and kicked at our locked bedroom door. Memory is an odd thing. Right now my heart is pounding, my whole body shaking, like some trembling animal cornered by mad dogs.

—·—·—

THE HAVEN
A Hospital for the Nonviolent Insane
Utrecht, The Netherlands

9 November 1890
Dear Mrs. van Gogh:

It is with deep regret I must inform you that your husband, Theodoor van Gogh, had a relapse yesterday, becoming totally disoriented and violent. For his own protection, we were forced to use physical restraints, in addition to sedation. Since The Haven is not equipped to handle manic patients, it was necessary to arrange for his transfer to the nearest public facility, The Utrecht Institute for the Insane. The director, Dr. Phineas Moll, requests you be informed of their "no visitors" policy. He also requests that your brother, Andries Bonger, make an appointment to provide The Institute with the patient's health history as soon as convenient.

Our office will be sending you a prorated refund for the month of November, from which the cost of the two attendants who escorted the patient to The Institute will be deducted. Your servant, *J. van de Meer*, Director

10 November

I have read Dr. van de Meer's letter over and over again, as though rereading it could change the horror. In Paris, it was easy for me to accept the idea of a Theo gone berserk, I knew what he'd just been through—the agony of losing his brother, the frustration of being unable to arrange posthumous exhibitions of Vincent's art. I could say to myself, "That is not my beloved husband, but a tormented stranger, out of his mind with grief."

But now—how can I possibly believe that my sensitive, gentle Theo could suddenly, inexplicably become a raving maniac, so dangerous to himself and others he must be locked away, even from those who love him. There must be some mistake. My Theo was so saddened by Vincent's death, he'd retreated into his own safe, silent world of grief. What nightmare could have caused him to come out screaming?

Anna, bless her, just came up with a decanter of port. It's late. I'm tired beyond belief. I have two choices—I can weep or I can sleep. I'm afraid if I start crying I'll never stop . . . better the wine.

—·—·—

ANTON BONGER
Insurance: Marine and General
Herengracht 204, Amsterdam

11 November 1890
The Utrecht Institute for the Insane
ATTENTION Dr. Phineas A. Moll, Director
Re: THEODOOR VAN GOGH

I am outraged by the cavalier way The Haven and The Utrecht Institute have conspired in the transfer of my son-in-law, Theo van Gogh. Why was neither my daughter nor myself consulted? Neither the van Goghs nor the Bongers are families without means. To commit my son-in-law to a *public* institution, with its mongrel mix of classes, just because Dr. van de Meer lacks the experience or knowledge required to handle an excitable patient, is no excuse. I insist you recommend a private hospital that could handle his case, or a competent private nurse. Let me hear from you immediately.

Yours, *Anton Bonger*

––·––·––

THE UTRECHT MEDICAL INSTITUTE FOR THE INSANE
Dr. Phineas A. Moll, Director

14 November
Dear Mr. Bonger,

In reply to yours of the 11th, re: your son-in-law, Theo van Gogh, I am enclosing the five-day summary prepared by the doctors in charge of his case. I think you'll find the answers to your concerns if you study it. You will note it's marked "Confidential." I trust you will not share it with anyone else.

Yours truly, *Dr. Phineas A. Moll*

Re: THEODOOR VAN GOGH. *Patient has no idea where he is. Speech is impeded; he becomes infuriated when not understood. He staggers, has difficulty walking. Face has a vacuous expression, with frequent tremors of eyelids, lips, and tongue. Pupils are uneven. In the five days since he was admitted, he required sedation three times, twice required seclusion in the isolation room, and twice tore off his clothes. He is an inaccessible, difficult, sometimes violent patient. His total condition is such that he is unfit for ordinary human contact or for private nursing. (Confidential 14/11/90.)*

––·––·––

THE UTRECHT MEDICAL INSTITUTE FOR THE INSANE
Interview with Andries Bonger re: Theodoor van Gogh, 17/11/90

We first reviewed the epileptic-type attacks experienced in recent years by patient's brother, an artist. There is evidence that this type of midlife mental disorder was not unknown in their mother's family. Vincent's attacks had continued for over two years. Bonger reports that between attacks, Vincent produced an amazing amount of paintings and drawings, all of superior quality.

Unlike Vincent, Theodoor's insanity manifested itself suddenly, with no sign of remission. Bonger, who had known both brothers well, observed that the two brothers' mental illnesses seemed to have nothing in common. (A fact I needed verified before I could confirm my initial evaluation.)

We then discussed the diagnosis which had appeared probable to me during the intake examination: paresis, the psychosis caused by widespread destruction of brain tissue occurring in cases of tertiary syphilis. Like most laymen, Mr. Bonger's knowledge of syphilis was fragmentary. He was aware of the primary stage when a painless chancre appears at the site of infection, and the secondary stage with a rash being the most common symptom. But was unaware of the noninfectious latent period which may last for years. You could see the relief on the gentleman's face when he realized that his sister must have married Theodoor during the latent period and that neither she nor her child could have been infected.

He then confessed that he knew both Vincent and Theo had contracted the disease from the same *maison de tolérance* in Belgium many years ago. Vincent had opted for the mercury treatment, while Theo, afraid of the time involved ("One night with Venus, a lifetime with Mercury"), had chosen the newer and quicker—but less effective—potassium chloride. I explained that the onset of paresis is usually insidious, but may be sudden or explosive following prolonged mental or physical stress, or an excess intake of alcohol. Mr. Bonger reported that all three of these had been present prior to Theodoor's mental collapse in Paris.

Finally, we discussed how much Mrs. van Gogh should be told. Her brother told me his sister is a well-educated, intelligent young woman who is deeply in love with her husband. He begged me to completely deceive her, saying she would see through a half-truth immediately. I added a line to the admissions report, stating that "Theodoor van Gogh's mental illness was caused by congenital disease, chronic ill health, overwork, and grief." Such a statement could also be used as cause on a death certificate.

Dr. Phineas A. Moll (Carbon of interview to A. Bonger)

JOHANNA VAN GOGH-BONGER
C/o Anton Bonger, Herengracht 204, Amsterdam

18 November
Director, The Utrecht Institute for the Insane

Dear Dr. Moll,

My brother, Andries Bonger, informs me that he met with you yesterday to provide you with a medical history of my husband. It's been ten days since my husband was committed. Do you feel you are now in a position to evaluate his condition and determine what kind of care would be best for him? Is there a private hospital that might be able to care for my husband, or a private nurse?

My brother was very impressed with your competence, and has suggested I follow your advice in this matter. It is extremely difficult for me to come to terms with the future, when it is so uncertain. Is it possible for you to give me a prognosis at this time? I would so appreciate it. *J. van Gogh-Bonger*

— . — . —

THE UTRECHT MEDICAL INSTITUTE FOR THE INSANE
Dr. Phineas A. Moll, Director

20 November 1890
Dear Mrs. van Gogh-Bonger:

In reply to yours of the 18th, the truth is I know of no private institutions that are equipped to take care of violent patients, or any nurse I could recommend. Around-the-clock attendants are a necessity, as are special facilities for the protection of the patients. For example, The Utrecht Institute has upholstered cribs available for patients having an epileptoid-type attack, and isolation rooms for patients who suddenly become manic. Specially trained physicians are available day and night. Your husband might not require such facilities now, but if the need should arise, we have the facilities and experts to care for him in a safe and humane way.

Your brother has indicated that you are a woman of education and intelligence. Therefore I shall be candid when replying to your request for a prognosis. First of all, I think you should be made aware of our diagnosis. Your husband's problems are both physical and mental. The body as well as the mind can accept only so much stress before irreversible damage occurs. It is with great regret that I must inform you that his chance of survival is very slim—a matter of months, not years. We will notify you if there is a chance of the family seeing him at the end. Sincerely, *Dr. Phineas A. Moll*

—·—·—

THE PERSONAL DIARY OF JOHANNA VAN GOGH-BONGER

22 November

"A matter of months, not years." Those words keep echoing, again and again, like church bells tolling the departed. "A matter of months . . . a matter of months . . . of months . . . months." And then what? I cannot imagine a life without Theo. My whole world revolved around him. I can no longer say, "How Theo will laugh when he hears the baby trying to talk" or "I must send Theo the article on Vincent's Memorial Corner." I must keep remembering— "A matter of months . . . only months."

23 November

For twenty-four hours I kept Dr. Moll's letter to myself, my own terrible secret. I knew that once I told the family, any illusions I had would dissolve. I could no longer daydream of receiving another letter: "Our deepest apologies—there was an error made—the prognosis given in our letter of the 20th was inaccurate—another file was substituted for Theo's—the clerk who was so careless has been dismissed." Father just destroyed my daydream. He asked me what was in the letter I received from The Utrecht Institute yesterday. I gave it to him to read. "A matter of months . . ."

25 November

I can no longer put off writing Mother van Gogh. "A matter of months, not years." But I can't bring myself to do it. She's close to seventy, is still in mourning for Vincent. Still? That was only four months ago! It may be cowardly, but what I will do is write Wilhelmina, ask her to tell Mother van Gogh at an appropriate time. The spoken word can be so much kinder and gentler than the written one.

27 November

Writing Theo, when I was not allowed to see him, kept him near me, kept me sane. Should I continue? It would only be a matter of months. If visitors are not allowed at The Utrecht Institute, I don't suppose letters are.

I know I'm refusing to face reality! Theo is in a place that has upholstered cribs, isolation rooms, and specially trained physicians available day and night. He is quite likely no longer able to read, let alone receive mail. The reality is I may never be able to bring him that packet of letters I've been saving for him. The little one is holding out his arms to me. I pick him up—but can't stop crying.

— · — · —

JOHANNA VAN GOGH-BONGER
C/o Anton Bonger, Herengracht 204, Amsterdam

12 December 1890
Dear Andries,

Father is furious at me—as usual. This time because of my absence at the family's St. Nicholas gathering. I'm told you suggested perhaps I did not want to burden everyone with my sorrow after hearing the bad news about Theo. It was more than that—my little one would have been the only child there without his father. I could never have joined in the laughter as the gifts were opened, the poems read. I could never have pretended surprise when Sinterklaas knocked.

Mother van Gogh hadn't seen her grandchild since he was born. Wilhelmina as well. We had a quiet St. Nicholas, just the four of us. We even laughed a lot. The baby was in one of his comical show-off moods, playing peekaboo, trying his best to walk. When I left for Leiden on the fifth, Father was away on business in The Hague. When I explained why I couldn't stay for the holiday, Mother said she understood—even asked if I needed money for train fare. Now Father is saying, "I cannot describe the embarrassment your absence caused your dear Mother. She is deeply hurt." I'm beginning to realize that putting his words in Mother's mouth is something Father does often. "Mother and I cannot imagine you would still want to nurse the baby yourself." "Mother is heartbroken because you declined all invitations." "Mother and I feel it our duty to insist on an engagement of several months."

Do you know I just realized I have never heard Father *discuss* anything with Mother. The only thing I can honestly say I know about her is that she never ever contradicts him. My wish, Andries, for the coming New Year— that I can finally get to know our mother! Help me if you can. *Jo*

— · — · —

THE PERSONAL DIARY OF JOHANNA VAN GOGH-BONGER

New Year's Eve

A new year—what will it bring? Not much happiness, I'm afraid. But Dr. Moll's candid prognosis has been a blessing in disguise. It gave me the opportunity to do some thinking about my future. Once Theo is gone, I wonder if it will be possible for me to continue living with my family. I almost wrote, "I wonder if it will be possible for me to continue living." But I know that is not an option. Theo is leaving me too many legacies. There is the baby to care for, and beside the child, Theo will be leaving me another task—the work of Vincent, to show it and let it be appreciated as much as possible. And yet another. Vincent's letters ought to be published. They're beautifully written, and will make a remarkable book. But not yet. Theo always said it would be an injustice to Vincent to create interest in his writing before the art to which he gave his life is fully appreciated.

Knowing how Father feels about Vincent's art, I don't see how I can continue to live at home while trying to arrange exhibitions of his paintings or publication of his letters. It's possible that once this Greek tragedy is finally concluded, Father's attitude may change. He may realize at last that I have a legacy I cannot disregard. How I hope so! If not, I must prepare to consider alternatives.

I will have to support myself, but must find some way without leaving my child in the care of others. One possibility is doing translations, another is running a boardinghouse. For the sake of the child's health, I'd like to bring him up in the country. It seems to me that all these new factories are making the air in Amsterdam unhealthy. Oh, Theo—so many decisions to make without you! Must stop now—the little one has just announced it's time for lunch.

20 January 1891

It's been two months since I received Dr. Moll's terrible prognosis: "a matter of months, not years." Father had dismissed it, saying he was not particularly impressed with Dr. Moll's competence. "Don't place too much faith in him, or you may well spend the rest of your life grieving for a husband who has not yet passed on."

Could it possibly be that Father was right? Could Theo possibly remain alive for a long, long while? Could his disease have been arrested, then slowly, very slowly, could his mind and body begin to heal? I had accepted that the end was near—but now I dare to hope.

25 January

I thought Dr. Moll had prepared me, but when the telegram arrived, I recall holding it and reading it over and over, as though it were written in hieroglyphics. Finally Father took it from me and read it aloud. From then on, everything is a blur. I don't remember anything except an interminable train ride with Anna, Mother, and Father. I have no recollection of how we got from the station to The Utrecht Institute—a rental carriage? I do remember an attendant escorting us down a long hall to what he called the "Family Room." We could hear faint screams coming from another area of the hospital.

In the "Family Room" the gas lamps had been dimmed. The bed was in the center so we could gather on both sides. I kept thinking it all looked like a stage set. Theo looked very pale and immaculate, as though he'd just stepped out of a bath, combed his hair, trimmed his beard, then donned a clean nightdress. I remember noticing that the pillow slip and bed linens appeared freshly ironed.

At first I thought we were too late. He did not seem to be breathing. Then he gave a sigh. That's when Mother van Gogh and Wilhelmina arrived. Mother van Gogh took me in her arms—Wilhelmina gave me a handkerchief. I hadn't realized I was crying. The attendant said, "Be careful what you say. We think that hearing is the last to go."

I bent over, kissed Theo on the forehead, then the cheek—then whispered in his ear. He gave another sigh. I smelled a faint whiff of urine. A minute or two later, the attendant said he was gone. It was almost midnight. Too late for the train. Father sent for a rental carriage.

The ride back seemed an eternity. I kept thinking, "That was not my husband lying motionless on those freshly ironed sheets, but a pale echo waiting to trail off into silence." I wondered about the faint screams we'd heard when we arrived.

— · — · —

THE UTRECHT MEDICAL INSTITUTE FOR THE INSANE
Dr. Phineas A. Moll, Director

PATIENT:	Theodoor van Gogh *Age:* 34	
23 January:	4 P.M.	Patient had a seizure, which was treated with difficulty
24 January:	2 P.M.	Another seizure, which did not respond to treatment
25 January:	9 A.M.	Now comatose: breathing irregular
	NOON	Still comatose: pulse difficult to detect
	4 P.M.	Telegrams sent to family. Wife and mother arrived in time
DECEASED:	11:50 P.M	25 January 1891
CAUSE OF DEATH:		Congenital disease exacerbated by chronic ill health, overwork, and grief.

Last Sunday, at the age of only thirty-four, and after the sudden culmination of a fatal disease, a Dutchman who had been the focus of the avant-garde art scene in Paris died. Theodoor van Gogh, who had for years managed the Goupil gallery in Paris, leaves behind an empty place in the world of art.

To the wide circle of militant French artists, the passing away of this courageous young man appears to be an irreparable loss. He, the art dealer, was in reality infinitely more artistic in his aspirations and actions than so many so-called artists with famous names, who in point of fact seek only to produce a marketable commodity, slavishly following the Academy's rules.

Van Gogh was very different. He was absolutely a man of convictions. The mezzanine of the gallery he managed on the Boulevard Montmartre was always assigned to work of the French Independents. Whoever visited Paris and wanted to see work done by Pissarro, Redon and Sisley, Signac and Seurat, or Monet and Degas, was forced to go to Theo Van Gogh. Those who had learned by experience not to go to the great department-store exhibitions of the Salon in order to see real art, found the newer, more eclectic art in the Goupil mezzanine.

There also one could occasionally see works by Theo's brother, Vincent, a little-known promising artist who predeceased him by six months. Of Vincent's work the art critic Aurier has written: "His color is unbelievably dazzling—the only painter I know who perceives the coloration of things with such intensity." With Theo gone, with no one to arrange reviews and exhibitions, Vincent's work is probably doomed to oblivion.

As for the other Independents Theo had encouraged and sponsored, the entire movement will probably be set back many years. Who is there who could continue his work with so much fortitude in the face of the Academy's criticism? Theodoor van Gogh's death means an irreparable loss for avant-garde art.

Jan Veth, Art Editor

27 January

Thanks to Dr. Moll's tactful wording of the death certificate, Theo's total mental collapse will not be a matter of public record. For myself, it's of no consequence, but when he's older it might matter to the little one.

I remember very little about the funeral this afternoon, except that it was raining—not a hard drenching downpour, but a gentle, steady patter. I remember Mother van Gogh holding the umbrella over both of us. Her dignity and courage set an example I could not but fail to follow. While I was burying a beloved husband, she, a widow of many years, was burying her second son. How I wish I knew the source of her courage! I remember waiting for Andries because the train from Paris was late. Everything else remains a blur.

30 January

I still feel dazed and numb, as though I were sleepwalking. Anna, bless her, has taken charge of the baby, brings him to me only for nursing. Father mutters about a wet nurse or a *kinder meid,* but Anna and Mother smile sweetly, and ignore him.

2 February

This morning we woke to a winter wonderland. Last night, a freezing rain—and now every tree and bush is outlined in ice. Today Anna insisted that we all needed fresh air. She bundled the little one into his carriage, wrapped in so many blankets he looked like an Egyptian mummy.

We had quite an outing—first to the rental bookstore to return a book, then to the laundry to pick up the dresses I'd taken to be dyed black. (The only black dress I have is the one Father bought me to wear to the funeral, and it's much too good for everyday wear.) On the way home we stopped at one of the outdoor kiosks, where we warmed ourselves with steaming-hot chocolate before returning.

3 February

Maybe it was our outing yesterday that did it, maybe it's the baby who has lately been in one of his playful moods, playing patty-cake and waving "bye-bye." I'm beginning to feel like myself again. But deep down, underneath it all, there is this emptiness, this pain. I never thought it would be like this. Doesn't it *ever* cease?

—.—.—

JOHANNA VAN GOGH-BONGER
C/o Anton Bonger, Herengracht 204, Amsterdam

4 February 1891
Dear Andries,

I hope you're not sad that you could not be reached in time to see Theo before he passed. He had been in a coma for two days, so it felt like saying goodbye to an almost empty shell. I've been in a daze all week, but now I'm beginning to consider the future.

If I had any doubts, I'm certain now that I can't live with the family much longer. Another terrible quarrel, this time over appropriate attire for a widow. Remember what I was wearing at the funeral? Father had sent Mother and Anna to Amsterdam's new department store to select a "suitable garment." They returned with that handsome bombazine dress lavishly trimmed with expensive black crepe, deemed proper for widows to wear during the year and a day of First Mourning. It fit perfectly, needed no alterations. When I glimpsed the bill, I was shocked. That dress cost more than my entire wardrobe!

I thanked Father for his generous gift, wore it to the funeral (after removing the padded bustle), then the next day took my own dresses to be dyed black. There seemed no point in putting them away. Custom dictates that a widow continue to wear black for Second Mourning, Half Mourning and Ordinary Mourning—a total of two and a half years. I did not see how I could afford an entire new wardrobe. (It's interesting that widowers are only required to wear black for three months.)

What a storm! Father is calling me ungrateful, cannot understand why I could not wear that costly bombazine dress while nursing and playing with the baby—not to mention changing his swaddling cloths! Father says Mother is wondering what her friends will think of her daughter wearing dyed dresses, like some pauper. (Mother actually says nothing.)

Why is it that everything I do, even something that seems eminently sensible, results in a family storm? I think Father has some secret dream of a docile daughter, a wet nurse at her side, fashionably dressed in crepe-trimmed bombazine, grieving the loss of her husband with the aid of smelling salts. You know that is not me!

There's something else that was been worrying me. Yesterday Father asked me where Vincent's paintings were stored. I pretended I didn't know exactly, replied, "Some art supply store where Vincent used to buy paints." Has he asked you? Why do I feel like I'm living on the edge of a volcano? How I miss my big brother! *Johanna*

— · — · —

ANTON BONGER
Insurance: Marine and General
Herengracht 204, Amsterdam

19 February 1891
Dear Andries:

Much as it is against my nature to interfere, I feel I must ask your assistance in helping Johanna accept her new circumstances. Wanting to give our girl some financial advice, I took the liberty of contacting our firm's Paris representative, instructed him to go to Tanguy's storeroom, inventory Theo's collection, and give me a professional appraisal. While Theo was alive, saving Vincent's paintings seemed not too unreasonable, especially since there were no storage fees. But now it is evident that Johanna simply cannot afford this type of sentimental gesture.

Our appraiser inventoried 204 paintings by Vincent, said their valuation was no more than ten guilders each—though he doubts if more than a few could be sold. Shipping them to Holland would cost more than they're worth! And where could she store them? The only sensible thing to do would be to destroy them. The wood in the stretchers, frames, and crates could be sold, providing Johanna with an immediate nest egg, perhaps a couple of thousand guilders.

Tanguy flatly refused to take the paintings out of their frames and off the stretchers without instructions from Johanna. And now Johanna stubbornly refuses to do it! Try to make her understand that a widow with her limited financial resources really has no alternative. *Father*

— · — · —

ANDRIES BONGER
22 Place de la Concord, Paris

20 February
Dear impractical little sister,

Are you sure you want to burden yourself with *all* Vincent's paintings? I would strongly suggest you keep the two dozen you like best for your own use, give a few to Père Tanguy, and then to provide yourself with a nest egg, take the wood from the remaining paintings and sell it.

With Theo gone, and no one to advise you on obtaining exhibition space, I really don't see how you will ever be able to build Vincent's reputation as an artist, though there is no doubt of his genius. Even Jan Veth said that without Theo, Vincent's work is probably doomed to oblivion. The paintings may never be worth more than a dozen guilders each, and with over 200 of them, finding storage space will always be a problem.

Think it over. Fondly, *Andries*

— · — · —

THE PERSONAL DIARY OF JOHANNA VAN GOGH-BONGER

20 February

When I refused to send Tanguy instructions to destroy Vincent's paintings, Father acted like he couldn't believe his ears! Asked how dare I question his judgment, especially after he had arranged for a professional appraiser to advise us.

"You foolish girl! The paintings are worthless, but selling the frames, stretchers, and crates would assure you a nest egg. Theo's savings account is a modest one—you'll soon need those extra guilders." I tried, but could not make Father understand that destroying Vincent's paintings would be like destroying the memory of Theo. No amount of money could persuade me.

22 February

Another dreary night. It's snowing, the wind is rattling the casement windows of our "cozy nest," while stray gusts slip through the cracks, shaking the drape's gilt fringe and making the gas lamp sputter. The baby fell asleep after nursing, oblivious to it all. On the desk in his study, Father has one of those new glass paperweights. When you shake it, a swirl of snow envelops the miniature house, trees, and people inside. That's how I feel right now, trapped in a never-ending storm inside a glass globe. I think Father would have accepted one of his sons defying him—but never a daughter. Well, this daughter has to find a way to escape being smothered in snow!

Until the baby is older, I can't teach, but I can cook. I could run a boardinghouse. At first, the housekeeping might leave something to be desired (some corners may be dusty), but the meals would be gourmet.

25 February

I ran into Mrs. Verkirk at the rental bookstore today. I recalled that last summer she had talked about vacationing at the Hotel Nieuw Bussum, where the ambience was delightful (lovely grounds) but the food left much to be desired. She said she knew of no boardinghouse in the village, said it could probably use one.

26 February

This afternoon I stopped by Mrs. Verkirk's to get more information. There are really two Bussums—the older country hamlet made up of Catholic tradesmen and farmers and the newer belt of villas called the "Spiegel," inhabited by Dutch Reformed commuters—most of them the wealthy of Amsterdam. As in many such towns-in-transition, the local notary has rental information. Do I dare write him? (There's not many guilders left in the Limoges cookie jar.) I guess it won't hurt just to inquire.

J. K. KLASSEN, Notary
Hotel Nieuw Bussum: Room 506

Dear Mrs. van Gogh-Bonger:
I know of only one villa for rent that might make a suitable boarding-house. Enclosed is a copy of the advertisement posted in the local town offices. Let me know when you and your brother would like to inspect it.

Your servant, *J. K. Klassen*

VILLA HELMA: Koningslaan 2-A
Designed initially to accommodate the original owner's married son and his family, Villa Helma is a charming smaller version of a large estate villa in Bussum's exclusive Spiegel section. Yellow brick with shuttered casement windows. Private garden.

GROUND FLOOR: (Unfurnished) Foyer with staircase. Small parlor. Spacious drawing room with dining area. Two glassed-in verandas. Large kitchen has sink with hand-pump and *kook kachel*. Ample cold cellars below.
SECOND FLOOR: Four bedrooms. Furnished with beds, chests, and armoires.
ATTIC: Servant's sleeping quarters furnished with cot and chest of drawers. Large dry and vermin-free space for furniture storage under the eaves.

———

ANDRIES BONGER
22 Place de la Concord, Paris

10 March 1891
Dear courageous little sister,
Villa Helma sounds like an excellent choice for a boardinghouse, small enough to be managed with two or three part-time servants. I'll be in Amsterdam on business next Friday, should be finished by noon. I could accompany you to inspect Villa Helma that afternoon. Should I write Mr. Klassen to arrange it? Let me know— *Andries*

J. K. KLASSEN: Notary
Hotel Nieuw Bussum: Room 506

15 March
Dear Mrs. van Gogh-Bonger:

I was pleased that you found *Villa Helma* to your liking, and suitable for your purposes. As we discussed, there is ample storage space in the cold cellar and the attic for your late husband's art collection.

Your brother's suggestion that the small ground-floor parlor could be turned into a bed-sitting room for yourself and the baby was a wise one. It will not only provide you with a private retreat, but also make the four bedrooms on the second floor available for boarders and guests. As a matter of fact, I may very well be your first applicant—the food at the Hotel Nieuw Bussum leaves much to be desired.

The painting and minor repairs agreed upon can be completed within a month, after execution of the lease. May I know your decision?

Your servant, *J. K. Klassen*

— · — · —

ANTON BONGER
Insurance: Marine and General
Herengracht 204, Amsterdam

16 March 1891
Dear Andries:

We have been doing all we can to comfort our Johanna in her hour of sorrow. Mother and I have told her she is free to remain with us as long as she wishes. Incredible as it may sound, Johanna, a penniless widow with a small baby, insists that she "prefers to be independent." "To give the child healthy fresh air," she is thinking of moving to Bussum—and to earn a living for both of them, she proposes to take in boarders. Our grandson being brought up in such an environment! Mother is in tears wondering how she can explain it to our friends.

Johanna knows nothing of household management. Her experience has been limited to a small apartment in Paris. How she expects to manage a villa, we do not know. It seems evident that the shock of Theo's passing has turned our usually sensible daughter into someone whose wild ideas can only end in disaster. She no longer pays the least attention to advice from me. Since she knew you as Theo's best friend, she may possibly equate a word from you with advice from a husband who is no longer here to guide her. Try your best— *Father*

—·—·—

ANDRIES BONGER
22 Place de la Concord, Paris

19 March
Dear determined little sister,

Are you certain you want to leave the security of our home in Amsterdam? With the baby so young, it may not be wise. Even with part-time servants, managing a villa will mean an enormous amount of work for you. I'll help you, of course, if you're *absolutely sure* this is what you want.

There are a few legal matters that must first be clarified: nothing complicated. It will take no more than a month to obtain the required papers for transferring Theo's bank account, his furniture, and his art collection. I can arrange to take a week's leave the middle of April. Shall we set April 18 as Moving Day? (To avoid a "scene" with Father, we can meet at the Amsterdam station.)

Unless you have second thoughts, and would like to put this off till the baby is older? Let me know— *Dries*

—·—·—

THE PERSONAL DIARY OF JOHANNA VAN GOGH-BONGER

21 March

I'll be moving to Bussum in less than a month! I couldn't have done it without Andries. I couldn't even have gone to inspect Villa Helma without him. Train travel is relatively new. Ladies seldom travel unescorted, women with infants almost never! (Father would have had apoplexy if Anna or Mother had offered to accompany me.) And I suspect Mr. Klassen would never have discussed the terms of the lease with an unescorted female.

27 March

Compared to our narrow canal house, the villa I've rented seems huge, although by Bussum standards, it's modest in size. How shall I manage? As Father keeps pointing out, I know little about housekeeping and nothing about gardening. *I shall simply have to learn.* My one concern is that with all the housekeeping worries, I must not neglect my most precious responsibility—my child. Or my second—somehow arranging for Vincent's work to be seen and appreciated as it should be.

2 April

Dries says he can spend a week helping me get settled. Then what? I wanted to be independent—but now that it's about to happen, I confess I'm terrified. Where does one find boarders? How does one arrange exhibitions for an unknown artist like Vincent? Whatever made me imagine I could make a living, let alone make Vincent famous? Oh, Theo, I need you so!

—·—·—

DE AMSTERDAMMER: WEEKBLAD VOOR NEDERLAND
From: *Johan Cohen Gosschalk,* Contributing Editor

9 April 1891
My dear Mrs. van Gogh-Bonger:

It was so gracious of you to take time to write and thank us for the Memoriam we recently published. Jan Veth received your letter just as he was leaving for Paris and requested I reply for him. I am also a contributor to this newspaper's Art Section and, like Veth, am an artist as well. When Jan Veth wrote, "With Theo gone, with no one to arrange reviews and exhibitions, Vincent's work is probably doomed to oblivion," he was obviously unaware of the devotion and determination of his widow. In response to your request, I would personally consider it a privilege to assist you.

It might be wise to forget for the moment exhibiting in Paris. In France, the ridicule and persecution of the Independents is now more intense than ever. It would be advisable to concentrate first on the Netherlands, contacting the few avant-garde galleries as well as the artists' associations. It may take a few years, but I am certain that eventually your brother-in-law's work will gain the recognition it deserves.

You mention that you will be moving to Bussum and opening a pension. Here is an opportunity to display as many of Vincent's paintings as you can, as a kind of small exhibition that gallery managers can come to see. Be sure to send me your address when you are settled. We often have occasion to recommend lodgings to colleagues with business here.

I had the privilege of meeting your late husband when he visited The Hague last summer. When we were discussing Vincent's work, he confided, "I put up with all sorts of things, cannot abandon Vincent no matter how difficult he is, because I think he may very well be a genius." I agree.

Don't hesitate to contact me when you're settled and ready to begin your quest for exhibition space. Sincerely, *J. C. Gosschalk*

—·—·—

THE PERSONAL DIARY OF JOHANNA VAN GOGH-BONGER

17 April: Amsterdam

A rainy, chilly April evening. Even the thought of that encouraging letter I received last week from one of the *Amsterdammer*'s editors is not enough to cheer me. If only Mother had been less lavish when she decorated this "cozy nest"! The dark velvet drapes, the matching plush upholstered sofa and chairs, the ornate gilt frames on the Goupil lithographs—all make this bleak April evening seem particularly depressing. My last night in the house of my childhood. I doubt I shall ever return. It saddens me to realize that the rift between Father and myself may very well be a permanent one. I have never seen him so angry!

Poor Mother and Anna are caught in the middle. Yesterday, when I was packing my trunk, they crept up the stairs like conspirators, carrying boxes of bed linens. "You'll need extra linens to furnish all those bedrooms," Mother whispered. "With all the children gone, we no longer use these. But don't mention it to Anton." I'm just beginning to realize that although Mother would never contradict Father, she listens to his tirades—then does as she wishes. I do hope there is some way she can come visit her grandchild once we're settled. And Anna—we've become so close! Right now I'm sure Father would never permit it.

Must stop now—the little one just decided he wants a midnight snack.

Later: I'd forgotten that today is our second wedding anniversary. What is left? I have Theo's furniture, Vincent's paintings, plus a small savings account of Theo's that will just about cover the cost of shipping it all. I have my husband's dreams, my husband's child—but no husband. Oh, Theo! I'm ashamed to admit I sometimes feel very angry with you for deserting me!

5

"—if only I had time to catch my breath!"

18 April 1891: MOVING DAY
Late afternoon: This place looks more like a furniture warehouse than a villa. Crates of furniture are now stacked all over the first floor—some opened, some not. Right now we'd be freezing if Mr. Klassen had not arranged for a shipment of anthracite and had fires going in every ground-floor *kachel.*

Mr. Klassen had met us at the station, key to Villa Helma in hand. At his side, two "locals"—a dairy farmer and his wife—both available for temporary employment. The entire shipment from Paris was waiting for us in the goods shed. Dries immediately hired the farmer and his wagon for transport and assistance in loading and unloading. I hired the farmer's wife to keep the baby out of mischief. (At fourteen months, he's a handful. I couldn't have managed to do a thing without Elly.)

So far we've managed to set up the baby's crib, the two beds in my bed-sitting room, the couch in the living room, the dining-room table, and a few chairs. But now we've a real problem. Elly made up the beds with the linens Mother gave me, but I can't find *any* of the blankets and quilts I left stored in Paris! I distinctly remember folding them neatly and packing them away in cedar chips, but in *what?* We may have to overnight at the Hotel Nieuw Bussum. We've already decided to treat ourselves to dinner there tonight. (The pantry is bare, the dishes and pots and pans are still in their boxes, and the hamper of sandwiches Mother provided has been empty since lunch.)

Later: Dries has just left for the station to meet Wilhelmina. "I'm afraid the years are finally catching up with me," Mother van Gogh had written. "So I'm sending Wilhelmina to give you the help that I cannot."

An hour later: The amazing Wilhelmina to the rescue! As soon as she arrives, she goes right to work, helping with furniture arrangement in my bed-sitting room. "My! This chest is so heavy you'd think it was made of English mahogany, not East Indies teak," comments Wil. (The two of us are trying to shove it into the space between the windows.) "Whatever have you got in it?" Of course! Quilts and blankets in every drawer. Mystery solved—tonight we'll sleep cozy-warm, lulled by the scent of cedar.

Evening: We are all so tired none of us feel like hotel dining. Elly informs us we can have *gebakken visch* with fried potatoes delivered hot from the fishmonger. Says if we want she can order it on her way home. We ask if she can pick up some bread at the bakery, coffee, tea, and a round of cheese at the grocer. She says she'll ask the fishmonger to add them to his delivery, then promises to be here early tomorrow in time to empty the chamber pots and relight the *kachels.*

Must stop—the little one wants his supper NOW. Bless Dries for uncrating the rocking chair before anything else.

19 April: MOVING DAY + ONE

At dawn today, the morning birds woke me—trills, twitters, and chirps interwoven with bits of melody in high C. I was startled. In the city, all one ever hears is an occasional pigeon. I swear I heard one bird that kept singing Theee-O! over and over and over. I knew then Theo wanted to hear from me. It's been almost three months since I last wrote. Why did I stop writing? We've been so close I can't believe he wouldn't hear me now. "Else what's a heaven for?"

Dearest one, writing you and sharing my thoughts with you was all that made the previous six months bearable. Can you think of any reason I must stop now? I've so much to tell you. Did you ever visit Bussum? It's a sleepy country hamlet twenty-two kilometers from Amsterdam which the railroad has been transforming into a rich commuters' settlement.

You'd like Villa Helma. The glassed-in verandas make it appear larger than it is. I intend to furnish them in an East Indies theme, with wicker furniture, straw matting on the floor, and lots and lots of house plants—cyclamen, geraniums, begonias, and hanging ferns everywhere. Our own furniture fits nicely in the small bed-sitting room and large living-dining room downstairs. Fortunately the upstairs bedrooms were let furnished. I only need to buy a *kapstok* for umbrellas and coats in the hall.

Just a small hedge and a low wrought-iron fence separate Villa Helma from the sidewalk along the Koningslaan. At first I wondered about privacy, but only the kitchen and entry hall overlook the street. My bedroom and the living-dining room look out on the verandas facing the gardens. We have the most marvelous flowering trees and bushes. I noticed a morello cherry. If it bears fruit this summer, I'll put up lots of the cherry compote you used to love. I saw some rose bushes also. But oh, Theo, no lilacs! (Perhaps it's just as well.)

The little one is babbling and sucking his thumb. Time for his breakfast. I'm still nursing him—but have also been giving him a little pea soup, strained vegetables, and mashed potatoes from the table. You should see your son now. This is no quiet, contemplative child, but a bundle of energy. He's into everything! I'll write again, my darling, tomorrow. It feels so good to once again share my thoughts with you.

20 April: MOVING DAY + TWO
Dear Theo,

I heard the Theo bird again this morning, so I know you are waiting to hear from me. Dries discovered why the uncrating of our furniture was taking so long. Our frugal farmer-helper had been taking each crate apart, carefully removing all the nails, then chopping it into small pieces so that we could use the wood for kindling. When Henk arrived today, Dries asked him to *first* empty all the crates, and *then* prepare them for kindling. In no time we had the Persian carpets laid down and the rest of the furniture in place. The empty crates were banished to the south veranda, where Henk could dismantle them. We can hear him whistling now as he attacks each one with hammer, saw, and ax.

We set up the kitchen next. There is now a forest of iron pots and pans hanging above the *kook kachel*. Later, while the little one napped, Elly and I went to the grocer to provision the pantry and cold cellar—then to the bakery to arrange for the daily order, which Elly can pick up each morning on her way here. And finally to the butcher and fishmonger to leave orders for next week's deliveries. Dries had opened a bank account for me, but I was worried because I had a limited amount of cash. Elly assured me each merchant would be pleased to let me charge everything.

Theo, I must confess that yesterday I was wondering how I would possibly manage without you. Today I don't feel quite so overwhelmed.

21 April: MOVING DAY + THREE
(The Theo bird calling again!) Dear Theo,

Finally Villa Helma is beginning to look like a home. Today we hung the curtains and drapes (I was worried about drafts on these chill April nights.) Also added typical Dutch finishing touches. The glass doors of the corner cupboard now reveal some of our treasured wedding gifts—the Limoges jars, the Delft and Dresden bowls, the hand-painted Oriental platter. In the dining room, we covered the table with an Oriental rug, and laid a small one on the tea table in my bed-sitting room.

Later: Tomorrow we've arranged for delivery of the crates of paintings—the last things still waiting in the goods shed. (It will seem strange hanging paintings without you to advise me.) I said no to decorated tiles or wallpaper, had the walls whitewashed to set off Vincent's brilliant colors. Theo, my beloved, once your treasured collection is hung, I won't ever again be lonely. You'll be there always, all around me.

— · — · —

ALETTA VONDEL-DIRKS
Villa Zundert, Koningslaan 11, Bussum

22 April 1891
Dear Jo-Jo,

Are you surprised to hear from me—your chatterbox school chum from so many years ago? We're neighbors! I live just down the road from you. How did I know you'd moved here? Dearest Jo, this is a very small town. The farmer Andries hired to move your furniture delivers milk to us each morning. And his wife, Elly, helps my Selma in the kitchen when we have company. (She'll deliver this letter to you.)

Oh, Jo-Jo—we still have so much in common. Did you know I married an artist? Hans specializes in portraits, is very successful (he's been called a modern Frans Hals), has almost more commissions than he can handle. Well! Before we start catching up on the years that have passed since our school days, I want to help you to get settled.

I understand you're turning Villa Helma into a boardinghouse. (I think you'd better call it a pension—that sounds classier.) You should have no difficulty finding boarders. I can think of at least two possibilities—Mr. Klassen, the notary (who you already know), and Mr. Wijnberg, the pharmacist, both of them bachelors. They've been complaining about the food at the Hotel Nieuw Bussum.

Because you're still in First Mourning, I guess I can't introduce you to the community by having a tea or any kind of social "do" for you. But if you can manage to come to church this Sunday, I'll introduce you around. I hope you have something to wear other than the dyed black dresses Elly told me you were wearing around the house. Something in bombazine or even zibelline? A good impression is important.

And don't be shy about mentioning that you're turning Villa Helma into a pension. After church, I want you all to come to Villa Zundert for lunch. I'll invite along anyone who seems interested in learning more about your facilities.

(You haven't hung any avant-garde *Parisienne* art in the drawing room or dining room, have you? Bussum is such a conservative town.)

Some refreshments after church. I think this would all be quite proper, don't you? And do bring your baby. Elly says he is a darling. I have a two-year-old myself. Dear Jo-Jo—can't wait to see you again! I'll send our carriage around at nine on Sunday to bring you to church. (Elly mentioned you didn't have one yet.)

I've put on a few pounds since school days. Marriage agrees with me, and Hans likes his ladies plump.

Underneath the avoirdupois is your loving school chum— *Letti*

24 April 1891
Dear Anna,

Let me know if receiving mail from me causes you difficulties with Father. I know you can't visit, but has Father also forbidden *all* communication?

Dries leaves Thursday. Wil is leaving the end of the month. But before you start feeling sorry for me, let me tell you who I learned also lives in Bussum. Remember my school chum Aletta Dirks? "Talk-talk Letti" we used to call her. She lives just a kilometer away on the Koningslaan. I heard from her three days after we'd moved in. She's still the same Letti, very generous, somewhat conventional, a little bossy, and underneath the chatter, a caring person.

The first Sunday after we'd moved in, Letti insisted I come to church with her and get introduced to the villa community. Before I knew it, I had two boarders—possibly a third. And now with Letti here, I also have a friend and confidante.

I hate to see Dries leave. I don't know what I would have done without him. We both never want to see another crate again!

Share this letter with Mother. How I miss you both! *Johanna*

—·—·—

25 April
Dear Émile,

Tell Père Tanguy that the paintings arrived here without a mishap. One of the *Amsterdammer*'s art editors advised Johanna to turn Villa Helma into a gallery for Vincent's art. We've just finished hanging as many of his paintings as we could. For her bed-sitting room, Jo wanted the three *Orchards in Bloom* painted in Arles, and above the baby's crib, the *Almond Blossoms*. Even though

I see little chance of success for Johanna's hope of making Vincent's art well known, I advised against storing the remaining paintings in the cold cellar because of the damp. So we lugged the crates up to the attic, and my back has been regretting it ever since.

Before I leave here, I want to inquire among the locals and arrange for household help for Jo. She already has two boarders starting the first of May. She has hired a part-time *femme de ménage,* but also needs a laundress and a gardener. Jo insists she can't afford a cook, but can manage herself. I'm just beginning to realize what a remarkable young woman my little sister has become. One cannot help admiring her courage.

I need to spend a day or two with my family in Amsterdam before returning to Paris. See you after that— *Andries*

———

THE PERSONAL DIARY OF JOHANNA VAN GOGH-BONGER

28 April

Theo, my dear— Not expecting any mail, I was surprised to find two letters in my box today. One from Bussum's burgomeister, Jonkheer Reinier van Suchtelen van de Haare. (I didn't make it up, that's his real name!) He sounds like a bore—very conservative, and proud of it, a caricature of minor Dutch nobility. I understand he's distantly related to the Queen. I'm told Jonkheer Reinier van Suchtelen van de Haare never lets anyone forget that fact! He welcomed me to Bussum and urged me to become involved in Bussum's Society for Beautification. (As though I had time!)

The other letter is from the pastor of our church. He's coming to tea today to ask a favor of me. *What* I don't know. But he ended with a quotation about "he who giveth being twice blessed."

Reverend B. C. Andresen
Dutch Reformed Church of Bussum

27 April 1891

Dear Mrs. van Gogh-Bonger,

I was delighted to see you at services last Sunday, and to be able to welcome you to the Dutch Reformed community in Bussum. As you undoubtedly are aware, until the recent development of the belt of villas Bussum was predominantly Catholic.

Naturally, we keep very much to ourselves. Like the Catholics, we have our own state-supported schools, and I was recently responsible for hiring a Miss Margaretta Koster to teach weaving and needlework in our newly opened girl's school. She arrives the fourth of May. Having interviewed her, I can personally assure you of her high moral character and respectability. I do *not* approve of unaccompanied single women lodging even for one night in a hotel. Would you accept her as one of your boarders without the usual interview? May I visit you at teatime tomorrow to discuss this, and one other matter too complicated to put in writing?

"He who receiveth is blessed; he who giveth, twice blessed."

Rev. B. C. Andresen

— · — · —

Villa Helma
A Boardinghouse for Gentlemen and Ladies
Koningslaan 2-A, Bussum

29 April

Dear Anna (Still no letter from you),

Wilhelmina leaves tomorrow. How I shall miss her! She is one of those quiet, efficient people who do everything without fuss.

Our boarders will be here in three days. Wil and I have been working from morning till night. The house sparkles with furniture wax, smells of fresh linen and flowers. In the upstairs bedrooms the beds are made, the armoires aired out and polished. In the downstairs hall, the shiny new *kapstok* stands ready to receive coats and umbrellas. Yesterday I initiated the *kook kachel* (I call it my black monster), baked two pound cakes and a raisin-and-currant *tulband,* and started a pot of soup stock. So I've desserts for the first two days, soup stock for a week. How I wish I could invite you and Mother to come for dinner! (The little one needs me; must stop for now.)

Later: Letti came by with her carriage and insisted Wil and I needed a day off, an outing in the country. She'd had her cook make a hamper of sandwiches for lunch, and off we went—three women, two babies, Letti's coachman, and a pair of bays. Our destination was the annual country fair in Laren, a town to the southeast. The motion of the carriage had rocked both babies to sleep before we went a kilometer.

It was one of those magical days in late April when the sky seems endless, the clouds pile high, the elms and the lindens wear their tenderest green, and the fruit trees are just beginning to blossom. We passed through Gooiland, a region of lakes and woods whose scenic beauty is beginning to attract the rich of Amsterdam. We felt rich too as we ate our picnic lunch beside a sapphire lake ringed with birches. The country air had made us ravenous. When we reached Laren we feasted again on hot chestnuts and spicy cakes.

The babies were enchanted by the organ grinder imported from Amsterdam. They were so funny—two tots who could barely walk themselves, bouncing up and down, trying to dance. Oh, Anna, how you and Mother would have laughed watching them!

Letti had a special surprise in store for me. There's a small art colony in Laren. In a corner of the fair, an exhibition of landscape paintings by Dutch Impressionists—the "Amsterdam School." And another group of artists known as the "Luministen." We chatted with a few of them. Most knew Theo—had visited his gallery in Paris, and one or two had heard of Vincent's work. It was good to be discussing modern art again, good to leave housekeeping worries behind for this one day.

How I wish I could afford a live-in maid! I can't get a thing done except when the baby naps. He climbs, and gets into all sorts of mischief! Maybe next year. Please do write if you can. (Has Father forbidden *all* communication?)

Missing you— *Jo*

ALETTA VONDEL-DIRKS
Villa Zundert, Koningslaan 11, Bussum

30 April 1891

Dear Jo-Jo,

Wasn't the Laren country fair wonderful? If I may say so, both our babies were absolute angels. Clap your hands and say "organ grinder" to my little one now and he starts dancing around!

Elly (who will bring you this letter) reports the only way you manage the baby plus the house is to never take a minute to sit down. That simply won't do! I'm truly cross with you, Jo. Reverend Andresen came by for tea today—as a matter of fact, he just left—and was very upset because he still hasn't found a home for the orphan girl Christina. He says you refused to consider his suggestion that you take her in as a live-in maid because you insisted you couldn't afford it.

My dear idealistic Jo—when will you accept the facts of life in the Netherlands in the Year of Our Lord 1891? Christina is fourteen, but her father sent her to work in a factory in Amsterdam when she was ten. When he died, she was sent to her grandparents to help out at their farm on the outskirts of Bussum. The grandparents died last month in a fire that destroyed everything. So now this good Christian girl is left alone with nothing and no one to turn to. She has an uncle in Amsterdam, but Reverend Andresen says he fears the uncle will send her out to earn money as a prostitute. And you dare to tell him that if you took her in, it would be "slavery"!

You need a "live-in" to do the early-morning chores before Elly arrives— bring fuel from the coal shed, get the kitchen *kachel* started, empty the chamber pots, wash the baby's swaddling cloths, wash the breakfast dishes, and a few other small chores. Christina needs a place to sleep and three meals a day. If it will make you feel better, you can give her a couple of guilders a month for pocket money and bring her to church with you on Sundays. Johanna, if you are not to work yourself to death, you must have some live-in help. Next time I see Elly I want to hear that Tina is in the attic bedroom and that you have apologized to Reverend Andresen. Oh, Jo—slavery indeed! You lived in France too long. Please forgive me for being bossy. *Letti*

2 May

Dear Theo— I can see that the protected life I led while growing up leaves me with a lot to learn about the problems of the poor. I still feel guilty expecting a child of fourteen to work for her room and board, but sending her into a life of prostitution with her uncle in Amsterdam is a horrendous alternative.

Rev. Andresen said he told Christina to consider his wife and himself her godparents. I am to feel free to consult them should any problems occur. I am to be assured that "He who giveth to the unfortunate will receiveth tenfold in the hereafter." That's nice, but all I want in the here and now is a little help with the baby and some of the household chores.

3 May

Dear Theo— Today my first two boarders moved in (Margaretta Koster arrives tomorrow) and I realized I didn't have enough quilts and blankets. Just as I'm resigned to ordering some from de Sinkel's. Henk's horse and wagon comes clanking up the Koningslaan with a delivery from the station. Your mother had emptied her blanket chests for me! "Now that the children are gone, I don't need all these," she wrote.

Now I can afford to furnish the verandas this summer, instead of waiting till next!

4 May

Theo, my darling— If only you could see me now, you'd be so proud of me. It's one thing to cook dinner for your husband and a few friends. If you burn the peas, the worst that can happen is that your husband will laugh and tease you unmercifully. Today was the first meal I cooked for all three boarders. Miss Margaretta Koster, the teacher, arrived this afternoon. She is one of those *very* pale blondes—one needs to look twice to be certain she has any eyebrows or eyelashes. She has a pale personality as well, is very shy. She doesn't talk, she stutters. On the other hand, Jan Klassen, the notary, is quite self-assured—a dandy with neatly trimmed, waxed mustache and pince-nez glasses. The pharmacist, Jeremiah Wijnberg, is a typical Semite—mournful dark eyes and a hesitant way of speaking. Maybe it's his flourishing beard, the words seem to have difficulty finding their way out of that dark tangle.

I discussed dietary needs with Mr. Wijnberg before he moved in. He assured me he did not "keep kosher" (I'm not sure exactly what that is) but requested I substitute "a little cheese or leftover fish, if it isn't too much trouble," when serving the others pork sausage or ham.

The fishmonger sent word he had some extra-large fresh pike—so that's what I served tonight. Vegetable soup followed by grilled pike, garnished with stewed onions and boiled potatoes. For a salad, finely cut cooked beets, with chopped apples and raisins. For dessert, egg custard sprinkled with cinnamon.

I let the baby join us this one time. Your son is a little piglet. He stuffed his cheeks so full of mashed fish and potato he couldn't swallow. And half the egg custard ended on his chin. Margaretta Koster was laughing so hard her cheeks turned pink and she forgot to stutter, while Mr. Klassen let the baby play with his glasses and tweak his waxed mustache.

Jeremiah Wijnberg whispered to me he had the perfect potion for pediatric tummy aches. (It has just occurred to me, it's going to be very convenient having a pharmacist in the house. The nearest doctor is in Hilversum.)

10 May

Today a letter from Johan Cohen Gosschalk in response to my note of last week. He says Villa Helma sounds delightful and he will not forget his offer to recommend my transient guest room to colleagues visiting from other countries.

"A great inducement for many will be a landlady who is fluent in English and French. Like most Dutch girls, I imagine you are able to speak German as well."

It will help me so much financially to keep that fourth guest room frequently occupied. I had felt hesitant about writing him, was afraid he wouldn't remember me. Wonder what he looks like—he sounds so nice.

VILLA HELMA
A Boardinghouse for Gentlemen and Ladies
Koningslaan 2-A, Bussum

14 May 1891

Dearest Mother van Gogh and Wilhelmina,

This is the first chance I've had in two weeks to sit down, let alone sit down and write. Between the baby and the boardinghouse, I've been busy from morning until night. But now, thanks to Tina, an orphan girl I've taken in, things are becoming a bit easier. At first I was extremely reluctant, feeling I would be taking advantage of her misfortune, but when her alternatives were explained to me, I relented.

Tina has only been trained to work in a mill and help on her grandparents' farm, so needs a great deal of instruction and supervision. But she's a willing, cheerful girl, and adores the baby, and I'm now glad I was persuaded. By next year, I should be able to pay her a little more than pocket money.

Right now I'm trying to figure out what to do with the milk my boarders ask for with their morning tea. Henk, who delivers milk daily, ladles it out from his open can into whatever container I provide. He assures me it's safe if you boil it. "Bring it to a boil three times, store it in the cold cellar for no more than one day in the container in which it was boiled." The baby appears ready to be weaned, and I wonder if he could drink boiled cow's milk. Elly tells me the odd taste can be disguised by chocolate or anise. Also, please send me your recipe for porridge. I caught my little devil trying to eat peat from the begonia pots on the veranda! Love to you both— *Johanna*

— · — · —

THE PERSONAL DIARY OF JOHANNA VAN GOGH-BONGER

5 June

Dearest Theo— It's been a while since I had time to write. These past weeks cost me such an immense effort learning the most ordinary household duties, I could think of little else. Though housekeeping and child care ab-

145

sorbed almost all my thoughts, that doesn't mean I haven't thought about you and missed you every single day.

Right now I'm envying you your childhood in the Brabant countryside! How I wish you were here to consult with Piet, our gardener. Being a city girl has its disadvantages. I solemnly nod whenever he comes into the house to explain what he's doing, to ask me to approve his plan for trimming the hedges, or to request that I order a load of cow manure (phew!) I respond, "That sounds like an excellent idea"—though I haven't the faintest idea if it is.

I manage quite a household: Elly is our part-time *femme de ménage;* Tina is our part-time *kinder meid* chore girl, and scullery maid; Maria is our one-day-a-week laundress; Piet, the one-day-a-week gardener—while I'm the seven-day-a-week cook and mother. I try to keep every morning free for the little one, who wakes up ready for mischief. I just realized I never call the baby Vincent. He's such a happy child, the name doesn't seem to fit. Have to go now, Theo. Right now, your son is happily trying to reach the dinner gong by climbing on the *kapstok!*

13 June

Oh, Theo, I never dreamt household management would be so difficult! Every day seems to bring another crisis.

Yesterday was wash day. As usual, Maria stripped the beds for the weekly laundering, then looked out the window and asked if I *really* wanted the bed linens hung outside today. I snapped, "Of course!" The sun was shining—just one small cloud on the horizon. I love the smell of sun-dried sheets. Only when it's raining do we hang them in the attic or on the veranda.

Next time when one of the locals asks what sounds like a foolish question, I'll pay attention. Five minutes after the sheets were on the garden clothesline, it began to pour. Five hours later it was still raining, and I was close to tears. Without my asking, Elly, who had been helping me prepare dinner, ran over to Letti's house and returned with borrowed linens.

I'm ordering extra linens from de Sinkel's tomorrow. (I'll have to charge them—my bank account is low.) How could I have been so foolish? I should have known that any boardinghouse requires more than just one set of sheets for each bed.

2 July

Christina greeted me this morning with the news that the coal bin was empty. Not wanting to awaken me, she decided the only thing to do was use wood kindling to build the morning fire in the *kook kachel.* Wood kindling costs four times as much as anthracite, burns three times as fast. Today my entire fuel budget for a month went up in smoke! Made arrangements with the anthracite dealer to deliver monthly, even in the summer. Explained to Tina that under *no* circumstances was wood kindling to be used for anything but *starting* fires. (I tell myself, *remember she's only fourteen.*)

12 July 1891

Today I discovered that our shy girls'-school teacher had the nerve to ask Tina to wash out her redheaded visitor's napkins every month. I'm appalled that Miss Koster would take advantage of the child! I let her know that I had no objections to having Tina spend her spare time as she chooses, provided she is compensated. I suggested that two guilders a month might be adequate.

Tina was delighted, of course. I made her promise she will refer all future requests from any of the boarders to me.

20 July

Theo— Today another crisis! An English couple on holiday, friends of Gosschalk, appeared at my door this afternoon. It seems they had written for a reservation, but I never received the letter. Since no guests were expected, the extra bedroom hadn't been cleaned in two weeks. Except for the baby, who was asleep, there was no one in the house but Christina and me. After serving tea, I excused myself, put on my apron, and became a *femme de ménage* with Tina as my assistant. In three-quarters of an hour, the two of us swept, dusted, and cleaned, made the beds, laid out towels, filled the water pitchers, even put a bouquet of fresh flowers on the table by the window. From now on, regardless of reservations, the transient bedroom is to be cleaned, and the towels and linen changed, just as soon as it is vacated.

2 August

More difficulties with my boarders. Oh, Theo! How I wish you were here. You'd have no problem handling them. I'm afraid I lack your quiet authority. First it was Mr. Klassen, twirling that waxed mustache of his and informing me he was visiting his mother in Haarlem for the next two weeks and expected a 50 percent reduction in the monthly room-and-board fee. I took a deep breath, and informed him that was fine as long as he stored his personal effects in the attic so I could rent the room. "And, of course, I can't guarantee it will be empty when you return." In the end he said he'd keep the room, but insisted on a 15 percent rebate for the two weeks' board.

I had the opposite problem with Mr. Wijnberg. I had a touch of catarrh plus a sore throat, and asked him to bring me Abbey syrup from the pharmacy. The next week the baby began cutting two more teeth and was feeling miserable. Mr. Wijnberg gave the little one a soothing potion that was positively magical. And he absolutely refused to let me pay for either! I'll deduct it from his room and board next month.

10 August

When she stopped by for coffee this morning, Letti told me she was afraid I was becoming a household drudge. (I'm afraid she's right!) Her remedy—next Sunday's Bussum country fair and band concert. We'll take the little ones, and bring Tina to watch them. Sunday lunch will be sandwiches. The boarders can picnic at the fair (as we will) or eat from a buffet I'll leave for them on the veranda. Who would have thought that one day I'd consider a picnic and fair the highlight of my week?

What has become of me? I used to love to read. Now my reading is confined to *The Netherlands Homemaker* and *The Gardener's Almanac*. I used to love to write. Now the entries in my diary are sparse. I rarely sit down and write out all my thoughts as I used to. I'm too tired at night to do anything but note the highlights (and the problems) of each day.

15 August

Theo dear— If it weren't for all the unexpected expenses, running a boardinghouse would be no problem. However, my inexperience has cost me dearly. At first I worried so much about paying the quarterly rent. I banked every penny my boarders paid me, until I had enough to cover the next payment. Which meant that for almost two months I purchased all our food on credit. I must be doing something wrong. I work so hard, but always seem to be in debt. Letti assures me that between commissions her husband lives entirely on credit, and that the wealthy owners of the largest villas have accounts they pay off when it suits them. But it still worries me.

17 August

Another decision to make, Theo. Mr. Klassen and Mr. Wijnberg asked today if I would give them a reduced rate if they roomed together. This would mean a smaller steady income for me, but would free a second bedroom for transients, who pay more. (Johan Cohen Gosschalk has been true to his word about recommending Villa Helma to foreign visitors. This summer, our fourth bedroom was almost always booked.) But I wonder about the wisdom of making the change with the vacation season ending.

I hate to bother him, but I do need Andries' advice. I hope he won't think I'm imposing, but I know he graduated top of his class from a Higher Burgher School that specialized in business management and accounting. I simply don't really know if I'm supporting myself. I'll send Andries my bills and receipts for the past three months, ask him to look at them and advise me.

— · — · —

ANDRIES BONGER
22 Place de la Concord, Paris

19 August 1891

Dear little sister who worries too much—

When I went over your books, I was amazed to see how often your transient guest room had been filled this past summer. You're building a reputation. Next summer, I'll wager, you'll be booked solid! I can't believe you've never met Johan Gosschalk. His recommendations made all the difference.

You're not yet making a profit, but you *are* supporting yourself. Your prices seem a little low, but instead of raising them, I suggest you serve lunch only on Sundays. Weekdays, none of your regular boarders come home for lunch, but you mentioned that every day after breakfast they'd help themselves to sandwiches from the buffet to take to work. They won't starve if you discontinue the sandwich buffet. Bussum's bakery sells sandwiches and filled hot rolls, as does the hotel. Serving only breakfast and dinners on weekdays will not only save more than a little money, but give you some much-needed free time.

By all means encourage Mr. Klassen and Mr. Wijnberg to room together. Your transient rooms can be filled by businessmen in winter, as well as by vacationers in summer. If you run short this first first winter, I'll loan you some money.

Don't worry—you're doing fine! *Andries*

—·—·—

THE PERSONAL DIARY OF JOHANNA VAN GOGH-BONGER

20 August

Did I think I was doing just fine? I reckoned without my dear Father, and I reckoned without the Dutch laws that seem to make it impossible for a woman to dare to live independently.

Today I received a letter from Father's attorney that my bank account in Bussum has been *frozen* "by order of the probate court of the Netherlands." I'm informed I also had no legal right to Theo's art collection (that no one else wanted), to the furniture in our apartment, or to Theo's savings account. It seems because Theo died without a will, I have no right to anything—I suspect not even to the few guilders in the Limoges cookie jar, all that's left of my own savings. How can I run a boardinghouse without a bank account? I have been depositing my boarders' rents in it. How can I pay the quarterly rent when it comes due? How can I pay for the food I have been purchasing on credit—the grocer, the butcher, the fishmonger, the baker? Of course, that is the point of it all. My dear Father does not want Vincent's paintings, Theo's furniture, or his savings account. He simply does not want me to be able to support myself by running a boardinghouse!

I'm informed that Father is applying to the court to be appointed executor of the estate. I'm certain the first thing he'll do is order Vincent's paintings destroyed and the wood from the stretchers, frames, and crates sold. He has also petitioned to be appointed guardian of the child. Will he hire a wet nurse and take the baby from me?

I feel so utterly helpless. The law is a mystery to me. Except that I'm beginning to understand that women are second-class citizens. Much the way the Jews were in Holland a century ago, before Napoleon changed the law—tolerated, treated not unkindly, but lacking most of the legal rights that ordinary citizens take for granted.

21 August

It's amazing how Father can turn his usually intelligent daughter into a babbling idiot. After a sleepless night. I remembered Andries had spoken of consulting a lawyer before shipping Theo's furniture and art collection to me. And there was something about legal details concerning transferring Theo's bank account. The sensible thing for me to do now is immediately send the letter from Father's lawyer on to Andries and ask him to handle it.

— · — ·—

W. J. Petersen and Son
Specialists in Estate and Probate Law
Prinsengracht 589, Amsterdam

18 August 1891
To: Johanna van Gogh-Bonger

This is to inform you that the bank account opened in your name in Bussum on 19 April 1891 with a transfer of funds from the Paris account of your late husband, Theodoor van Gogh, has been frozen by order of the probate court of the Netherlands, and may no longer be accessed. Under Dutch law, no female may open a bank account alone. All females are allowed only joint accounts: with their husbands if married, or with their fathers or nearest male relative if single, divorced, or, as in your case, widowed. In addition, the funds already withdrawn to pay for villa rent and shipping charges must be immediately replaced.

Because Theodoor left no will, under Dutch law his son is Theodoor's legal heir, not you, and all money, furniture, and artworks left by him are his son's property, and may be disposed of only with the advice and consent of the executor of the estate.

Your father, who has retained us for the purpose of being appointed the executor of your late husband's estate, has generously asked us not to bring charges against you, since he is certain you were unaware that under Dutch law you had no claim to the estate, and had no knowledge that you were breaking the law when you accessed the Paris bank account and took possession of the furniture and art collection.

We will contact you as soon as the courts have appointed your father the executor of the estate and guardian of the child, the latter a necessary step since you are still under thirty and are legally a minor. Yours truly, *W. J. Petersen*

— · — · —

ANDRIES BONGER
22 Place de la Concord, Paris

23 August 1891
My poor little sister who finds the law a mystery,

What a week of torment and distress you must have had! I blame myself as much as Father. What with all the excitement of moving, I mistakenly felt it was not necessary to burden you with information about the legal precautions I had taken to protect your interests.

Before transferring Theo's savings account and shipping his furniture and art collection to the Netherlands. I arranged to have his estate probated in France. Here, as you know, legal adulthood is defined as age twenty-five, not thirty. *That* takes care of your son's guardianship. The baby has dual citizenship. And to keep you in compliance with Dutch law, your bank account in Bussum was opened as a joint one, with a male relative (me) as your silent partner. (I should have told you.)

I turned the letter from Father's attorney over to my own, who immediately sent a rejoinder full of all sorts of pompous legalese. I'm certain Father will not pursue the matter, because to do so would mean a lawsuit with its attendant publicity, unheard of in a "family of our standing." And I very much doubt that Father will be angry with me for aiding and abetting your steps toward independence. He wants no confrontations right now. He's urging me to return to Amsterdam and join him in the insurance business, and I'm seriously considering it. Mother keeps telling me it's time I married and settled down. I'm seriously considering that too!

There's a girl in Amsterdam, Henrietta Hansel, who so far cannot bring herself to think of moving to Paris. She's very close to her mother and the only thing holding her back is the idea of living with no relatives or friends nearby. But if I move back to Amsterdam . . . If Henrietta says "yes," my favorite sister must come to the wedding. And that will require a reconciliation with the family. I know this last incident caused you much anxiety and some sleepless nights, but now that you've established your right to a life of your own, you can afford to be gracious. Please! For my sake— *Dries*

—··—··—

VILLA HELMA
A Boardinghouse for Gentlemen and Ladies
Koningslaan 2-A, Bussum

28 August 1891
Dear Mother van Gogh and Wilhelmina,

This past week there were some complications because Theo didn't leave a will. But the lawyers have finally finished their wrangling, and all is well. Andries arranged to have the estate probated in France instead of the Netherlands. Otherwise I would have nothing, not the small savings account Theo left, or the art collection, or even our furniture. Now half the savings account and half the paintings go to me, and the other half is to be held in trust for our son. Moving expenses and the three months' advance rent on the villa have pretty much decimated my half of Theo's savings account.

The reason I'm explaining my finances to you, Mother van Gogh, is that I know that since his father died, Theo had been sending you a little something whenever he could, and I worry because I can't continue. What I can do is send you a painting from my half of the art collection, to sell now or keep for a future emergency. Right now the painter whose work brings the highest prices is Monet. He's very popular in America. Monet gave Theo one of his first sunrise paintings. If you need money now, see what Goupil's will offer you. Theo was sure Monet's work would double in value during the next five to ten years, so keep it if you can. But if you need to sell it now, I can always send you another.

I'm also sending you one of Vincent's flower studies painted in Paris when he was learning the Impressionist techniques, and a small watercolor of your garden in Nuenen. Theo thought Vincent's work done in Arles and St.-Rémy will eventually be the most valuable, but when she was here Wilhelmina assured me that the flower studies would be more to your taste. My love to you both, *Johanna*

— · — · —

VILLA HELMA

A Boardinghouse for Gentlemen and Ladies

Koningslaan 2-A, Bussum

30 August 1891

Dear Anna,

Not one letter from you since I wrote to you last April—I gather Father has forbidden it. I feel like a Catholic who has been excommunicated! Were you and Mother aware of Father's latest attempt to punish me for daring to defy him? He tried to get himself appointed "executor of Theo's estate" (what there is of it) and "guardian of Theo's child" (who is incidentally my child too).

Thanks to Andries, he didn't succeed. Andries said he doubts Father will pursue it further, and now that I've established my rights, I can afford to be gracious. Anna, I don't want to be gracious. When someone tries to take away my baby, I'm not a very forgiving person. I'm not a very good Christian. I don't believe in turning the other cheek. Dries mentioned a reconciliation so I can attend his wedding, if, as, and when Henrietta Hansel says "yes." I don't want a reconciliation.

If I sound bitter, Anna, I suppose it's because I am. My love to Mother— *Jo*

THE PERSONAL DIARY OF JOHANNA VAN GOGH-BONGER

2 September

I've just finished packing the paintings for Mother van Gogh in one of the crates. They'll send her a notice when it arrives at the Leiden station.

15 September

Today, a letter from Johan Cohen Gosschalk assuring me he will recommend Villa Helma to businessmen this winter now that I have two transient rooms to let. But he declined my invitation to spend a few days here as my guest. What can I do? I feel so indebted to him but can't think of any other way to show my appreciation.

4 October

No Theo bird calling this morning—he must be wintering in the South of France. Just as well—I try to write only happy things to Theo. Right now, all I can think about is that today is my birthday, and I am living with strangers who don't know, and wouldn't care if they did. Not a soul wished me a happy birthday today. All these strangers require of me is that breakfast be on time, so they won't be late to work.

I suppose part of my blue mood is the prospect of Fall Cleaning. Every spring and fall, Mother would marshal her assistants (usually my sisters and me) and tear the house apart, beating every rug, laundering every drape and curtain, attacking any lurking spiderweb and dust ball. The bedrooms can wait until spring for thorough cleaning, but my latent housewife's conscience tells me the downstairs cannot be neglected any longer.

I feel like a general marshaling his forces for the attack. Maria said she had some extra time and could manage laundering the downstairs drapes and curtains next week. Elly will scrub down the kitchen, including the *kook kachel,* and Tina will empty the cupboards, wash all the shelves and the dishes. I have assigned myself the task of waxing the wood furniture. (I love the look and smell of polished wood.) Since Moving Day, there's never been time for more than a feather duster. I've asked Piet to help with the heavy work, moving the furniture, beating the rugs.

I know I must have forgotten something. If only Mother, or even my older sister, were here to advise me! Two degrees—one in English literature, one in language—are of no use to me in this instance. I wanted to be independent, and I'm discovering the price—to spend one's birthday alone, worrying about Fall Cleaning.

Later: The post just arrived . . . a letter from Mother van Gogh wishing me a Happy Birthday. As usual, she begins "Just a little word to cheer you—" Now I feel so ashamed because I was feeling sorry for myself. It's just that at times I feel lonely and lost—then once again become angry at Theo for deserting me.

As I leaf through this diary, this past summer appears like one crisis after another. Sometimes it seems as though I were on some kind of nonstop carousel—if only I had time to catch my breath! Then the little one holds out his arms to be picked up and hugged, and it all becomes worthwhile.

6

"What is it I'm afraid I'll discover?"

ANNA BONGER
Herengracht 204, Amsterdam

20 October

Dear Jo,

We can imagine the pain and anxiety Father's legal maneuvers caused you, but please, we beg of you, don't let your justifiable anger destroy the opportunity to be reconciled with the family.

Since September, Dries has been coming home almost every other week. He looks so happy, we're sure Henrietta said "yes." If you are invited to the wedding, if you are invited to join the family on St. Nicholas, please, please *accept!* Mother says to tell you that we have your wedding portrait to look at, but no likeness of the little one. We keep trying to imagine him—is he walking? talking? is he weaned yet? (At this age babies change so fast.)

We wanted to, but there was no way that Mother and I could have written before. Even this letter is a daring action. Remember—do *accept!* Love, *Anna*

—·—·—

ANTON BONGER
Insurance Marine and General
Herengracht 204, Amsterdam

27 October 1891

Dear Johanna,

It is with great pleasure that I inform you of your brother's coming marriage to Henrietta Hansel. I am happy to announce that he will be leaving Paris permanently before the end of February, and after the wedding, will participate in the Amsterdam office of my insurance business. Andries assured me that you were aware of his affection for Henrietta, that you knew he was contemplating the move to Amsterdam, and that therefore this news would come as no surprise. Andries has expressed a strong desire that you be reconciled with the family, so that you may be included in the wedding festivities next February.

Your mother, as always generous and forgiving, suggested that you be invited to our traditional family gathering on St. Nicholas Eve. Henrietta and her family will also be joining us. Your dear mother is most anxious to renew her acquaintance with her grandson, as am I. We hope you will accept this invitation in the reconciliatory spirit in which it is tendered. *Father*

— . — . —

THE PERSONAL DIARY OF JOHANNA VAN GOGH-BONGER

28 October

Father is impossible! He couldn't resist including a hidden knife in his reconciliatory letter—"Your dear mother is most anxious to renew her acquaintance with her grandson, as am I." (If I could, I'd send his grandson to the festivities and I'd stay home!) No use being as mean-spirited as he is. I'd hurt too many people I love—my brother, my mother, my sister. I'll go, but I'm *not* looking forward to it.

— . — . —

ANNA BONGER
Herengracht 204, Amsterdam

5 November 1891

Dearest Jo—

Mother and I held our breaths until you accepted Father's invitation "in the reconciliatory spirit in which it was tendered." It may be hard for you to believe, but Father really loves you. The problem is he's so sure he knows what's best for you (and for everyone!)

What a difference your "yes" made. Believe it or not, Father *suggested* I write this letter to let you know how pleased we all are that you'll be with the family on St. Nicholas Eve. Uncle Dirk has agreed to play Sinterklaas, has already procured an elegant bishop's costume, complete with staff and miter, its red velvet robe trimmed with *genuine* white rabbit's fur. It feels so good to be able to say, "See you in Amsterdam on December 5th." What a joyous St. Nicholas this will be! Love, *Anna*

The Personal Diary of Johanna van Gogh-Bonger

10 November

Dear Theo— I have been dutifully preparing for our Eve of St. Nicholas festivities, though my heart isn't in it. I'm embroidering handkerchiefs for the adults, will make fudge for the children, and will follow tradition, writing a poem to go with each gift.

I was wondering what the little one should wear, until I read an article in the *Homemaker.* "Physicians report an alarming number of injuries due to toddlers tripping over the skirts of their traditional embroidered baptismal gowns, often worn for special events long after baby starts walking. The conscientious mother will put away the long gown before the child is two and substitute more suitable attire." They suggest pinafores for little girls, sailor suits for little boys. There goes my budget! Father, I'm sure, will be pleased to see *me* in the bombazine mourning gown he gave me a year ago. If I can only get through the evening without a quarrel, I'll be grateful.

Theo, my darling, remember our second St. Nicholas together, when we celebrated with a bottle of Chardonnay? It was snowing, and you wouldn't let me go skating on the Seine. It seems like a century ago, not just two years. Why am I crying?

5 December: 10 P.M.

Dear Theo— I just returned from our St. Nicholas reunion in Amsterdam. Our son fell asleep in the rental carriage on the way home, so stuffed with holiday goodies, I was afraid if I hugged him he'd burst! He didn't even wake up when Tina and I undressed him and put him in his crib. I must confess I worried unnecessarily about the tension involved in a reconciliation with Father. When we arrived, the first-floor drawing room was overflowing with conversation. Father was busy talking to Mr. and Mrs. Hansel. My brothers, Dries and Willem, were talking to Henrietta. My sisters, Anna and Katja, were exchanging recipes.

Mother swooped down on my little one with exclamations of joy. At first he looked startled, but then I suspect something about her began to seem familiar. When Anna carried him triumphantly around the room for everyone to meet, he became his most charming show-off self. Later, when Sinterklaas arrived amid a shower of candy, he joined Katja's twins in scrambling for the sweets. Unfortunately, when Sinterklaas sternly asked if he'd been a good boy, he buried his face in my skirt and began to cry. (He stopped when offered solace in the form of more candy.)

Oh, Theo! Your son is becoming a little person. He's no longer an infant. I wish you could have seen him in his sailor suit. I heard Father and Uncle Dirk arguing over who will take him to the Punch and Judy show at the Dam on his third birthday. Mother and Anna kept hinting they'd be delighted to take care of him any afternoon that I'd like to come to Amsterdam to shop. Theo, I must confess it feels good to have a family again!

When it came time to leave, I thanked Father for his gift, and I then realized gratefully that those were the only words we had needed to exchange during the entire afternoon and evening.

—·—·—

ANNA BONGER
Herengracht 204, Amsterdam

7 December 1891
Dear Jo,

What did you think of Andries' bride-to-be? Did you ever see such huge violet eyes? And blond curls? And isn't it amazing how much Henrietta looks like a younger version of her mother?

Do you remember *anything* she said? I never do. I hear you've invited them to Villa Helma for dinner this Sunday. I want a full report. We had the Hansel family over last Sunday and the only thing I can remember Henrietta saying was that the baked ham was delicious. Mother says I'm being unkind, that talking a lot does not necessarily mean one has a lot to say. (She *looked at me* when she said it.)

I'd be interested in hearing Henrietta's reaction to Vincent's work and the modern art on your walls. Love, *Anna*

VILLA HELMA
A Boardinghouse for Gentlemen and Ladies
Koningslaan 2-A, Bussum

11 December

Dear Anna,

Dries says Henrietta is an only child. Can you imagine how she feels being looked over and judged by a family as large as ours? (Especially when some of us are not as kind as we might be.)

What did I think of her? She's one of the most beautiful young women I've seen in a long time! Beautiful people are sometimes very shy. She didn't have much to say during dinner this Sunday. How could she when Andries and I were gossiping about the Paris art scene and our mutual friends there? I'm ashamed of myself. It had been so long since I had a chance to really talk to Dries—I forgot to be a good hostess, to include Henrietta in the conversation.

It's true I can't remember anything she said, but that's because we didn't give her a chance to say anything! I'm really disappointed with you, Anna. Just because Henrietta is quiet doesn't mean she has nothing to say. Andries is not the kind of person to fall in love only with external beauty. If he cares for her, he must have found her a beautiful person inside. Let's wait to judge her.— *Jo*

— · — · —

HENRIETTA HANSEL
Paulus Potterstraat 25, Amsterdam

3 January 1892

Dearest Jo,

I do hope it is permissible for me to address you by your nickname. After all, we will very soon be *sisters-in law!* It's been such a *rush* getting everything ready by the 11th of February. Mother found a *charming* town house with a delightful rear garden on the Paulus Potterstraat *just two blocks* from hers. We've been going there almost daily, arranging furniture and adding those *finishing* touches that make a house a home. Papa bought me a teak curio cabinet to hold my collection of carvings—mostly *adorable* ivory monkeys and elephants from the Dutch East Indies. I had my heart set on hanging Indonesian batiks—an East Indies wall decor that has become so *very fashionable* in Amsterdam. Then I remembered Dries had written saying he wanted to hang his collection of modern art.

He mentioned three artists (no one *here* ever *heard* of them): Odilon Redon and Émile Bernard and some painter named Cézanne. Oh, Jo! Whatever shall I do? All my life I have been dreaming (as all Dutch girls do) of a *home of my own* in which I could entertain family and friends. Of course, it will be Andries' home too. One solution to our dilemma has occurred to me. There is a nice sunny room on the fourth floor which I thought I would make into a *cozy study* for Andries. He could decorate it with *any avant-garde art he wants*. Of course, I doubt if his entire collection would fit in one room—but couldn't he hang *some* in the stairwell? Dearest Jo, you've been *so* nice to me. Will you back me up if he asks your opinion?

I know how much he values it. Fondly, *Henrietta*

— · — · —

VILLA HELMA
Koningslaan 2-A, Bussum

4 January
Dear Henrietta,

Regarding your "decorating dilemma," I really do think this is something you should discuss with Andries, and would consider it most inappropriate for me to offer you or my brother any advice. As you said, it will be his home as well as yours.

Please excuse the brevity of this note—I wanted to reply by return mail, before you wrote to Andries. As ever, *Johanna*

25 January 1892

Dear Theo— It's been a year ago today. I keep trying so hard not to feel sad. If you had to leave me, couldn't you have waited until spring? When the tulips bloom? But now! . . . all morning, the smell of snow . . . hovering on the horizon, ominous-looking dark clouds. Tomorrow is laundry day. We'll have to hang the sheets in the attic. Even the glassed-in verandas will be too cold.

Tomorrow begins my nine months of Second Mourning. Sinterklaas gave me another dress from de Sinkel's—this time, thank heavens, not one made of costly bombazine, but of the less expensive, more practical zibelline. I guess Father finally understands the life I lead, that even Sunday meals don't cook and serve themselves!

31 January

Today we celebrated the baby's second birthday. Just a small party with Letti and her own two-year-old. The little one was so comical—strutting around saying, "No baby! No baby! I'm two!" Letti insists that now that he's two, I really must stop calling him "the baby" and "the little one." But how can I call this happy child Vincent, a name so tinged with tragedy? I could call him by his middle name, Willem—or perhaps Vinnie? I like Vinnie!

Later: Henk just delivered a parcel from the afternoon goods train. For Vinnie's birthday, Mother sent a winter coat and leggings. Father sent a drum! (I'll have to hide it when the boarders are home.) I'm glad I'm reconciled with the family. Little boys need doting grandfathers—and practical grandmothers as well.

2 February

In just nine days Andries will be married. I so hope he'll be happy with his beautiful Henrietta. Only to my diary would I say this: *Henrietta seems somewhat conventional for him.*

Dries says he is afraid her idea of "modern" art is Millet's idealized peasants or Rosa Bonheur's bucolic cows. If she's willing to learn, as I did—she'll find her life so much richer for it.

VILLA HELMA
Koningslaan 2-A, Bussum

8 February

Dear Andries and Henrietta,

We're all looking forward to your wedding. I debated bringing little Vinnie (that's what I call the baby now), then decided to bring Tina along as *kinder meid*. She is now spending every spare moment making a blouse to go with the pinafore Sinterklaas gave her. We are hoping Vinnie will nap while we're in church. My two-year-old is too young to sit still during one of Reverend Bruyn's two-hour sermons, but not too young to enjoy your wedding feast afterwards. So add another place (and a high chair) at the table for the van Gogh-Bongers and Tina. We're all coming! My best, *Jo*

— · — · —

THE PERSONAL DIARY OF JOHANNA VAN GOGH-BONGER

12 February

Dear Theo,

Now I understand why people cry at weddings—they're crying for the "might have been." I used up three handkerchiefs yesterday when Dries got married, because I was thinking of you, my darling . . . How we missed our "wedding night" . . . How we made up for it the next morning! Theo dearest, I must stop now. I'm starting to cry again, and I have no clean handkerchiefs left.

— · — · —

ANTON BONGER
Herengracht 204, Amsterdam

12 February 1892

Dear Johanna,

While we were delighted to have Vincent Willem (I do NOT approve of your calling him Vinnie) attend his uncle's wedding feast, Mother and I feel it is our duty to point out the necessity of improving the child's deplorable table manners. Children without the manual dexterity to handle tableware must be taught to accept being fed. A child who is allowed to attempt independent feeding before he is old enough will think he can do anything he chooses before he has mastered the necessary skills. If Theo were here to guide you, I wouldn't dream of interfering. As ever, *Father*

—·—·—

THE PERSONAL DIARY OF JOHANNA VAN GOGH-BONGER

12 February

There he goes again! Father manages to put a dark cloud of criticism over the happiest occasion. He doesn't approve of his grandson's table manners, and he doesn't approve of my calling him Vinnie, instead of Vincent Willem. Oh, Theo! If only you were here to "guide me" so he *would* stop interfering.

15 February

Dear Theo—Just realized that this is the first week since Moving Day that I had time to read *The Chronicle* from cover to cover. Previously, my mind was so filled with household worries, I read nothing except homemaking and gardening publications, and an occasional *Amsterdammer.* Between child care and running the boardinghouse, my days are full, but now my nights are free. It's time I started thinking about exhibiting Vincent's paintings. Theo, I haven't forgotten. Vincent's work, and all your Impressionist treasures—to show them to an often uncaring world, that also is my task. I'm not sure I know exactly how to proceed. Do you think it would be presumptuous if I asked Gosschalk how to go about it? He did offer to help.

—·—·—

DE AMSTERDAMMER: WEEKBLAD VOOR NEDERLAND
From: *Johan Cohen Gosschalk,* Contributing Editor

16 February 1892

Dear Mrs. van Gogh-Bonger,

Stopped by the newspaper office today and found your note saying you were now ready to start arranging for exhibition of Vincent's work, and reminding me of my offer of guidance. As I said, I would consider it a privilege to assist you in any way possible. In the same mail, a letter from Bernard mentioning that you had approved his plans for a Vincent exhibition at the new Le Barc gallery in Paris. I wish you had consulted me. The French critics are unlikely to review a small retrospective so long after Vincent's death. I'll mention it in my column, though I doubt it will help.

It is unfortunate that Isaacson, who for years had been the Paris correspondent for several Dutch art journals, returned to Holland last year. He has always been a Vincent admirer. Don't hesitate to approach him for assistance in arranging exhibits. A painter himself, he'll be able to introduce you to the gallery owners in Rotterdam, Amsterdam, and The Hague. Also, don't hesitate to enlist the assistance of the well-known Symbolist painters Roland-Holst and Jan Toorop. While I specialize in portraits, and Isaacson in biblical scenes, Roland-Holst and Toorop feel that Vincent is one of them, an artist whose success will further their own Symbolist movement. Both of them are not only artists but also influential critics.

My suggestion: Invite them all to a weekend exhibition at Villa Helma. Cover the walls with Vincent's paintings. Wine them, dine them, then ask for their ideas.

I know I've said "no, thank you" to your previous invitations, but please do include me this time. I wouldn't miss it for the world! As ever, *J. C. Gosschalk*

— · — · —

VILLA HELMA
Koningslaan 2-A, Bussum

17 February (Delivered by Elly)
Dear Letti,

Can you spare Elly for two days next week—on the 21st, and 22nd? I will be having as my guests four art critics who want to see Vincent's work. This is the first showing I've had, and I must confess I'm more than a little nervous about it.

Gosschalk arranged it all, and though I've corresponded with him for almost a year, I've never met him. I've heard that despite his gray hair, he's

younger than me. Received his Ph.D. in law from the University of Amsterdam, but instead of a legal career, chose to involve himself in the arts. He's
considered a brilliant young man. An artist himself, and a writer as well, he is
a genuine admirer of Vincent's work and from the beginning was interested in
helping me. He appears to know everyone involved in the Netherlands art
community, and I feel very fortunate in having him as an adviser and mentor.
Drop by for coffee tomorrow and we'll have a good gossip— *Jo*

—·—·—

THE PERSONAL DIARY OF JOHANNA VAN GOGH-BONGER

23 February 1892

Theo dear— Your wife has just learned the first principle of being a successful art dealer. Until now I did not realize how important the right contacts can be! I had been feeling a little afraid of appearing unladylike and
aggressive, but was advised by Gosschalk to contact some of Vincent's admirers and invite them to Villa Helma for an "Art Exhibit in the Country." Of
course, I invited Gosschalk as well. (He turned out to be both charming and
attractive; his jet-black eyebrows contrasting with his gray eyes and prema-
turely gray hair.)

When I went to meet them at the station, it was another grim and dreary
February day. I had told Tina to build a fire in every *kachel*. When we arrived,
Villa Helma was aglow with warmth—and with *color*. I had taken down the paintings from your Impressionist collection and displayed nothing except Vincent's
work throughout the house, including the transient guest rooms. How encouraging it was to hear exclamations of admiration! (Till now almost everyone
in Bussum looked upon Vincent's paintings as a source of amusement.)

I didn't even need to ask—there was much advice about where and when
to seek exhibitions. Isaacson said there was a cancellation in the winter exhibition schedule at ARTI, the artists' association in Amsterdam with its own
galleries. He's on the board of directors, can try to arrange a showing of Vincent's drawings as a substitute. Jan Toorop said he was certain he could
arrange a spring exhibition in the galleries at PULCHRI, The Hague's artists'
association.

Roland-Holst said he would put in a word for me at Buffa in Amsterdam and Oldenzeel in Rotterdam, two excellent avant-garde galleries. All agreed that in addition to each of them interceding on behalf of Vincent's work, I must write to the galleries myself, mentioning their names. "Roland-Holst suggested I write you," etc. I shall be busy with correspondence for the next several weeks!

Sunday: Letti and her husband joined us for dinner. You could see that they were impressed when they heard these well-known artists and critics being so very enthusiastic about Vincent's work. My three regular boarders, who had referred to Vincent (behind my back) as the "mad painter," uttered not a word during the entire meal. I served a fifteen-pound roast. Had to use all the leaves in our table to accommodate the ten of us.

27 February

Things have been happening so fast, I am breathless. Almost immediately after spending the weekend in Bussum, Isaacson arranged the promised exhibition of Vincent's drawings at the ARTI in Amsterdam. Fortunately, Letti's husband knew of a local carpenter who had been taught how to construct frames and crate artwork. Yesterday, the living-dining room at Villa Helma was transformed into a carpenter's workshop, with much measuring, sawing, and nailing. (Vinnie adored all the noise and confusion.) There was barely time to clean up the room before dinner and deliver the crates to the goods shed at the station. No time to cook—we had leftover potatoes and smoked sausage, with Gouda for Mr. Wijnberg.

_ _._ _

DE AMSTERDAMMER: WEEKBLAD VOOR NEDERLAND
From: *Johan Cohen Gosschalk,* Contributing Editor

28 February 1892
Dear Mrs. van Gogh-Bonger,
    Another exhibition possibility just occurred to me. The next time you're in Amsterdam, stop by the Wisselingh gallery. They exhibit only the finest

artists, many of them French: Corot, Monticelli, and Michel, for example. If they agree to show some of Vincent's paintings, it would be quite a triumph.

Had lunch yesterday with P. L. Tak, editor of *The Chronicle*. (As you know, I have been doing a series of portraits for that publication.) He was complaining about the difficulty of obtaining adequate translations for his new series of French and English short stories. I mentioned your degrees in English and extensive knowledge of French. He asked me to find out if you'd be interested in doing some translating for him. It would be one way of earning extra money should you require it. Drop him a note and mention my name if you're interested. As ever, *J. C. Gosschalk*

— · — · —

THE PERSONAL DIARY OF JOHANNA VAN GOGH-BONGER

3 March

This afternoon Henrietta is showing off her new home with a tea for the family and a few intimate friends, and of course I must go and admire the bride's town house. I wonder what I shall find hanging on the walls—Indonesian batiks or paintings by Cézanne, Redon, and Bernard? (My guess is the fashionable batiks.)

Left Vinnie with Anna and Mother while I went to the Wisselingh gallery, bringing two of Vincent's small paintings to show them. They asked to keep them for the afternoon, suggested I come back.

Later: Good news—Wisselingh will take half a dozen paintings, not to hang all at once but to rotate. And more good news! When I returned home, there was a letter from Jan Toorop saying that PULCHRI, The Hague's artists' association, had finally decided to schedule a Vincent exhibit next May. Toorop asked if I wanted him to supervise the hanging. Indeed I do!

6 March

Thanks to Roland-Holst, there will soon be ten of Vincent's paintings on exhibit with Buffa in Amsterdam and twenty with Oldenzeel in Rotterdam. All this crating and shipping is an unexpected expense. Earning extra money is now a real priority. I'll contact *The Chronicle* about doing some translating. When I shall find the time, I don't know. The baby and housekeeping take the whole day. I shall simply have to learn to do with less sleep! For dinner tonight, once again *gebakken visch* with fried potatoes. I've promised my patient boarders a goose this coming Sunday.

—·—·—

ANTON BONGER
Insurance Marine and General
Herengracht 204, Amsterdam

9 March 1892
Dear Johanna:

P. L. Tak lectured at this month's meeting of our Literary Society, and I was shocked when he mentioned that you will be translating some English stories for *The Chronicle*. Really, Johanna, this is the lowest kind of literary work! This is not what we had in mind when your mother and I hired tutors so that our daughter could obtain the equivalent of a university education, something very few girls in the Netherlands are privileged to do. We were so proud when our daughter passed the government examinations A and B in both the English philological and literary sections, certifying her to teach in any school in the Netherlands.

Do you think it is unreasonable for us to expect our Johanna to make us proud by becoming a poetess herself, or perhaps even a novelist—just as your sister Anna, who studied in the conservatory, is now an accomplished pianist, and your older sister Katja, who studied at Mrs. Selton's Art Academy, is now an accomplished watercolorist? Even teaching as you did before your marriage was an acceptable profession. But translating! There may be some money in it, but it's an occupation totally without the aura of accomplishment expected of young ladies of your class.

It would be foolish for me to forbid your continuing to translate for *The Chronicle*. But I do indeed hope you'll begin to appreciate the educational advantages your mother and I have given you at great sacrifice, and reward us by involving yourself in more appropriate, ladylike pursuits. All I suggest is that you ask yourself if you are not being selfish and unreasonable. *Father*

11 March

I suppose I must resign myself to Father being constantly critical of everything I do. Our reconciliation did not change either of us. He will be eternally disappointed with Vinnie's "table manners" and my own "unladylike pursuits." (How I would love to become a poetess instead of a translator, to give readings at the various literary society teas. But that would not put a single guilder in my pocket, would it?)

—·—·—

Anna Bonger
Herengracht 204, Amsterdam

25 March 1892
Dearest Jo,

Don't mention this to Father, but Mother and I surmised it would be both difficult and expensive purchasing art journals in Bussum. Knowing you'd want to start a scrapbook, we've been collecting the reviews and articles that have been appearing concerning Vincent's work. As you may have guessed, Mother's rheumatism keeps her housebound in the winter. So I scout the newsstands and bookstores, while she supplies the guilders via some creative bookkeeping with the household account. Here's the first batch—we'll send along more as they appear.

Your loving conspirators, *Anna and Mother*

3 March: Amsterdam

Not new to the avant-garde art scene, but new to the Netherlands, Vincent van Gogh's drawings, now on exhibit in ARTI, are often primitive, sometimes awkward and childlike. Both passionate and uncontrolled, his art is a mixture of good and bad qualities. Unfortunately, neither has priority.

Etha Fles: *De Algemene Handelsblad*

10 March: Rotterdam

The Oldenzeel gallery in Rotterdam, long known for its courage in presenting the individualistic in art, is now showing twenty paintings by a Dutchman whose unconventional approach to art will undoubtedly cause much controversy. Vincent van Gogh's approach is neither a superficial search for originality nor a lack of technical control, but the product of an inner vision that is at once both passionate and abstract. Here is a talent bordering on genius!

J. J. Isaacson: *De Portefeuille*

12 March: Rotterdam

The condition of Vincent van Gogh's mind that led to such a tragic end prevented him from thinking and feeling soundly. Here we see the creations of a sick mind.

David van der Kellen: *Nieuws van den Dag*

15 March: Rotterdam

If the unfortunate painter had lived, perhaps he might have succeeded in developing what is simply a remarkable effort into a mature and beautiful art. There are two tragedies revealed in the Vincent van Gogh paintings now hanging in the Oldenzeel gallery: the one of a sick genius who reaches for the sun like a child, and the tragedy of the loving brother who believed in him.

A. C. Loffelt: *Weekblad voor Rotterdam*

21 March: Amsterdam

This March, Amsterdam art lovers have the opportunity to preview the work of the Symbolist painter Vincent van Gogh in three galleries. The drawings of this tragic genius have been on exhibit in the ARTI since the first week in March, while ten of this brilliant colorist's paintings are on display at the avant-garde Buffa gallery, and the elite Wisselingh has half a dozen more.

In The Hague, PULCHRI plans a small retrospective in May, while the Kunstkring plans a large retrospective with close to a hundred paintings the following month. These retrospectives have been long overdue.

A year and a half after his death, we are now realizing that Vincent van

Gogh was a unique pioneering figure in the art world—a solitary genius standing alone to struggle in the night, creating the art of the future.

Johan Cohen Gosschalk: *De Amsterdammer*

23 March: Amsterdam

Vincent van Gogh's art defies conventional criticism. His work reflects a rare passion, a seldom seen fervor. Without thought as to what would happen to himself or to his work, this genius traded his very life and soul for his art. Some may call him mad—he seems to me a saint.

Frederik van Eeden: *De Nieuwe Gids*

Jo: I checked the French journals searching for some mention of the retrospective you said Émile Bernard had arranged at the new Le Barc gallery in Paris. Couldn't find a thing. Finally ran into Johan Cohen Gosschalk and asked him if he'd come across any reviews. Mr. Gosschalk told me that the French critics had totally ignored the exhibit. What a shame, after all the expense of crating and shipping!

I can't tell you how happy it's made Mother to know we're once again a family. She's so enjoyed helping you with the reviews. (I think she likes the thrill of deceiving Father.) Please, let's never become estranged again. Love, *Anna*

— · —

VILLA HELMA
A Boardinghouse for Gentlemen and Ladies
Koningslaan 2-A Bussum

2 April 1892
Dear Mr. Cohen Gosschalk:

Have you seen the reviews of Vincent's work? There were far fewer unfavorable ones than we expected. Naturally your own and Isaacson's were wonderful—but I was somewhat surprised by Frederik van Eeden elevating Vincent to sainthood. (Vincent would have been embarrassed.)

I was just thinking of you, and how like a magician you've been—or with your almost-white hair, perhaps a benevolent Sinterklaas might be more accurate. Whenever I have not known where to turn, or how to proceed, Johan Cohen Gosschalk appeared to point the way. I remember your first letter, written in response to my plea to Jan Veth for guidance. My whole family, even my brother Andries, had been advising me to give up my idea of an independent life. No one but you felt that an inexperienced widow with a baby had a chance of succeeding.

I'll never forget that Sunday at Villa Helma, listening astonished as the artists you'd recommended planned where and when Vincent should be exhibited. At the time, it seemed like a miracle. I felt it was time I let you know how much your assistance has been appreciated. Sincerely, *J. van Gogh-Bonger.*

— · — · —

DE AMSTERDAMMER: WEEKBLAD VOOR NEDERLAND
From: *Johan Cohen Gosschalk,* Contributing Editor

4 April 1892
Dear Mrs. van Gogh-Bonger,

Your charming letter of appreciation was unnecessary. So far as I am concerned, what you are doing is saving for posterity the work of a major talent. My own work may be nothing whatever like Vincent's (I fear my pastel portraits and watercolor landscapes will forever remain anchored in the past), but that does not mean I cannot recognize the art of the future when I see it. Helping you has been its own reward. As ever, *J. C. Gosschalk*

— · — · —

ANNA BONGER
Herengracht 204, Amsterdam

18 April
Dear Jo—

Have I ever told you how proud I am of you, Jo? Already Vincent's work is becoming known and appreciated at least among the avant-garde. There's no doubt in my mind that he will eventually be famous. Dutch women aren't expected to accomplish such things or to support themselves as you do.

Watching Father try to dominate your life made a deep impression on me. I'm no longer the sweet acquiescent little sister you came home to two years ago. Father would probably disown me if he knew, but I've become quite radical in my thinking. Lately I've found women who think as I do. I've been going to the box-lunch meetings of a Women's Federation connected with the Socialist Party.

Aletta Jacobs, the first Dutch woman physician, the first woman who was *ever* permitted to study in a Netherlands university, will be speaking at our meeting next Thursday. Come with me—Mother could take care of Vinnie.

I've been telling her I belong to a weekly sewing circle, but I'm sure she's not fooled. Being a woman today means learning to live with deception.

Love, Anna

— · — · —

VILLA HELMA
Koningslaan 2-A, Bussum

19 April 1892
Dear Anna—

What a coincidence! I have been meeting with a small women's discussion group in Bussum. We've come to the conclusion that the Socialist Party offers the only hope for women in the Netherlands. We're all planning to go to your box-lunch meeting to hear Aletta Jacobs. Is it true that she's actually opened a Birth Control Clinic in Amsterdam? What a courageous woman! I'm looking forward to Thursday. *Johanna*

— · — · —

THE PERSONAL DIARY OF JOHANNA VAN GOGH-BONGER

26 April

These past two days I have been leading a double life. With one part of my mind I continue the correspondence concerning exhibitions of Vincent's work and also attend to household duties and my child. Another part of me has been trying to sort out all the ideas stirred up by Aletta Jacobs' speech.

Until I moved to Bussum and became aware of the tragic options available to orphan girls like Tina, and the twelve-hour workdays of farm women like Elly, the problems of strangers, of anyone outside our own church and class, did not concern me. I had always accepted my place in Dutch society as my God-given right.

The family was the center of my existence, a warm cocoon that nourished and protected me. Once I emerged from it, I changed so much. Marrying Theo changed me—he introduced me to so many new ideas, new ways of looking not only at art but also at life. Now with Theo gone, I've been forced to learn how to deal with the uncaring world outside. I've had many helping hands—Anna and Wilhelmina, Letti, Elly, even Tina and Maria. I look at the list, and realize that half of them do not belong to "my class," have not had the education that permits me to lead an independent life.

Something must be done about the status of women in the Netherlands. Women's discussion groups like ours can do nothing BUT discuss. If we are going to really accomplish anything, it can only happen if we are permitted to vote. Aletta Jacobs told us she checked the voting laws and *nowhere is gender mentioned.* Next year she intends to attempt to register and vote as a "resident." Wouldn't it be wonderful if she gets away with it?

— · — · —

ALETTA VONDEL-DIRKS
Villa Zundert, Koningslaan 11, Bussum

27 April 1892
Dear foolish Jo-Jo—

Have you gone out of your mind? Elly tells me you went to Amsterdam to hear that outrageous woman who wormed her way into the Groningen Medical School and has been stirring up trouble ever since. What in heaven's name possessed you? Women like Dr. Jacobs are considered beneath contempt by most decent, well-bred people. Really, Jo! Don't you realize that Bussum's villa population is made up of the cream of Amsterdam society—all very wealthy and conservative. Your despairing *Letti*

VILLA HELMA
Koningslaan 2-A, Bussum

28 April (Sent via Elly)
Dear Letti—

Our Bussum women's discussion group started out as half a dozen women meeting to discuss books we'd read, and evolved into a discussion of the plight of working-class women. While the group is small (this is, after all, a small town), its members are all from what you term "Bussum's villa population, the cream of Amsterdam society."

Do join us here next Thursday at three. We'll be discussing how decent girls are being forced into prostitution. A female servant who is seduced or even raped by her employer, and then dismissed, needs legal means of gaining financial support for her child, or prostitution is her only alternative. Do come—I've always known that beneath that frivolous front, Letti hides a quick mind and a warm heart. Love, *Johanna*

— · — · —

ANTON BONGER
Herengracht 204, Amsterdam

5 May
Dear Johanna:

Mother mentioned that Anna had received a letter from Katja last week, while I was in The Hague on business. Naturally, like any concerned grandfather, I was anxious to learn how the twins were doing. While searching Anna's desk, I was shocked to come across a note from you reminding Anna of a meeting of the Socialist Party's Women's Federation. I have long resigned myself to *your* wild ideas, but am outraged that you should attempt to proselytize your innocent sister. Anna has always been a model of feminine modesty and Christian decorum. How dare you introduce her to an organization that discusses prostitution while professing to help the unfortunate!

There are many acceptable charities with which cultivated women from a

179

family of our standing can associate themselves. But the Socialist Party! I know for a fact that their Women's Federation is made up of wild-eyed feminists and suffragettes, most of whom have spent time in mental institutions. Let me assure you that you will never enter this house again unless you *cease* this outrageous conduct. *Father*

— · — · —

VILLA HELMA
A Boardinghouse for Gentlemen and Ladies
Koningslaan 2-A, Bussum

7 May 1892
Dear Father,

I did not "proselytize" Anna. Anna has a mind and heart of her own. We each joined the Socialist Party's Women's Federation separately. I think you would be quite surprised at how many women from "families of our standing" are members.

Father, I love and respect you, but will not permit you to tell me how to think or act. Nor will I submit to separation from my mother and my sister. My family, including you, means too much to me, and to my child. I regret angering you, and hope you will come to realize that the Women's Federation is made up of sincere women who work only for causes which are noble. *Johanna*

— · — · —

ANDRIES BONGER
Paulus Potterstraat 65, Amsterdam

9 May
Dear Jo:

Father showed me your response to his outrage at your new political affiliations. How proud I am of you. My little sister has finally grown up! As usual, Father asked me to intervene. Previously when he asked me to interfere in your decisions, I'd simply ignore it. That was easy enough to do when the request was in a letter. But this time I felt it necessary to flatly refuse. I told him I felt he had no right to tell you or Anna how to think. I wish Henrietta could emancipate herself as you have. She's so utterly dependent on the approval of other people. She's still very young. I keep telling myself to be patient—perhaps in time. Love, *Dries*

—·—·—

Villa Helma

A Boardinghouse for Gentlemen and Ladies

Koningslaan 2-A, Bussum

12 May 1892
Director: Family Planning Clinic

Dear Dr. Jacobs:

I never dreamt that women working together could really make a difference until I heard your speech at the Women's Federation last month. I've been trying to figure a way I might help. My time is limited. I'm a widow with a two-year-old son, whom I support by running a combination pension-boardinghouse and by doing translations for a literary magazine.

In addition, I am obliged to arrange posthumous exhibitions of the artwork of my brother-in-law—a legacy left me by my late husband which cannot be ignored. To date, the only contribution I have been able to make to the Federation is to allow the Bussum chapter to meet in my home.

Would translations from foreign medical journals be of help to you? This is something I would be able to do. I so much want to assist in whatever way I can.

Sincerely, *J. van Gogh-Bonger*

FAMILY PLANNING CLINIC
Nieuwstaat 309, Amsterdam

13 May

Dear Mrs. van Gogh-Bonger,

I cannot tell you how encouraging it is to receive a letter of support and offer of assistance like yours. It makes up for the frequent vituperation one must endure. Thanks for offering to translate medical articles for use in the clinic. This would be a valuable contribution, and very much appreciated.

There is no need for you to apologize for not having time to be more active in the Women's Federation. Just holding the Bussum chapter's meetings in your home is a great service. Many women report that this is something they are unable to do because of their unsympathetic husbands. We each do what we can. I'll get the articles that require translation ready. The next time you're in the city, stop by the clinic to pick them up, I look forward to meeting you.

Sincerely yours, *Dr. Aletta Jacobs*

— · — · —

VILLA HELMA
A Boardinghouse for Gentlemen and Ladies
Koningslaan 2-A, Bussum

15 May 1892

Dear Dr. Jacobs,

I'll be in Amsterdam for the Women's Federation box-lunch meeting next week, when we'll be discussing the newly formed "Committee for the Amelioration of the Social and Legal Position of Women in the Netherlands" (a convoluted way of saying that we need to change the Dutch laws that make a husband's power over his wife absolute—or a father's over his daughter). I'll pick up your medical journals then.

I am fascinated by the idea of a Family Planning Clinic. This is a concept that is new to me. I lived in London briefly, and in Paris for two years, and am unaware of similar clinics in either city. Although I've heard there were methods of preventing conception, I'm ignorant as to exactly what they are. If you have any brochures that explain it, I'd very much appreciate your sending me one.

Looking forward to meeting you next week.

Sincerely, *J. van Gogh-Bonger*

— · — · —

"To save women from the bondage of unwanted pregnancies"

FAMILY PLANNING CLINIC
Nieuwstaat 309, Amsterdam
Sponsored by the Dutch Malthusian League

Free information on "the safe period" and "withdrawal"
Free information on the newest, most proven methods of birth control:
The "Womb Veil" or Cervical Cap . . . The Mensinga Pessary
Vaginal Sponges . . . Sheep-membrane Condoms . . . Syringe Douches
Fees for the above devices based on ability to pay
Dr. Aletta Jacobs, Director

— · — · —

THE PERSONAL DIARY OF JOHANNA VAN GOGH-BONGER

19 May 1892

What a nice visit I had with Aletta Jacobs. I feel like I've made a real friend. Dr. Jacobs says it's not surprising that I was unaware of similar Family Planning Clinics in Paris or London. Until now, birth control information has been quietly disseminated by gynecologists and midwives. She believes the Family Planning Clinic in Amsterdam is the first of its kind!

However, preventing conception is not a new idea. Some of the clinic's methods date back to Roman times. Unfortunately, many people believe that Dr. Jacobs is the devil incarnate, introducing dangerous new ideas.

VILLA HELMA
A Boardinghouse for Gentlemen and Ladies
Koningslaan 2-A, Bussum

20 May 1892
Dear Anna,

You'll really enjoy this. Letti's husband has recently been appointed to the Town Council. He's been giving Letti hilarious reports on our esteemed burgomeister. At each meeting Burgomeister van Suchtelen presents every council member with a white Gouda pipe and a pot of tobacco—but no documentation for the agenda items. He wonders why anyone would need any information in order to vote "no" on giving a franchise to an electric company? Why pay a fortune for electricity when gas is so cheap? At the last meeting someone mentioned the Family Planning Clinic, and when van Suchtelen understood what it was, he almost had apoplexy. He has been gathering information for a WARNING to the ladies of our community which he intends to incorporate into a Letter to the Editor. Hans had given Letti a copy, which she brought to our Women's Federation meeting. You could hear our laughter clear across the Koningslaan as Letti read it aloud:

Letter to the editor: Weekblad voor Bussum
I have just been informed that Aletta Jacobs, Holland's infamous feminist physician, has opened a birth control clinic in nearby Amsterdam. Any decent woman who goes there is taking her life in her hands. I have consulted two prominent physicians, both of whom have informed me that these immoral experiments for the prevention of conception are a hazard to female health.

Those daring to attempt to subvert nature's plan can expect severe illness, even death, from acute and chronic metritis, leucorrhoea, menorrhagia, and histeralgia as well as hyperaesthesia of the generative organs, ovarian dropsy, and ovaritus. Frequent side effects are mania leading to severe melancholia, and a most repulsive nymphomania, often resulting in suicide. As your Burgomeister, I feel it is my duty to inform the Ladies of our Community of the dire consequences of birth control. *Burgomeister van Suchtelen*

The letter may be funny, but it has the potential for great harm. We voted to distribute fifty Family Planning posters to counteract van Suchtelen's letter. Everywhere he goes—to the post office, the town offices, the railway station, our esteemed burgomeister will be confronted with his nemesis. We know he'll have them taken down, but as fast as he takes them down, we'll put others up! It feels so good to plan on *doing* something instead of just talking.

My love to Mother. *Johanna*

—·—·—

THE PERSONAL DIARY OF JOHANNA VAN GOGH-BONGER

21 May 1892

Today a letter from Johan Cohen Gosschalk telling me he had seen Vincent's exhibit at PULCHRI in The Hague and was somewhat disappointed because it was not well lit. Gosschalk reports PULCHRI hasn't yet switched from gas to Edison bulbs. Being an artist-owned gallery, they don't have funds for modernizing.

25 May

Another letter from Gosschalk, asking about next month's exhibit in The Hague's Kunstkring gallery. This will be a major retrospective. They've agreed to eighty-nine pieces. If I don't have enough frames, Gosschalk suggested a firm in Amsterdam. He says to mention his name and ask for their special "artist's discount."

Gosschalk puzzles me. He is always so helpful. Several times I've told him I'd like to show my appreciation by having him spend a few days at Villa Helma as my guest. He came to Villa Helma for the first showing of Vincent's work, but since then my invitations are invariably ignored. Maybe he simply doesn't enjoy the country?

VILLA HELMA
A Boardinghouse for Gentlemen and Ladies
Koningslaan 2-A, Bussum

15 August 1892
Dear Aletta Jacobs:

The members of the Bussum chapter of the Socialist Party's Women's Federation have asked me to convey their congratulations on the occasion of your forthcoming marriage to the journalist Carel Victor Gerritsen. We know that for several years you have both kept a "Free Union" as a way of protesting Holland's humiliating marriage laws, and respect you for living your convictions. How wonderful to learn that the "Free Union" of two such remarkable human beings will soon result in what will surely be a remarkable child. I want to add my *personal* best wishes. *Johanna*

— · — · —

ANNA BONGER
Herengracht 204, Amsterdam

25 September
Dearest Jo—

This past summer, Mother's rheumatism disappeared along with the ice on the canals and has yet to reappear. (Every winter Father tries to turn her into a permanent invalid, but she always frustrates him by recovering in the spring.)

Do you realize that on October 4 you have a very special birthday— you'll be thirty, legally an adult! Mother and I want to celebrate by taking you to lunch at the Hotel Krasnapolsky's new Winter Garden. Its glass roof, murals, mirrors, and flowers make it a spectacular setting for a special guest— and, dear Jo, you are very special to us. No excuses—like Villa Helma's Fall Cleaning or Vincent's coming retrospective at the Panorama gallery. Mother says she won't take "no" for an answer. Love, *Anna*

VILLA HELMA
Koningslaan 2-A, Bussum

27 September

Dear Anna,

I accept Mother's luncheon invitation with pleasure. I was wondering when I'd have the occasion to wear the elegant dress Father gave me for my three months of Half Mourning. (How does one "half mourn"?) Although I removed the padded bustle as usual, a dress of black silk trimmed with jet beads will surely turn heads at the Winter Garden!

After lunch, I need to make a condolence call. Perhaps you'd like to go with me, Anna. Did you hear? Aletta Gerritsen-Jacobs had a baby girl who lived only one day. It was one of those heartbreaking infant deaths. Apparently healthy, the baby simply stopped breathing in the middle of the night. When Vinnie was born, I was aware of such tragedies. That first week, I remember waking up almost every hour all night long, just to be sure he was breathing. Until next week— *Johanna*

—·—·—

THE PERSONAL DIARY OF JOHANNA VAN GOGH-BONGER

New Year's Day 1893 [Three months later]

Dear Theo— Yesterday Letti and I took our three-year-olds ice-skating for the first time. Hans was a little timid, but not Vinnie. He loved it, as long as he could hold my hand or clutch my skirt. Only the promise of hot chocolate made him agree to come home before dark. Elly had a steaming pitcher and a plate of sugar cookies waiting for all of us. It was bedtime before Vinnie's bright red cheeks faded to pink.

7 January

Dear Theo— Andries just left after a Sunday visit. Once again, Henrietta was unable to join him—"a previous engagement." I feel so sad. I have the impression that Dries' marriage is a disappointment to him. He and Henrietta do not appear to have shared interests, to have the kind of marriage that you and

I enjoyed. Henrietta has no interest whatever in modern art—her calendar is filled with spectator social events such as the theater, the opera and concerts, where one goes to be seen. Henrietta is a remarkably attractive young woman, but I have the feeling that Andries does not even enjoy her physically. I keep wanting to say to him that if he feels that way, perhaps Henrietta does too. They could talk it over. But we've both been brought up to believe that, for our class, any discussion of that kind of intimacy is unacceptable.

The lower classes can be forthright to the point of vulgarity regarding their sex lives—they live in such restricted quarters that privacy is impossible. But a cultivated man like Dries cannot describe his feelings. To be upper-class is to live a lie. We think one thing, say another. I wonder what the consequences of such deception are.

8 January

Just last week I read an interesting article by a young Austrian student of Charcot's named Sigmund Freud. He theorized that Charcot's success in curing hysteria by hypnosis proves there is an uncharted part of the mind which he tentatively labels the "subconscious." All the thoughts repressed, the words left unsaid, slumber there, waiting for release. If that is so, the "subconscious" of any upper-class European must be like a giant Pandora's box, waiting to be opened.

For example, I worry that Dries may satisfy his needs in the Amsterdam brothels. I could not bear it if he were to contract syphilis, which is now almost endemic in all our cities. A young country girl, a virgin mistress, would be far safer. And yet I dare not speak to him about it—another taboo. I'm not without my own repressed thoughts. Now that Vincent's work is beginning to be appreciated, Gosschalk is urging me to proceed more quickly with the letters. For almost two years I've been organizing them, trying to put them in chronological order—Vincent was exceedingly erratic about dating letters, and Theo simply threw them in the desk drawer.

To tell the truth, I have yet to really read them thorough. Why do I keep putting this off? What is it I'm afraid I'll discover? And if the unspeakable should appear, will I have the courage to accept it? Or will I shove it into my own "subconscious"? I wonder.

20 January

January is such a difficult month. I always feel as though I'm on an emotional seesaw. On the 25th there's the anniversary of Theo's death. Each year I relive that terrible night in the "Family Room" of The Utrecht Institute for the Insane. A week later I must force myself to at least look and sound happy in time for Vinnie's birthday celebration on the 31st.

25 January

"—mental illness caused by congenital disease, chronic ill health, overwork, and grief." The wording of Theo's death certificate still troubles me. Every year at this time, I take that piece of paper out. I puzzle over it—then, as Freud would say, "shove it back into my subconscious." Oh, Theo! I was there beside you when you died, but I still don't understand what it was that killed you.

7

"Not yet, there's more. And there was!"

VILLA HELMA
A Boardinghouse for Gentlemen and Ladies
Koningslaan 2-A, Bussum

15 February 1893
Dear Mother van Gogh,

I've assured Vinnie that two *very* important guests will be on next Sunday's afternoon express from Leiden. Henk's milk cart would never do, or even a rental fiacre. You and Wilhelmina will be transported to Villa Helma in an elegant carriage (borrowed from my neighbor Letti).

I think you'll like Bussum. The original old section, with its tiled-roof cottages, winding dirt lanes, marshes and sandpits, seems to me reminiscent of the Brabant countryside. The newer section of villas was laid out by a consortium of wealthy entrepreneurs who realized Bussum's potential once the railroad made commuting to Amsterdam a journey of no consequence. The "locals" are not too fond of the newcomers, but tolerate them because they can make a small profit selling building supplies and labor. In the new section, the streets are broad and tree-lined, and the villas, very elegant. Villa Helma is comparatively modest in size, but seems larger because of the glassed-in verandas.

Wilhelmina must have told you I turned the front parlor into my own bed-sitting room. There's a daybed for special guests like yourself who might find stairs difficult. The living-dining room sometimes seems crowded, but luckily I have congenial boarders and guests. Be prepared for much laughter and good conversation. I've been so fortunate. My two transient bedrooms are booked solid from June through August, and with the most interesting people: artists (word has gotten out that this is a villa filled with modern art) and poets and writers, as well as foreign vacationers.

I'm busy from morning till night—but my life is not an unhappy one. There is this sense of fulfillment every time I ship a crate of Vincent's paintings off to an exhibition, or mail a translation to *The Chronicle*. (The translations pay for the crating and shipping.) All the reviews have not been favorable, but his work is now known, not ignored. An art editor at the *Amsterdammer* has been my adviser and mentor. Without Gosschalk's guidance, I'd never have made it this far.

You're both expected to stay on until Friday, when Henrietta has invited us all for lunch in her Amsterdam town house. (Prepare for a feast. She so enjoys any kind of entertaining.) At the station, look for the fanciest carriage in the lineup. I'll be in it, along with a three-year-old lad who looks forward to a hug! Jo

— . — . —

The Personal Diary of Johanna van Gogh-Bonger

25 February

Dear Theo— Through Vincent's letters I am getting a sense of what it must have been like for you to be an art dealer with the Academy controlling the art market. I understand now your frustration, even depression. Vincent understood too. He writes from Arles: "Dear Theo— You talk of the emptiness you feel everywhere. Nonetheless, I'm convinced that the time in which we live represents a great and true renaissance. The worm-eaten Academy may still be alive, but is, through your work as an art dealer, becoming truly impotent."

I know how you must have felt, because now I too have had to become an "art dealer." At first it was heartbreaking—the mixed reviews Vincent's work received. But I could not give up. And it is happening at last—a slow but sure appreciation of Vincent's art. Gosschalk advises I concentrate now solely on large retrospectives, such as the 89-piece exhibit shown in The Hague's Kunstkring last spring and the 112-piece one that created such a stir in Amsterdam's Panorama this past December. Gosschalk assures me such exhibitions are seeds that will shortly bear international fruit. He's already received requests for my address from Ambroise Vollard in France and Paul Cassier in Germany. Just last summer, the Art Department of the University of Amsterdam sponsored an exhibition surveying Dutch painting of the past decade, and *two* of Vincent's paintings were included! There is talk of a similar exhibition at the Rijksmuseum. What a triumph that would be if they would exhibit some of Vincent's work—even if only temporarily! I'll ask Gosschalk to tactfully look into it.

ANTON BONGER
Insurance Marine and General
Herengracht 204, Amsterdam

3 March 1893
The Rijksmuseum, Amsterdam

Dear Mr. van Emde:

    I regret having missed this past month's meeting of our Literary Society when you presented your paper "Contemporary Dutch Art," which I hear was well received. This cough that has plagued me most of the winter seems unwilling to evaporate as it should, even though I try to forgo or at least cut down on spirits and tobacco. Our mutual friend, I. K. Drukker, reports you noted my absence because there was some discussion of the painting of my daughter's brother-in-law, Vincent van Gogh. Even though we are distantly related, as a cultivated Dutchman who is proud of his country's art and has donated frequently and substantially to our illustrious Rijksmuseum, I feel compelled to urge you *not* to consider displaying any of van Gogh's paintings. They were not well received even in France, where his brother managed one of the esteemed Goupil galleries.

    When my daughter's husband passed on, I contacted our insurance firm's Paris representative, instructed him to go to the art supply shop where the paintings were stored, inventory them, and give me a professional appraisal. He reported they were not worth as much as the stretcher bars and crates that held them. And this less than three years ago! Since then a conspiracy of wild-eyed Symbolist painters, such as Toorop and Roland-Holst, have been promoting Vincent, hoping acceptance of his work will lend validity to theirs.

    We have been pleading with our daughter to give up her dream of turning her unfortunate brother-in-law into a famous artist, but her grief and devotion to her late husband have warped our usually sensible girl's judgment. It saddens me to see her continue to waste money she can ill afford on crating and shipping to little-known galleries, in the vain hope that one day his work will someday hang in a museum.

    We have tried to make her understand that Vincent's work would be totally out of place in an exhibition of Dutch masters. Can you imagine those wild smears of color hanging, even for a few weeks, in the Rijksmuseum, where masterpieces by Rembrandt, Rubens, and Frans Hals are displayed? It would be an insult to our illustrious heritage! Yours sincerely, *Anton Bonger*

— · — · —

DE AMSTERDAMMER: WEEKBLAD VOOR NEDERLAND
From: Johan Cohen Gosschalk, Contributing Editor

15 April 1893
Dear Mrs. van Gogh-Bonger,
    I am totally perplexed. I have been in contact with the Rijksmuseum's director concerning the possibility of including some of Vincent's work in their 1894 *Survey of Recent Dutch Painting*. Despite Vincent's many enthusiastic reviews and growing reputation, Mr. van Emde is adamant about refusing to even discuss it.
    He admits he has never seen any of Vincent's work, but insists what he's heard of it is sufficient for a negative decision. (It's as though Vincent's paint was infected with the Pox!) Sorry for the disappointing news. As ever, *J. C. Gosschalk*

— · — · —

[The following winter] *Mrs. van Gogh: Did you see the enclosed letter to the editor by van Eeden?* —Gosschalk

February 1894
EDITOR, DE NIEUWE GIDS
    An unfortunate reflection on the inability of the Rijksmuseum to recognize the geniuses among us is the museum's consistent unwillingness to exhibit any painting by Vincent van Gogh. Without the least care of how critics in high places regarded his work, van Gogh struggled to present his version of beauty and truth, his devotion to the common man. Often sharing his few crusts of bread with the less fortunate, van Gogh's selflessness was legendary. Was Vincent not one of that noble and immortal race which the common people call madmen but which some consider saints? That his work should

be denied space in our national museum's *Survey of Recent Dutch Painting* is indeed a sad commentary on its curators. *Frederik van Eeden, 2/10/94*

— · — · —

The Personal Diary of Johanna van Gogh-Bonger

15 February

I do wish van Eeden would stop elevating Vincent to sainthood. What can I do? Write and say, "You're mistaken. Vincent was a very selfish man. He accepted Theo's financial assistance as his due, constantly complaining it was not enough. After sharing with the unfortunate, he would write saying he needed money for food and paints. What would Theo do? Send him the money! Which one was the saint?"

20 February

Today a letter from Gosschalk urging me to start work in earnest on Vincent's letters. He mentions there's a new American invention which would be faster than copying them by hand. (Few people can decipher Vincent's scribble.) Gosschalk writes: "The Remington writing machine requires some practice, but learning new things does not appear a problem for you." He says the *Amsterdammer* just ordered half a dozen. If I'm interested he'll arrange to have one sent on a trial basis.

17 April

Theo dear— Last night I cried myself to sleep, because I knew today was our wedding anniversary, and although I tried and tried, I could not recall your face, your voice, your touch. It's been months since I've written you, and I'm ashamed to confess weeks since I even thought of you. I'm spending every spare minute working on Vincent's exhibitions, Vincent's letters. In my mind's eye and ear I can see and hear him quite clearly. But *you* seem to be fading! When I'm involved with the Vincent legend, you seem to slip away. Oh, Theo, don't let Vincent come between us!

25 April

Dear Theo— As time drifts by, as I immerse myself in Vincent's career, keeping the two of you separate becomes more and more difficult. I have decided I must write you often, share things with you, so you'll stop "fading."

Your son started kindergarten this year. Of course, a small town like Bussum didn't have one of the new preschools, but Letti and I talked Reverend Andresen into adding a morning kindergarten to his boys' school, now that there are four little boys in our church between the ages of three and five. It was interesting to learn that little Vinnie's teacher says he appears to have a real talent for numbers and is quite mechanically inclined, but shows little evidence of a talent for art.

7 May

Dear Theo— I knew Father was interested in Amsterdam's children's recreational activities such as the marionette show on the Dam, but didn't realize he had a membership in the zoo. A trip there was Father's belated birthday gift to "Vincent Willem" (Father still insists on calling him by his full name.) Neither Letti nor I was invited to accompany them, but little Hans was. Now the two of them constantly play "ZOO" in our glass verandas.

After school one hears much creeping and growling among the ferns and begonias!

20 May

Our honorable burgomeister has finally agreed that the glare of electric lights might not turn this country village into a den of iniquity, and gave the much-discussed franchise to the Hollandse Electriciteits Mij. I expect we'll all start staying up later now, as they do in Amsterdam. Letti's husband is still a member of the Town Council. He reports that Gouda pipes are still distributed with the agenda, but no documentation. Van Suchtelen considers any request for information new faddism, like the trend to shorten the workday. (He asks what would a laborer be doing with his time if he did not stay on the job until eight at night? A six-day week keeps him out of trouble. And why would a good wife need any more education than the special courses like weaving and needlepoint provided in our schools for girls? And who needs those newfangled telephones? Anyone who can afford one can also afford a boy to run errands and deliver notes.

15 October 1894 [The following fall]

What is this world coming to? In France, Alfred Dreyfus is being tried for treason. Zola writes that it's a trumped-up case. There are unbelievable reports of anti-Semitic riots in Paris and even Algiers . . . mobs roaming the streets screaming, "Down with the Jews!" and desecrating synagogues. No one seems to have the courage to object except Zola. I wonder how Mr. Wijnberg feels about it? Or Israels? Or Cohen Gosschalk?

22 November

Today Andries warned that I must keep track of every one of Vincent's paintings sold. At the time I inherited them, Vincent's paintings were considered worthless, and fell in the category of minor household decorations to be divided equally between the wife and the son. Now that Vincent's reputation is slowly being elevated, I may be putting myself in the position of eventually not owning any of them—simply because I am a woman. Vinnie is only four now, but if prices for Vincent's work continue to rise, the entire collection may be declared "works of art" belonging to the eldest son.

It's ironic, isn't it? I never wanted to profit from Vincent's art, but I did want to feel free to share it, to sell it to the art galleries and museums of the world.

14 September 1895 [Ten months later]

Today Andries and I went to the grand opening of the Stedelijk. It's only a short distance from the Rijksmuseum, at the other end of the park. The new Stedelijk looks like a miniature Rijksmuseum, a steepled and turreted brick castle dedicated to ART, but less baroque and less pompous than its royal predecessor. The new city museum has well-lit rooms—the Edison bulbs are a great improvement over gas lamps.

Dries suggests that one way to protect myself legally would be to open a separate bank account for sales as well as expenses incurred by Vincent's exhibitions. We might eventually have enough to rent the Stedelijk for a huge retrospective! How wonderful to imagine all of Amsterdam promenading *past* the mighty Rijksmuseum with its gas lamps, on their way to see the van Gogh exhibition in the well-lit Stedelijk!

———

VILLA HELMA
A Boardinghouse for Gentlemen and Ladies
Koningslaan 2-A, Bussum

15 November 1895
Dear Mother van Gogh,

When you and Wilhelmina visit us next week, you'll find that more than just your grandson has grown in the past couple of years. Bussum is no longer a sleepy country village. Every year sees another park laid out, another lane widened into a street, another villa built. By far the grandest has been built by the Amsterdam hotel owner Krasnapolsky. They say he has two full-time maids and showplace gardens! Around the Komvan Biegel Park, the land was recently subdivided for a number of villas. Frederik van Eeden, the art critic, built one, and Jan Veth, known for his portraits and art reviews, built another. Bussum now has a small enclave of artists and literati.

Last year the township purchased land for the new Wilhelmina Park, named for the Queen of course. (However, I confess I told little Vinnie it's named for his Aunt Wilhelmina.) The intention is to hold the town's annual fair there, as well as band concerts in summer. There's a pond for skating in winter. They are talking about lighting it with lanterns at night!

Your grandson is becoming as adept at skating as he is at hoop rolling. Why can't he enjoy some quiet, contemplative recreation? Like poetry or sketching. Something that doesn't add another gray hair to his mother's head.

I look forward to your visit for a special reason. I'm still going over Vincent's letters, trying to put them in order. I'll have no problems with the later ones—the ones from Arles, St.-Rémy, and Auvers. I can easily correlate the events in Vincent's life with the events in mine. But I've so many questions to ask about his earlier life—preaching to the miners in the Borinage, taking art lessons in Brussels, teaching in a boys' school in England. His life is a kaleidoscope. There's much I need to know in order to fit the pattern together. I'm counting on your help. My love to you both, *Jo*

—··—·—

THE PERSONAL DIARY OF JOHANNA VAN GOGH-BONGER

6 September 1896 [The next year]

Today the much-discussed Suffrage Extension Bill finally passed. Twice as many Dutch citizens now have the right to vote—but as yet only male citizens. When Aletta Jacobs attempted to vote two years ago as a "resident," they simply changed the registration requirements to read "male resident."

10 November

I couldn't identify that ringing I kept hearing, suddenly realized it was the new telephone installed last month. (Our esteemed burgomeister had no opportunity to object when the government took over all the private phone companies and installed a nationwide system.) I still forget the phone is there, don't realize I can use it to order *gebakken visch* delivered from the fishmonger, instead of sending Tina out.

1 December

We have yet to fully realize the potential hazards of our new telephone. Letti and I were chatting away when we heard a click—and realized that one of the parties on our line had been listening in. Well, I suppose everyone in Bussum now knows that the Reverend Andresen finally gave his permission for Tina to marry Piet. (Letti and I had spent an afternoon with Reverend Andresen. We finally convinced him that at eighteen his godchild was not too young to get married—in fact, she was too mature *not* to get married.)

Tina wants to continue working for me. As a wedding gift, I have promised to turn her attic room into an apartment. Now that we have electricity, water mains, and plumbing, it will cost practically nothing to add another sink and lavatory. Tina and Piet want to save their salaries so they'll have a "nest egg" when they're ready to start a family. (I'm taking them to Aletta's Family Planning Clinic this Friday.)

25 February 1897 [Two months later]

Tina made a beautiful bride! My seven-year-old Vinnie was heartbroken, kept saying, "Why couldn't she have waited till I grew up?" Reverend Andresen invited everyone (including the couple's Catholic friends) to stay for a small reception after church. (I baked three *tulbands* to go with the wine and bought a round of Gouda to serve with the crackers.)

29 April 1897

Everyone is talking about Zola's courage in insisting that Dreyfus was convicted on forged evidence. His article in *Aurore* headlined "J'Accuse!" has stirred up another storm of anti-Semitism. I'm so glad I'm no longer in Paris.

6 September 1898 [Five months later]

It seems as though every man, woman, and child in the Netherlands has converged on Amsterdam today for Wilhelmina's coronation, and the opening of the Rembrandt exhibition at the new Stedelijk. At eighteen, our Queen is so much like her mother—dignified yet unpretentious, regal yet gracious. Since the royal barge was scheduled to pass in front of the canal house balconies on Herengracht, all the Bongers met there for lunch. Dries and I left early to be among the first to follow the Queen when she transferred from barge to carriage at the Museumplein dock. (Henrietta remained behind, pleading a headache.)

At the Rembrandt exhibition. I glimpsed the back of a gray head some distance ahead and said to Dries, "That's Cohen Gosschalk. Let's catch up." Dries wondered how I could recognize someone from just the back of his head. (Frankly, I wonder myself.) It's been several years since I've heard from Gosschalk. I finally gave up on inviting him to Villa Helma.

The three of us spent a pleasant hour immersed in the wonders of Rembrandt. "He died penniless just 229 years ago," Gosschalk observed. Then added with a chuckle, "But, of course, Rembrandt did not have a determined sister-in-law like Johanna." (*Not* Mrs. van Gogh-Bonger, but *Johanna*—a slip of the tongue?)

3 October

Today a letter from Gosschalk asking if "Mrs. van Gogh-Bonger intended to go to the opening of Vincent's retrospective in The Hague's Arts and Craft gallery." He has promised to review it for *De Amsterdammer*. Would I honor him by allowing him to escort me? I'm to phone him at the newspaper to let him know.

Of course I will. I really enjoyed seeing him again at the Stedelijk. But I wonder—will I *ever* understand that man?

THE PERSONAL DIARY OF JOHANNA VAN GOGH-BONGER

31 December 1898

The end of the year—endings are always somewhat sad. Gosschalk, as expected, wrote a brilliant review of Vincent's retrospective. I haven't heard from him since.

The forty-four pieces were shipped back from The Hague last week. There are times I wished I had taken Dries' advice against keeping Theo's entire collection. The Arts and Craft exhibition was just a *fifth* of what I have stored under the eaves. Other times, I bless Dries for storing the paintings, not in the cold cellar, but in the attic. There's no sign of mold or fading, and Tina's cat promptly dispenses with any stray mice.

25 January 1899

I had a nightmare last night. I swear I wasn't even aware of the date, but I suppose my "subconscious" knew it was the anniversary of Theo's death. I saw him again, just as he was the night he died, looking pale and immaculate, damp hair combed, beard trimmed. Again I heard him sigh, and smelled a faint whiff of urine. But he didn't die. He opened his eyes—but *there were no eyes under the lids.* I bent over to look more closely. Inside his head—nothing! Then incredibly a trail of small white worms crawled out of his mouth, his nostrils, and the empty holes where his eyes should have been. I woke to find my nightdress damp with perspiration, my cheeks wet with tears.

28 January

We had a hard freeze last night, and Vinnie is beside himself with joy because the canals will soon be safe for skating. I told him if the canals froze before his birthday, as a special birthday treat he could skip school and we'd visit Mother van Gogh and Aunt Wilhelmina in Leiden. No child knows the meaning of skating until he's skated on Leiden's Galgenwasser at the mouth of the Rhine.

2 February

That same nightmare over and over again! It's getting so I'm afraid to sleep. Just read an article based on Freud's forthcoming book, *The Interpretation of Dreams.* It left me as puzzled as ever. It is certainly not an unfulfilled wish, and hardly a suppressed desire. Freud speaks of the images in dreams as being symbolic, but I can't imagine what white worms crawling out of an emptied head could possibly symbolize. Now, why did I write "emptied" instead of "empty"? According to Freud, every slip of the tongue has a hidden meaning.

20 February

Our visit to Leiden was delayed by some of Pasteur's germs, which we battled for almost two weeks with Abbey syrup and all manner of cough and sore throat remedies supplied by Mr. Wijnberg. Vinnie is now barely speaking to him. (Nine-year-olds are not noted for their patience.) The ice was so good this year we could have made the entire journey on skates. The Hollandsche Society had put up fingerposts at all crossroads and ditches, with notices to mark the dangerous thin-ice places. I promised Vinnie that if his elementary school grades were good, he could skate the whole way before he went on to a *gymnasia.* This year, we took the train, skating only from Leiden to the Galgenwasser. Mother van Gogh and Wilhelmina came by carriage to join us at Vink's famous outdoor café.

It was quite a sight to see the skaters sitting at those little tables with bowls of steaming pea soup in front of them. With the Galgenwasser frozen, not only skaters but also pedestrians from Leiden and nearby villages had flocked to the café to watch the skating. It was like a carnival. The ice was dotted all over with tents, flags, even sleighs. Along the banks, vendors with tables in little tents sold milk boiled with aniseed and sweet cakes.

Later: I had been sitting at a table chatting with Mother van Gogh and Wil, and suddenly realized it had been five or ten minutes since I last caught sight of Vinnie. "He's probably hidden behind one of the tents. Mustn't let them see I'm worried," I said to myself. I skated twice around the Galgen-wasser before I found him—sitting on a gray-haired man's shoulders, laughing and calling to me, "Mama! Look who I found!" I felt like spanking them both! Gosschalk explained he'd been invited to lecture at Leiden University, and afterwards couldn't resist a visit to the Galgenwasser on borrowed skates. There seems to be no escaping that man!

22 February

Again the same nightmare. This time the white worms keep multiplying as they crawl out of Theo's open eyes and mouth, then all over his head—multiplying and multiplying until it looks like he is wearing a squirming gray wig. How horrible! Once again I wake to find my cheeks wet with tears, my nightdress damp.

— · — —

DE AMSTERDAMMER: WEEKBLAD VOOR NEDERLAND
From: Johan Cohen Gosschalk, Contributing Editor

22 March 1899
Dear Mrs. van Gogh-Bonger,

Eight years ago when we started seeking ways to get Vincent's work exhibited in Holland, did you ever dream that by the turn of the century you'd have so many requests for major exhibitions in France and Germany, as well as the Netherlands, it would empty your attic storerooms? It will really be difficult deciding what to send where, and I'm glad you felt free to request my assistance.

I could get away on Sundays. If we could start next Sunday and work straight through until Villa Helma's busy summer season, you'd have plenty of time to get the frames and crates made before the shipping deadlines. The only way I can envision organizing so many exhibitions is to get all the work brought downstairs, and group the actual paintings visually, taking subject matter, color, and technique into consideration. Could we work in one of your glass verandas?

As a start, could you mail me a list of the exhibitions and their dates, so I have some idea of what we need to do? I'll arrive on the nine o'clock next Sunday if that is convenient. You say you feel overwhelmed. No need to. This is one project which will be a pleasure! Sincerely, *J. C. Gosschalk*

— · — · —

VILLA HELMA
A Boardinghouse for Gentlemen and Ladies
Koningslaan 2-A, Bussum

25 March 1899
Dear Mr. Gosschalk,

You've no idea how grateful I am for your offer of assistance. Here's the list of exhibitions: Next year Paul Cassier in Germany wants to plan a major Vincent retrospective, the first of a series of annual exhibits. At the same time, Durand-Ruël is taking a huge gallery at the Paris Centennial, where he wants to show the finest work of all the Independents. Later that year the Bernheim Jeune gallery is planning a major van Gogh retrospective, and shortly thereafter Ambroise Vollard wants to feature paintings from Auvers. Meanwhile, all the avant-garde galleries in Amsterdam. Rotterdam, and The Hague constantly request anything I can spare.

Vinnie looks forward to seeing you, asks can he help? *J. van Gogh-Bonger*

— · — · —

THE PERSONAL DIARY OF JOHANNA VAN GOGH-BONGER

8 May 1899

Dear Theo— We're almost finished planning Vincent's "Turn of the Century" exhibitions. The first Sunday, all 200 paintings were brought downstairs and stacked in the south veranda. Gosschalk is amazing with children.

He explained it all to Vinnie and Hans as though they were adults. Yesterday I heard Vinnie tell his friends, "We can't play in the south veranda. Those paintings are *very* valuable. Hans and I are only allowed to work there."

And work they have—holding each painting up for us to study, then propping each against a wall as directed. Gosschalk and I sit back like Salon judges, sipping coffee and discussing the merits of each grouping. Gosschalk has made our young assistants feel proud of helping. The boys look forward to Sundays and so do I. This project which I thought would be overwhelming has turned out to be very enjoyable. I'm sorry we're almost finished.

— · — · —

VILLA HELMA
A Boardinghouse for Gentlemen and Ladies
Koningslaan 2-A, Bussum

10 May
Dear Anna,

Just received the announcement of your solo performance at the Amsterdam Conservatory of Music. (Father must be so proud. The Conservatory invites only its most talented alumni to participate in its concert series.) I do apologize for neglecting you and the family these past couple of months. Gosschalk and I have been spending every Sunday planning Vincent's "Turn of the Century" exhibition schedule. Even Vinnie and Hans Vondel have been helping us.

But no work for us *that* Sunday. We're all coming to Amsterdam to hear you play. In fact, we'll be bringing along an entire cheering section from Bussum for our favorite pianist—Gosschalk, Letti and her husband, Vinnie and little Hans, as well as Dries and Henrietta. (I phoned Dries so he couldn't say "no.") Have the box office set aside tickets in my name for eight adults (I'm including Mother and Father, of course) and two children. Gosschalk has made reservations for all of us for supper at the Winter Garden afterwards. I just mentioned I wished I could afford it, and he offered.

It will be a big day for Vinnie and Hans too. Like Father, Gosschalk has a membership in the zoo and will take the boys there in the morning (something he has been promising them as a reward for helping organize Vincent's exhibitions). By concert time, we figure they'll be so tired they'll sit quietly like little gentlemen, and by suppertime, we hope the Wintergarden's 350 Edison lamps will leave them speechless. Actually, they're well behaved for nine-year-olds (though I'm sure Father will find something to criticize). Love, *Jo*

———·—·—

ANNA BONGER
Herengracht 204, Amsterdam

20 May 1899
Dear Jo—

What's going on with you and Gosschalk? It's not nice to keep secrets from your little sister! I tried questioning Letti. She says she has been curious too—but all she'd been able to find out from little Hans is that he and Vinnie are always with the two of you on Sundays, working on Vincent's exhibitions until dinnertime. I'm told that after dinner Gosschalk smokes one cigar, then takes the six o'clock back to the city.

That doesn't sound very romantic, but I know what I saw at the Wintergarden—the way he looked at you, the way he tucked one of the roses from the table in your hair, even the way he arranged for our supper after the concert, as though he were one of the family. Answer me, Jo! Otherwise I'll phone and discuss it with you on your *party line*. Your curious sister, *Anna*

———·—·—

VILLA HELMA
A Boardinghouse for Gentlemen and Ladies
Koningslaan 2-A, Bussum

22 May
Anna dear—

There's nothing to be curious about—Gosschalk and I are just very good friends. I've known him over eight years. Though I haven't had the occasion to see much of him, we've corresponded often concerning Vincent's career.

From the beginning, Gosschalk has been my adviser when it came to promoting Vincent's work. Once when I wrote him a letter of appreciation, he said it was totally unnecessary, that he considered helping me a privilege because he shared Theo's belief that Vincent was a genius.

Anyhow, your romantic imaginings are just that—*imaginings*. And, dear sister, I would be more than happy to discuss my relationship with Gosschalk on our party line. We are simply good friends with just one thing in common, our admiration for the art of Vincent van Gogh. Now that we're almost finished with arranging Vincent's "Turn of the Century" exhibitions, I'll probably never see him except at an occasional gallery opening. Love, *Jo*

— · — · —

ARTI
The Artists' Association of Amsterdam
presents an exhibition of
CONTEMPORARY PORTRAITS
featuring the work of
Johan Cohen GOSSCHALK, Jan VETH, and Hans VONDEL
2 July to 5 August 1899
Opening reception Sunday, 2 July, from 2 until 5 p.m.

— · — · —

DE AMSTERDAMMER: WEEKBLAD VOOR NEDERLAND
From: Johan Cohen Gosschalk, Contributing Editor

15 June 1899
Dear Johanna,

The reason I didn't mention the enclosed ARTI announcement when we were working on Vincent's exhibitions is that I had completely forgotten about it till the gallery manager phoned last week! Fortunately I had portfolios full of portraits, simply needed to get some framed.

I hope you'll find time to come to the opening, since you know all three artists. My favorite Indonesian restaurant is the one across from the ARTI gallery. How do you feel about going there for rijsttafel afterwards? We could ask Letti and Hans, and Jan Veth and Veronica to join us.

There's one other thing I've been wanting to ask you, but lacked the courage—would you permit me to do your portrait? Nothing pretentious, just a simple pastel or watercolor sketch. I know that summer is Villa Helma's busy season, but it shouldn't take long—just a few sittings. I'd appreciate it so much. *Gosschalk*

—·—·—

VILLA HELMA
A Boardinghouse for Gentlemen and Ladies
Koningslaan 2-A, Bussum

20 June 1899
Dear Gosschalk,

Of course I'll "find time" to come to your ARTI opening! And Letti and Hans said rijsttafel at the Indonesian restaurant afterwards sounds like a wonderful idea. Be certain you mention it to Jan Veth next time you see him at the *Amsterdammer*.

And of course I say "yes" to my portrait. I loved the sketch you did of Mother van Gogh when she visited last year. Villa Helma's transient guest rooms are booked solid in July, but both Mr. Klassen and Mr. Wijnberg are vacationing July 7 through 22. I had no clear idea of what you meant by a "few sittings," so offered them a reduction in rent if they would permit me to let you use their room during those two weeks.

Vinnie says "come for a *long* visit." Even if you don't need that much time, we hope you'll come for the entire two weeks. I have been puzzled. I felt so indebted to you for all your advice and assistance. The only thing I could offer in return was a vacation at Villa Helma. Do you realize how often you ignored my invitations in the past? I hope you won't say no this time. *Johanna*

8 July

Mr. Wijnberg and Mr. Klassen left yesterday after work. Last night Tina and I thorough-cleaned their room, changed the sheets and laid out clean towels. This morning I put fresh water in the pitcher by the towel rack, fresh flowers on the table by the window, then hung one of Vincent's *Iris* studies beside it.

I feel so foolish—like Madame Bovary preparing her boudoir for a lover. And it's only Johan Cohen Gosschalk, my familiar mentor and adviser of eight years. Vinnie's excitement and anticipation must be contagious. Yes—that must be it.

I can hear the Henk's milk cart rumbling up the Koningslaan, then Vinnie's whoops of joy. Gosschalk evidently didn't wait for a rental carriage, but got a ride from the station with Henk. I must stop blushing like a schoolgirl, so that I can go down and greet our guest.

9 July

Last night we had my special rabbit stew, simmered for hours with leeks, carrots, and potatoes. I ordered little hot rolls from the bakery to scoop up the gravy. Everyone seemed to like it. Gosschalk took three helpings. (When we'd finished, there was barely enough stew left for Tina and Piet and only two rolls.)

10 July

I posed for my portrait this morning. I don't have to sit absolutely still. Gosschalk says that's why many portraits look stiff, stilted. He says he thinks I'm going to be a very unusual subject, because there's a sadness in my eyes that's always there, no matter how much I smile. (I looked and looked in the mirror, but I couldn't see it.)

11 July

Vinnie insisted we explore Wilhelmina Park this afternoon. They now have introduced five ducks in the lake and one black swan. The baby ducks, a dozen of them, were comical to watch. Vinnie worried out loud about what they'd do in the winter when the lake becomes a skating rink. Gosschalk assured him the ducks and the swan would be wintering in the south of Spain. Vinnie is trying to be very grown-up, to play host and see that everything is to Gosschalk's liking. My son appears to be completely enamored of our guest. It's embarrassing. Vinnie keeps treating him as though he were my suitor. How silly—me, a widow-lady in her thirties.

12 July

I'm trying to recall if I've ever been alone with Gosschalk before. There were always other people around—at the original showing of Vincent's work here at Villa Helma, at the Stedelijk, at the various exhibitions.

We're seldom alone now. At mealtimes there's my four transient boarders (two Frenchmen and an English couple) and my permanent boarder, Miss Margaretta Koster. Mornings are spent on the portrait. Gosschalk tries a different pose every morning, says he is trying to eliminate the sadness in my eyes. When Vinnie comes home after school, he always has plans for entertaining Gosschalk while I cook dinner—a walk along one of the trails laid out by our burgomeister's Beautification Society, a game of horseshoes, a game of darts, and, in the evening, whist, checkers, or chess.

Sunday I am planning a sandwich buffet on the veranda and have invited Hans and Letti, Jan Veth and Veronica, to join us for lunch. Johanna—confess! It's apparent that you are *avoiding* being alone with Gosschalk.

15 July 1899

Today I had the strangest experience while sitting for my portrait. This was the first time Johan tried a full-figure pose. I could literally *feel* his eyes on me, following the curve of my cheek, lingering for a moment on my lips, my throat, tracing the curve of my bodice, sliding down and encircling my waist. I had to hold my breath to keep from crying out.

Johanna—face the truth. Your letters to Theo are no substitute for being held, caressed. Does Gosschalk feel the same way? I doubt it. I must be very careful not to embarrass him, not to show him how I feel.

17 July

All day yesterday and today I concentrated on being very proper, cool, and correct, as befits a widow-lady in her thirties with a nine-year-old son. I sensed Gosschalk seemed puzzled at first—then became cool and correct himself. And this evening, after Vinnie had said his good-nights, asked if I'd like to take a walk. Though I wanted to say "no," I didn't see how I could refuse. After half an hour of strolling and desultory talk, we found ourselves back in Wilhelmina Park. The ducks were nowhere to be seen, but the moonlight was tracing ripples of silver in the wake of the barely discernible black swan. A fish splash, a frog sound, the scent of water hyacinths, the whistle of the ten o'clock to Amsterdam—a scene staged by a magician just for the two of us. When Gosschalk put his hands on my shoulders and drew me toward him, the very proper, cool, correct widow-lady in her thirties . . . simply *disappeared.*

18 July

Today we took a picnic lunch to Wilhelmina Park. In daylight it seemed an ordinary place. But as soon as the black swan appeared, as soon as Johan touched me, the magic returned. How fortunate that Vinnie's school does not begin its summer break until August. I am happy to have Vinnie keep Johan entertained while I cook dinner, but I cannot bear to share him any other time. We have only three days left. There's so much to plan, to decide. I'm glad Vinnie likes Johan—it would be terrible if he didn't. But I'm discovering how possessive I can be. Vinnie seems to want to stay up forever after dinner. It's so frustrating!

21 July. Dear Theo,

I've sometimes wondered what someone would think if they found this diary with all these letters to you in it. It may seem insane, but it is my way of *staying* sane. For the past couple of years, I've been telling you how sad I was because you seemed to be fading. But, Theo, today of all days, when I am writing what will probably be my last letter to you, I can see you very clearly.

Theo, my dearest, you are not for one minute to think that my loving Johan means that I love you any less. In a strange way, he seems like an extension of you. From the very start Johan shared your belief in Vincent's genius. You know how much he's helped me. He's been responsible for much of the success of the Vincent legend. Theo, you left me two responsibilities—Vincent's art and our child. I think your son recognized that he was approaching the age when he needed a father before I did. He practically adopted Johan. Johan is younger than I, and I'm glad. I was always worrying whether I could keep up with Vinnie, wondering who would explain sex to him, and whether I could skate with him from Bussum to Leiden as I'd promised. I could just see myself, finally reaching the Galgenwasser, sitting down for a bowl of Vink's pea soup—and never finding the strength to get up again!

I doubt I'll need to write to you again, because half an hour ago, Johan and I left the announcement of our engagement at the printer's. Dearly beloved—please be happy for me. We had enough tragedy, you and I. Now for me, a new beginning.

Announcing the betrothal of
JOHANNA GESINA BONGER of BUSSUM
daughter of Anton and Hermine Bonger of Amsterdam
and widow of the late Theo van Gogh of Paris
to JOHAN HENRI COHEN GOSSCHALK of AMSTERDAM
son of Saloman Cohen of Zwolle and the late Christina Cohen-Gosschalk
Reception for friends and family
the ninth of September 1899 from ten until five
at Villa Helma in Bussum

——

VILLA HELMA
A Boardinghouse for Gentlemen and Ladies
Koningslaan 2-A, Bussum

30 July 1899
Dear Grandmother van Gogh and Aunt Wilhelmina,
    Mother was about to write a personal note to include in this annowncement of our betrothal (Correction: Mother says it's HER betrothal, not mine.) I asked if I could right instead to show you how much your grandson's hand-

rightting and spelling has improved. I think I wrote OUR betrothal because I like Johan Cohen Gosschalk so much. And fond as I am of Mother, lately I've wished I had a father. He'll be a wonderful one!

If he hadn't preposed on his own, I think I would have begged him to ask her. Mother told me that Gosschalk will actually be my STEP-father, said I should be sure to tell you that Theo will always be my father, you will always be my own paternal grandmother and will always have a special place in our hearts. Aunt Wilhelmina too!

I hope you're both coming to the resception. They've ordered wonderfull cakes, cookies, and pies and dozens of little sandwiches. My best friend, Hans Vondel, and I bought identical long-trowser suits for the occassion. (Hans likes my new father as much as I do.) I used to feel sad when anyone mentioned Theo. I was so young when he went to heaven, that try as I might, I could not remember him at all. So I feel like this will be my first father. I love you, Grandmother, and can't wait to see you September ninth. Sinserely yours, forever your grandson, VINNIE

— · — · —

VLLA HELMA
A Boardinghouse for Gentlemen and Ladies
Koningslaan 2-A, Bussum

31 July
Dear Anna,

Was it only two months ago I scolded my sister for her romantic imaginings, assured her that Gosschalk and I were "merely good friends"? Anna dear, I wasn't lying to you—I was lying to myself.

The truth is, I think I was attracted to Gosschalk from the moment we met. For years I had made overtures of friendship, disguised as rewards for his helping me with Vincent's exhibitions. And for years he rejected all overtures. He seemed determined to keep our relationship businesslike and platonic. I still cannot figure out what changed his mind. What does it matter—he did!

I was somewhat disappointed that you were out when we called to tell the family about our engagement. Not too disappointed, because now I can chat with my little sister privately.

Without a murmur, I let Johan take over my life, even including managing our betrothal reception. Johan overheard Elly and me planning the refreshments and said, "I simply won't have my Jo making sandwiches and baking pies and cakes for a party in her honor. Make out an order for the Bussum bakery, and another for sandwiches from the hotel and have them send the bills to me." How did he guess I felt overwhelmed by the thought of providing even simple fare for fifty guests? I think my intended knows me better than I know myself! Love, *Jo*

— · — · —

DE AMSTERDAMMER: WEEKBLAD VOOR NEDERLAND
From: Johan Cohen Gosschalk, Contributing Editor

31 July 1899
Dear Dad,

Well—it's happened. As you can see by the enclosed announcement, your son is getting married. I can just hear Mother saying "Finally!" And then when she found out who it was: "I knew it! How could he be expected to find a nice Jewish girl with all those artists and writers he spends time with?" I know she never quite forgave Grandmother Rachel for leaving me enough money to be able to follow my artistic and literary inclinations. And I've always been sorry about the disappointment I caused her when I never practiced law after getting my degree.

How I wish she were still alive so she could meet my intended. Johanna van Gogh-Bonger is the daughter of an insurance broker and the widow of a Paris art dealer. Since his death, she has been supporting herself by running a pension-boardinghouse in Bussum, which has become a gathering place for the literati and intelligentsia of Amsterdam. She is attractive, charming, intelligent, educated, a fabulous cook—and, Dad, I cannot keep my hands off her!

We met eight years ago when she was still in First Mourning. For me, the physical attraction was so immediate and powerful, I did not dare let myself be alone with her. It's been a long wait. She has a nine-year-old son of whom

I am very fond, who has recently made an excellent chaperone (which I very much needed), at the same time demonstrating what it would be like if we three were a family.

Dad, you and I have always been able to talk frankly about sex. You taught me that for Jews it was a "mitzvah," a celebration, while for Gentiles it was often a sin. I think my Johanna has a surprise in store for her. I am under the impression that her first husband was somewhat in awe of her innocence, that their loving involved a lot of petting, stroking, gentle teasing, and much laughter. My Johanna has only played at lovemaking. (Her idea of being seductive is to stretch out like a kitten.)

The first time I kissed her, she seemed to be somewhat startled by the intensity. Though she doesn't know it, I suspect Jo has yet to be totally aroused. I can't wait to see the look on her sweet face when it happens!

Because she is a widow, and because of our difference in religion, we don't feel a formal wedding with its double ceremony and a reception the day before would be appropriate. When we're ready, we intend to quietly slip away to the Town Hall for a civil ceremony. So we've invited *all* our friends and relatives to the engagement reception on September ninth.

Afterthought: Johanna just pointed out it's a long train journey from Zwolle to Bussum, says we must invite you to come the day before. (It's very convenient being betrothed to a lady who runs a boardinghouse.) Phone me at the Amsterdammer and let me know what train to meet.

— · — · —

VILLA HELMA
A Boardinghouse for Gentlemen and Ladies
Koningslaan 2-A, Bussum

2 August 1899
Dear Anna,

Oh, Anna, I'm not as independent as I thought! Johan is now happily rearranging my life, and I love it. He insists he does not want me to work, made me promise not to accept any future reservations for transient guests, and not

217

to look for another boarder to replace Miss Koster, who is leaving to get married next month.

Johan wants to build a villa designed especially for us, with a cottage on the grounds for Tina and Piet. Mr. Wijnberg and Mr. Klassen can remain at Villa Helma until the new house is built, but after that I'll be cooking only for friends and family.

Oh, Anna, I never dreamt I could once again be so happy! Don't forget you've promised to provide music on September ninth. Love, *Jo*

— · — · —

VILLA HELMA
A Boardinghouse for Gentlemen and Ladies
Koningslaan 2-A, Bussum

10 September 1899
Dear Mother van Gogh,

When you phoned and said your physician had insisted on bed rest after you fell yesterday, I promised you a full report on our betrothal reception. Herewith!

Villa Helma was a mass of fall color inside and out. Piet had coaxed our bed of chrysanthemums into full bloom, and there were enough to cut for the house. Vinnie and Hans, looking very grown-up in their long-trouser suits, greeted guests, took their coats and hats, and helped Elly keep the refreshment tables filled. Johan had hired a carriage to meet all incoming trains. We borrowed extra plates and champagne glasses from the hotel, but Tina still had to keep washing and drying, as some guests departed and new ones arrived.

Our guest list was an extraordinary mixture. There were, of course, the Bongers (all conservative burghers, except Dries and Anna), plus the entire Amsterdam art community, as well as the small enclave of artists and literati living in Bussum. We also invited our esteemed Burgomeister van Suchtelen as well as the Reverend Andresen—and then, to liven things up, the "infamous" Aletta Jacobs and her husband, as well as the members of the local Socialist Women's Federation and their husbands!

Johan and I had been wondering how such diverse groups would manage to retain their civility, but it all worked out very well. The avant-garde gravitated to the refreshment tables on the verandas, while the conservatives seemed drawn to the more formal dining-room table, with Anna's études floating in from the pianoforte by the windows. (I noticed Andries sampling the refreshments on the veranda, while Henrietta socialized at the dining-room table.)

My father and Johan's got along splendidly, once they discovered a mutual friend in Zwolle, who insures his shipments through the Bonger firm. I think Father convinced Mr. Cohen he should consider insuring his own. (Mr. Cohen is a merchant in butter. I just hope we don't have a hot summer!)

Mother and Father were disappointed you could not attend, and Vinnie was heartbroken. Since no bones were broken when you fell, I'm hoping you and Wil can plan to visit three weeks from now, in time for my birthday celebration.

(I promised Vinnie he could wear his long-trouser suit for you.) Let us know what your doctor says. *Johanna*

— · — · —

THE PERSONAL DIARY OF JOHANNA VAN GOGH-BONGER

8 October

Johan just phoned for a rental carriage so we could take Mother van Gogh and Wilhelmina to the station. Having them here made my birthday special. I asked Johan to give me his portrait of Mother van Gogh as a birthday gift—just a pencil sketch, but it's an amazing likeness. She looks as though she were about to speak, perhaps to say, "This oval silver frame is pretty, but much too fancy for someone like me."

9 October

Margaretta Koster left after her bridal shower last Tuesday, and Vinnie has just finished moving his things into her room, seems quite excited at the prospect of having the upstairs room for his very own. (Wait till he sees the bedroom that Gosschalk designed for him in the new villa!)

With only two boarders remaining, Villa Helma seems curiously empty.

I'm not used to cooking for so few people. Oh well, Gosschalk will be moving in next week, and with his appetite, I will need to plan meals as though I had a full house!

12 October

Today my pretty little bed-sitting room is now quite definitely a bedroom for a man and his wife. Johan brought with him a large four-poster. He has just finished setting it up, with sheer curtains all around, under a layer of brocade that will keep out the winter chill. (Tina and Piet were happy to get my former bed.) Gosschalk also brought a small chest full of art supplies and books. He has hung his clothes next to mine in the armoire, and has just laid out his shaving brush, razor, and strop next to the water pitcher. I suddenly realize that though we've had no time for a civil ceremony at the Town Hall, Johan intends to sleep here, with *me*—tonight!

13 October

With Theo I presumed I was an experienced young lady because I had read *Madame Bovary* and *Nana*. With Gosschalk I learned I really knew nothing. Quietly, relentlessly, he led me to places I never knew existed. And every time I felt I'd reached the end, he drew me closer and began again—and again—and again.

At one point I moaned and cried out, and he closed my lips with his and murmured, "Not yet, there's more." And there was!

8

"And I haven't told you how much I love you . . ."

THE PERSONAL DIARY OF JOHANNA GOSSCHALK-BONGER

1 January 1900

The first day of the twentieth century—the speed with which new ideas, new inventions have been changing our lives! Was it only ten or fifteen years ago that barricades went up along the new railroad tracks? They were there to protect the livestock and people (babies especially) from the supposed health hazards of the new steam engines. Dr. Aletta Jacobs says the real health hazards are the smokestacks in our cities. She claims there's a definite correlation between the increase in factories in Amsterdam and the increase in consumption.

Fifteen years after it was built, Amsterdammers still complain that the new Central Station blocks the view of the harbor. (They can no longer sit at a waterside café and watch the ships sail in—those riding low, usually laden with treasure from the Indies.) The railway station is an enormous edifice, built to last centuries—no amount of grumbling will remove it.

The thing I've noticed most is the way the world has been shrinking. Between the telegraph, the telephone, and printing presses, no one can keep a secret very long. When the Yaqui Indians in Texas proclaim independence from Mexico, I read about it in the local newspaper just a day later. We learn that in America prisons and orphanages will serve turkey dinners on Christmas Day. And the next day we read that in India hundreds of thousands die as the famine continues, while in China thousands of angry Boxers are massacring foreigners. Last week three missionary families living near Shanghai were beheaded!

Today's *Amsterdammer* reports that a wave of strikes is spreading through Europe: coal miners in Belgium and Germany, steelworkers in Vienna, glassworkers in Brussels. The workers' demands for an eight-hour day and safer working conditions are being ignored. I'm not so certain I shall like this new century.

16 January

Today Vinnie laid the cornerstone for our new villa, looking very solemn and important. Piet and Tina were there, of course, checking the surveyor's stakes where their little cottage will go, and Reverend Andresen stood by to say a prayer and bless our new hearth. (He would have had apoplexy if he knew we weren't married yet—we've never got around to going to the Town Hall because it's closed every evening and weekend.) Johan asks if I mind living in sin. I tell him I love it, but that he'd better take an afternoon off before we go to the Paris Centennial in April.

What will he do when it's time to check into the hotel in Paris? Count on the French being *laissez-faire?*

— · — · —

VILLA HELMA
Koningslaan 2-A, Bussum

20 January 1900

Dear Anna,

Yes, of course, we'd love to have you and Mother come next week to celebrate Vinnie's birthday. I'm so glad you thought of it. The Bussum bakery disliked my order for a small birthday cake. For me too, the bigger the party, the better.

I'm afraid Johan will want to monopolize the two of you by showing you the blueprints for our new villa. He has been driving poor Mr. Bauer, our architect, crazy. He insists on a home combining every modern convenience with "the country charm that typifies the Bussum villa community"—and wants everything done *yesterday!* Already in place are water mains, sewer lines, and phone and electric lines.

Electricity is indispensable for pumping water to an upstairs bath or commode, as well as for reading and working at night. But I still like the soft light of an occasional gas or oil lamp. A telephone is a wonderful convenience, but sometimes I long for those informal days when friends "dropped by" for tea, or even dinner, because there was no way to call ahead.

As for our new villa, Johan insists on satisfying my every desire—a big, sunny kitchen with an ample root cellar, a living-dining room spacious enough for large gatherings (he asked how many women usually came to our Women's Federation meetings), and because I enjoy Villa Helma's glassed-in verandas, we're to have the same kind. I feel like a princess awaiting her dream castle. Anna, whatever did I do to deserve such happiness?

Later: The mail just arrived with our official passes to the Paris Centennial. I have been invited as "the representative of the late Vincent van Gogh," whose work is being exhibited in the *Survey of Impressionism* at the Palace of Fine Arts. Johan has been invited as my "escort." The Centennial opens April 14. The Durand-Ruël opening is a "white tie" by-invitation-only gala. Letti has already agreed to house and feed Vinnie while we're gone.

Looking forward to seeing you on the 31st. Love, *Jo*

— · — · —

HOTEL PARISIENNE
29 Boulevard Montmartre, Paris

14 April 1900
Dear Vinnie and Hans,

The Centennial is as amazing as we expected. Larger than any previous European world's fair, it covers 547 acres!

Vinnie would have been astounded by the strange and magnificent effects produced by electricity in the Château d'Eau and Hall of Illusions. Most of the nations represented have their own palaces along the Quai d'Orsay, and there were not one, but two palaces of fine arts on the Champs-Élysées. Hans would have loved the exotic exhibits presented by France and England as well as the Netherlands, featuring costumes and handicrafts from their colonies. We've been collecting postcards and souvenirs for you both.

The Durand-Ruël opening is tomorrow night. Today I'll be showing Johan my favorite Montmartre haunts. Tomorrow will be spent immersed in art exhibits. We're taking the express home on Tuesday. Love, *Mother*

— · — · —

THE PERSONAL DIARY OF JOHANNA GOSSCHALK-BONGER

15 April—Paris

This morning I showed Johan all my Paris memories. It felt like going back in time—our flat on the Cité Pigalle with the chestnut trees in blossom and the three windmills whirling away on the top of the hill. . . . In the rear garden, one of the lilac trees is gone, but the others are in full bloom. The Goupil's gallery, where a Monet exhibition is their Centennial feature (was it only a dozen years ago that Theo fought to show just a *few* Monets upstairs in the mezzanine?).

After lunch we stopped by Père Tanguy's. He rushed up, and like a true Frenchman, kissed us both. Père had some unusual work by an artist named Picasso in the window, a pair of sad-looking clowns—perhaps traded for art supplies? I can still hear Père's wife screaming: "Cash—pay cash! We can't eat paintings!"

Later we wandered the side streets, found ourselves on a bench in a little park that looked somehow familiar. Across the street I saw the barred windows of The Asylum for the Deranged! I started to cry. Johan took me in his arms, whispering, "It's over, all over. Long ago and and far away." For the first time in years, I was at peace.

—·—·—

HOTEL PARISIENNE
29 Boulevard Montmartre, Paris

16 April: After midnight
Dear Andries,

Just returned from the opening of Durand-Ruël's *Survey of Impressionism.* Every important artist of that era was represented. We heard so many compliments on Vincent's paintings, not only by his contemporaries but by the many international guests as well. What a triumph! Johan was all smiles. We had spent one entire Sunday deciding which paintings to send, which paintings were Vincent's very best.

Dries, you would have enjoyed the opening reception—it was like a gala reunion with all our Impressionist friends, now ten years older. A few looking fat and prosperous, but most still lean and hungry in their rented top hats and tails.

If it weren't for his flowing white beard, I might not have recognized Pissarro—he's aged so much! Bernard told me Pissarro's eyes are now so painful he must restrict himself to street scenes painted from his Montmartre window. And poor Renoir's fingers are so arthritic there are days he cannot paint at all. Monet is enthusiastic about a new series of water lily studies he's begun. Says the subject is so fascinating he could easily devote the rest of his life to it. Cézanne sends you his regards.

When Durand-Ruël strutted around proclaiming himself the savior of the Impressionists, I recalled his refusal to rent his gallery to Theo for a posthumous van Gogh exhibit. I started to say, "But don't you *remember?*" when Johan interrupted firmly with "I believe my Jo needs another glass of champagne."

We're returning Tuesday. So much to tell you. Would you like to come for dinner Wednesday? *Jo*

—·—·—

THE PERSONAL DIARY OF JOHANNA GOSSCHALK-BONGER

18 April—Bussum

It felt so odd being on The Netherlands Express with no nursing baby to interrupt our enjoyment of the sunny French landscape, and nothing to worry about except the Dutch wind and rain awaiting us. In Bussum, on our way home from the station, Johan insisted the carriage take a short detour to inspect the new villa. (We've only been away five days!) No sooner are we home than Johan is on the phone to our architect, complaining about the lack of progress.

Bauer reminds him that we lost fourteen days' work in February and March due to inclement weather, and assures him that such delays had been factored into his schedule. Because it had no root cellar, Tina and Piet's one-room cottage is close to completion. Bauer still anticipates a mid-August completion date for everything.

Poor Bauer! Working with an artist is not easy. Johan cannot understand why it is not possible to build something as fast as one can draw it. He is so impatient for us to be settled in our very own villa. I keep telling him that I would be happy living anywhere, as long as it is with him. But I don't think he believes it.

VILLA VINCENT
Regentesselaan 39, Bussum

20 August 1900
Dear Grandmother van Gogh and Aunt Wilhelmina,

We moved into our new villa last week. I have my very own bedroom with *two* beds in it so that I can have my best friend, Hans, sleep over anytime I want. Father had bookcases built above the beds (I think he's trying to encourage me to read more) and a wall of cork put in behind my desk so I can tack up anything I want.

Villa Vincent is filled with bathrooms—upstairs, a large one at the end of the hall, downstairs a small lavatory next to my father's study. He put a daybed in it, so you can sleep downstairs when you visit, and needn't climb any stairs.

Father and Mother have been very lovey-dovey since we moved. I think they finally went to the Town Hall and got married—which was a big relief to me. I do hope you will come visit us soon. Did you know they named our new house Villa Vincent after your son, the artist? (Please note how my spelling and handrighting have improved.) I love you both very much. Sinserely yours, VINNIE

— · — · —

VILLA VINCENT
Regentesselaan 39, Bussum

27 August
Dear Andries,

My efficient husband had ordered this new stationery before Villa Vincent was ready for occupancy. I think it was his not so subtle way of reminding poor Mr. Bauer of his mid-August deadline. It's been two weeks since we moved. Already I feel as though we'd lived here forever. Remember the terrible amount of work it was getting settled in Villa Helma? A week of transporting crates, opening crates, dismantling crates. Another of arranging furniture, hanging drapes, hanging pictures, lugging crates of them upstairs. (How's your back been lately?)

Johan is amazing. Before Moving Day, he had decided where every piece of furniture would go. Since it was less than a mile, there were no crates—we just wrapped everything in quilts and made trip after trip in Henk's cart.

Johan is a competent painter and an excellent writer—but his real genius lies in organization. In five days we were completely settled. Vinnie had already asked Hans to "sleep over" and we had invited our Bussum circle of friends to a buffet Open House after church on Sunday. With no vacationers in transient rooms, I realize I can now invite friends and family to visit during the summer. How about next week? Or the next? Anytime Henrietta is free. Just let me know. Love— *Jo*

— · — · —

THE PERSONAL DIARY OF JOHANNA GOSSCHALK-BONGER

1 January 1901: After midnight:
Happy New Year! The last guest has departed. Mother and Father have retired to the guest room, Anna and Wilhelmina have retired to Vinnie's room (Vinnie has left to "sleep over" with Hans) and Mother van Gogh long ago went to sleep on the daybed in Johan's study. My husband just asked me if I wasn't a little tipsy. I vehemently denied it. But I lied. I may not be totally inebriated, but as the old year was about to depart, I've been saying my farewells in a rosy glow.

This New Year celebration was a happy compromise reached by Mother and me last December. I wanted to invite the family to Villa Vincent for St. Nicholas, but Mother wouldn't hear of it. It's turned out well. Along with my family, most of the Bussum villa community joined us tonight. (This is all I can write now. Johan has just closed the brocade drapes on our four-poster, leaving one side open a few inches. Who could refuse such a not-so-subtle invitation?)

Morning: I highly recommend champagne as an aphrodisiac. But now I must rise, and after transforming from paramour to cook, begin preparing breakfast. (Letti and Hans will be joining us, along with the boys.) This seems like my old boardinghouse days—cooking breakfast for nine adults and two ravenous ten-year-olds.

THE PERSONAL DIARY OF JOHANNA GOSSCHALK-BONGER

23 January 1901

This morning's papers are full of news of the end of an era—"England's staunchly conservative and unswervingly moral Queen Victoria died yesterday at the age of 82." I'm glad we got married before Victoria became a ghost who could haunt us.

21 April [Three months later]

Today Andries came for dinner—he'd just returned from Paris, brought back a catalogue and report on the Vincent retrospective at the Bernheim Jeune gallery. The 65 paintings were grouped according to the places where they were painted—Paris, Arles, St.-Rémy, Auvers. Andries says the show was a color spectacle!

In June, Ambroise Vollard's gallery will be devoted to the debut of an unknown young Spanish artist, Pablo Picasso. If what we saw of his work in Père Tanguy's window is typical, Johan feels this is a young man to watch.

31 January 1902 [The next year]

Vinnie is beside himself with joy, and I am barely speaking to Johan, who, without consulting me, gave our son a *bicycle* for his birthday. They may be called "safety bicycles," but rubber tires or not, I don't trust them. I keep telling everyone I distrust *any* mode of transportation that's smaller than a horse! I considered divorce, but decided against it, because I need Johan to fulfill my promise to Vinnie to let him skate all the way from Bussum to the Galgenwasser before graduating.

DUTCH REFORMED CHURCH SCHOOL OF BUSSUM
Reverend B. C. Andresen, Director

10 October 1902

Dear Mrs. Gosschalk-Bonger,

As the school year draws toward a close, I feel the need to discuss with you the future of your son, Vincent Willem. As we have noted in previous reports, your son is an exceptional student. Although he exhibits no talent for art, he is remarkably intelligent, with a decided aptitude for science and mathematics.

His teachers have requested I urge you not to prepare him for the classical university education that would be expected of a young man of his background. They feel he would be a mediocre student at best, but will perform in an outstanding manner in a college such as Delft that specializes in the sciences. I am told that in Amsterdam there are one or two higher burgher schools which prepare their students for the entrance examinations for a technical university such as Delft.

I realize it's been less than two years since you and your husband moved into your new home. We wanted to give you plenty of time to make an informed decision. Commuting is one possibility, boarding in Amsterdam, another.

"Blessed is he whose children prosper." *Rev. B. C. Andresen*

—·—·—

THE PERSONAL DIARY OF JOHANNA GOSSCHALK-BONGER

15 October

Johan and I have been discussing the problem of Vinnie's future. If he has no aptitude for a classical university education, Johan says it would be cruel to force him into an unsuitable mold. I was amazed at Johan's swift determination to abandon Villa Vincent, in which he has invested so much thought and love, and consider renting a town house in Amsterdam. "It will be only for a few years. Vinnie is too young to live apart from his parents." I have never loved Johan so much! It's such a wonderful feeling to realize that he loves Vinnie as though he were his own son.

VILLA VINCENT
Regentesselaan 39, Bussum

16 October

Dear Grandmother van Gogh,

I'm so worried, and I have no one to talk to. I pretended to be reading, but I was really listening when Mother and Father discussed moving from Bussum. Reverend Andresen says there's no upper school in Bussum suitable for me, and suggested one in Amsterdam. *I don't want to go to a school in Amsterdam!* But nobody is asking *me.* Mother says we lived in Paris and Amsterdam when I was a baby, but I don't remember living *anywhere* but in Bussum. All my friends are in Bussum.

I don't think there are any ponds or lakes to skate on in Amsterdam, just canals. And the streets are too narrow for hoop rolling. The buildings are narrow too—all squinched together with no grounds or woods or trees to climb. And stairs so steep you wouldn't believe it!

I have until the end of the year to change their minds. Would you right and tell them that it's not fair to separate me from my friends? If you tell them how misrable I'd be in Amsterdam, they might change their minds.

Counting on your help— VINNIE

— · — · —

ANTON BONGER
Insurance: Marine and General
Herengracht 204, Amsterdam

30 October 1902

Dear Johanna:

Anna tells me that you have asked her to look for a town house in Amsterdam where you and your family might live after the first of the year. I was appalled when Anna explained the reason for the contemplated move. You have scarcely settled into the villa that Gosschalk designed especially for his bride. Now, less than two years later, you're considering moving because supposedly no higher school in Bussum is good enough for Vincent Willem.

You've been told that the lad is not a good candidate for a classical education. I have never been a snob about education—your brother Andries has done very well for himself with the business education he received in a higher burgher school. While your brother Willem may have been offered a teaching position when he graduated from the University of Amsterdam, as you well know, in Holland teachers' salaries are *not* munificent. From a practical standpoint, there's no need for your son to obtain a university degree if he hasn't the inclination. When the time comes, between the Bonger and the van Gogh connections, he should be able to find a financially advantageous position that interests him.

I made inquiries about the Delft University of Technology and was told that it was originally a school of ceramics, was given university status only sixty years ago. I was also informed that there are indeed a couple of good higher burger schools in the city that specialize in science and math. The entrance examinations are said to be quite difficult. If you insist that nothing else will do, my grandson could always board with us during the week, and spend Sundays with you. Children must learn that the world does *not* revolve around them—and the sooner, the better!

If Theo were here to advise you. I'm sure he would agree. *Father*

— · — · —

VILLA VINCENT
Rengentesselaan 39, Bussum

5 November 1902
Dear Father Bonger,

Jo and I appreciate your offer of room and board for Vinnie, while he attends school in Amsterdam next year, but must decline. We consider that at his age it is very important that our son maintain close contact with his parents. Many people consider twelve the age of maturity, with no more growing up to do. Jo and I both feel it's only the beginning. We are a family—and until Vinnie enters the university, we feel it is very important that we live together as one.

He has already applied to and been accepted by an excellent higher burgher school that specializes in math and science. Vinnie is finding the prospect of being separated from his childhood friends very distressing. If he were separated from us as well, it would be a disaster. Thank you for your concern. *Gosschalk*

—·—·—

ANNA BONGER
Herengracht 204, Amsterdam

15 November
Dear Jo—

I think I've found the perfect town house for you—on Jan Luykenstraat. By Amsterdam standards it's fairly large. You'll be able to hang almost all of the van Gogh collection that you now display at Villa Vincent, and there's plenty of attic storage for the balance.

It's a quiet, tree-lined residential street, within sight of the Rijksmuseum (come to think of it, almost everything is within sight of that towering castle). A fairly new town house with inside plumbing and all modern conveniences. The canal boat dock is within walking distance, as is the horse tram that goes to Central Station. I've two other houses to show you, but they can't compare to this one.

Father is still grumbling about no one taking his advice, keeps saying you are both catering too much to your son, and will end up "spoiling" him. (Mother, of course, simply nods and says nothing.) Secretly I think he was pleased to hear that Vinnie passed the entrance exams to one of Amsterdam's most prestigious higher burgher schools—without any tutoring!

It will be wonderful having my big sister just a tram ride away!

Love, *Anna*

V. W. van Gogh
Jan Luykenstraat 44, Amsterdam

2 February 1903

Dear Grandmother van Gogh and Aunt Wilhelmina,

Now that we've moved to Amsterdam, I'll have lots of letters to write. Mother gave me this ruled stationery for my birthday. (We both agreed my handwriting was not quite good enough for plain paper.) This seemed a good time to drop my nickname, and use initials as grown-ups do. Vinnie is really a little boy's name—but if I let people call me Vincent Willem, as Grandfather Bonger does, people might confuse me with your son, the artist. I would certainly not wish to be mistaken for an artist, since I am studying to be an engineer. I like my new school very much, and have made lots of friends. I've asked them all to call me V.W. Though I won't mind if *you* continue to call me VINNIE.

—·—·—

Johanna Gosschalk-Bonger
Jan Luykenstraat 44, Amsterdam

10 January 1904

Dear Letti,

I've missed my favorite chatterbox. You come to town so seldom. It doesn't seem as though we've lived in Amsterdam over a year. I can't believe we ever thought of this move as a sacrifice being made for Vinnie. Johan seems relieved to give up commuting He walks to the *Amsterdammer,* often comes home for lunch. Vinnie bicycles to school. When the canals are frozen, he often skates there. He seems so happy in the new school—I think it's the first time he's ever been challenged. He appears to be quite popular. The phone is constantly ringing: "Is V.W. home?"

As for myself, I just realized that this is the first time since I was a girl that I really *enjoyed* the city. When I stayed with my family after Theo's collapse, there was the baby to care for, the constant quarreling with Father as well as the constant worry about Theo. Now Anna and I are reveling in the museums, the galleries, the theater and opera. To balance our life of pleasure, one morning a week we do volunteer work at Dr. Jacobs' Family Planning Clinic, often have lunch together.

Need to say goodbye for now. Johan just phoned to say he has a surprise for me. He's taking me and Vinnie out for Indonesian rijsttafel to celebrate. It's all very mysterious—celebrate *what?* When I know, you'll know. Love, *Jo-Jo*

—·—·—

THE PERSONAL DIARY OF JOHANNA GOSSCHALK-BONGER

11 January 1904

Ever since the Stedelijk opened, Johan and I have been dreaming and hoping we could arrange to rent the museum's galleries for a really comprehensive Vincent retrospective. And today Johan is making that dream come true. After the steady growth of Vincent's reputation over the past ten years, you'd think I'd have no doubt as to the success of such a venture. But now that the contract has been signed, I'm terrified. We have enough friends and admirers to fill the galleries on opening day, but after that? Will attendance dwindle during the ensuing two months? Will the exhibit enhance or diminish Vincent's reputation?

The bank account I opened for the proceeds from sales of Vincent's work is now a substantial fund—but will it be enough? Johan insists I must stop worrying, especially about money, says he's prepared to cover any deficit. He insists we shouldn't skimp on anything, including the catalogue. He'll write an introduction and a biographical essay for it—I'm to outline all the facts I want included.

I'm to think of this exhibition as the ultimate fulfillment of Theo's dream. Five hundred paintings and drawings by Vincent van Gogh! Is there enough time as well as money to pull it all together by July 1905?

JOHANNA GOSSCHALK-BONGER
Jan Luykenstraat 44, Amsterdam

15 June 1905

Dear Letti,

Neither Johan nor I realized how much work would be involved in mounting a retrospective in a museum. At first it was lists—making lists of what paintings we had, and what were owned by other people. Then I had to write, asking if the work could be borrowed for the show. When Johan noticed my hands beginning to shake from all the typing, he hired a secretary for me. The past month, as the borrowed paintings started to arrive, our town house began to look like an art warehouse!

As I write, every gallery in the Stedelijk is being painted. At first Mr. Vehmeyer, the curator, wanted to just "touch up" the walls, but Johan insisted on a *total* paint job. Right now we're both so tired, I worry we may sleep through the Opening.

Do come early. We're counting on your chitchat to keep us awake!

Love—your school chum who misses you . . . *Jo-Jo*

—·—·—

V. W. VAN GOGH
Jan Luykenstraat 44, Amsterdam

23 June 1905

Dear Grandmother van Gogh and Aunt Wilhelmina,

I'm so glad that Mother asked the Bongers to invite you to stay with them when you come for the opening of Vincent's retrospective. I don't know where we could find room for any guests. Our house is a mess! There are paintings and drawings stacked all over the place. 1,500 catalogues were delivered yesterday. Ten dozen bottles of champagne for the opening were delivered today. My best friend, Hans, and I have been practicing carrying trays of glasses (filled with water) and saying, "Would you care for some champagne, sir?" (or madam). Mother says that at fifteen we're old enough to help out.

The two of us are helping Father hang the artwork. There were 474

pieces to be hung! Father also hired a couple of the museum's regular instal-
lation staff. Hans and I do the carrying and holding. They do the hammering.

Don't forget I'm using my initials. It would be so embarrassing to have to
keep saying, "No—I'm not Vincent van Gogh the painter." At the opening,
don't accept champagne from anybody but . . . VINNIE

—·—·—

ANDRIES BONGER
C/o Émile Bernard, 206 Rue Noir, Paris

10 September 1905

Dearest little sister who constantly amazes me,

People are still talking about the Stedelijk exhibition. Did I ever suggest
you dispose of Vincent's paintings because, without Theo to guide you, I saw
no chance of them being worth more than a dozen guilders each? I reckoned
without my sister Jo's perseverance. Continue to keep accurate accounts. After this major exhibition, these paintings will no longer be classified as "minor household decorations."

Rumor has it that the Stedelijk's curator was not all that enthusiastic
about your exhibition project, that Cohen Gosschalk called on influential
friends to intervene. So the galleries were made available to you for two
months during the summer vacation doldrums. But during those two
months, two thousand people flocked to see Vincent's work, and the curator
is now wishing he'd charged admission!

As you can see by my letterhead. I've made arrangements to stay in
Bernard's apartment whenever business takes me to Paris. Henrietta and I
have separated—amicably, but irrevocably. I'm sure you guessed, and I appreciated your not bringing it up at the Stedelijk opening.

My best to Johan, and to you.

Andries

THE PERSONAL DIARY OF JOHANNA GOSSCHALK-BONGER

12 September
    Dries was right—of course I guessed that his marriage was over. I knew
he'd tell me when it felt comfortable. But now that he's put it into words, I
feel so sad for him. He writes "amicably, but irrevocably." The two words
seem to cancel each other out. *Something* must have happened to make him
feel that total separation was necessary. I wonder if he'll ever tell me what it
was. Why do I have the feeling that Johan knows more about it than I do?

- - · - · -

JOHAN COHEN GOSSCHALK
Jan Luykenstraat 44, Amsterdam

13 September 1905
Dear Andries,
    Jo just told me you and Henrietta have separated. Is this because of the
document she found in your desk? Henrietta contacts us so seldom, I was
certain her letter to Jo contained nothing more personal than an invitation to
one of her benefit receptions—so I opened it. When I saw what it did contain, all I could think of was how happy I was that I had been able to inter-
cept it.
    I can imagine how you feel. If Jo ever decided to clean out my desk dur-
ing Fall Cleaning, I'd be furious. I might not leave her (she's wonderful in
bed), but I would certainly tie her to our four-poster and never speak to her
again before bedtime.
    Did it ever occur to you that perhaps Henrietta may not have really read
the document she found? That she did not fully understand its implications,
did not intend to be cruel? Well—I'm sure you know Henrietta better than I do.
    The only thing for you and I to do is to make believe none of it hap-
pened. It was a private paper for your eyes only. I saw it by accident, and have
promptly forgotten it. It's now safely put away with my own private papers.
Jo will never see it. If you want it, just ask. I'm truly sorry about your marriage ending. As ever, *Johan*

1 January 1906

Dear Dries,

A new year—and it looks like my brother will never leave Paris. The family missed you on St. Nicholas. I hope the uncomfortable possibility of meeting Henrietta did not deter you. Henrietta has quietly broken with the Bongers. After Mr. Hansel passed away last fall, Mrs. Hansel moved in with Henrietta, and I hear that the two of them are inseparable. Poor sad Henrietta! All the while you were waiting for her to grow up, she was waiting only for her mama.

Right now, I myself have never been more content. I don't need to do a thing anymore about promoting Vincent's art—just wait for exhibition requests, ask Johan to help me select the appropriate paintings and drawings, and send them off. Now that the exhibitions are running smoothly, I've promised Johan I'll concentrate on the letters. But there are always so many other interesting things to do—art openings, poetry readings, the theater, concerts. Once a week, Anna and I work as volunteers in Aletta Jacobs' Family Planning Clinic. Once a month we go to the Socialist Women's Federation's box-lunch meeting. Anytime Letti comes to town, we lunch in the Winter Garden, sometimes accompanied by two handsome young men—our sons.

Vinnie is doing very well in school, should be ready to take the entrance examinations at Delft in two years. His friends will be doing the same. I'll feel better about Vinnie living away from home if he has friends he can turn to.

A confession—Johan is my best friend; I need no one else. Sometimes it scares me. My love, *Jo*

THE PERSONAL DIARY OF JOHANNA GOSSCHALK-BONGER

10 June 1907 [Eighteen months later]
    Today a phone call from Aletta Jacobs. She noted that when Johan picked me up at the clinic yesterday, he coughed a great deal and couldn't catch his breath after climbing the stairs. I noticed it too. He also has lost his spectacular appetite and has been losing weight. Aletta advises a checkup without delay. But Johan flatly refuses, says all he needs is a vacation. I'm worried sick!

—·—·—

FAMILY PLANNING CLINIC
Nieuwstraat 309, Amsterdam
Aletta Jacobs, M.D., Director

14 June 1907
Dear Johanna,
    Don't be upset because your husband insists there's nothing really wrong with him that a vacation wouldn't correct. I find that men will rarely admit to serious illness. And he's right (about the rest). If what I suspect is wrong, rest is the first thing any physician would prescribe. Also getting away from the city.
    Hasn't he exhibited in Laren occasionally? I know there's quite an artist colony there. In addition to air that is not befouled by factories and trains, Laren's elevation is high, by Dutch standards—well above sea level. If you can't convince him to totally abandon Amsterdam, a summer house in Laren would be a wise alternative. If you sell the house in Bussum, you could easily afford it.
    Rest, a slower pace. No more 474-piece retrospectives such as he organized at the Stedelijk. I know that wasn't your idea. There are some men who can't resist a challenge, and I'm afraid your husband is one of them (as was mine). Try to convince him to relax, to slow down. And do seriously consider a summer place in Laren.
    Call me anytime you want to talk— *Aletta*

21 August

Dear Hans,

Grandmother van Gogh died two days ago. (Father says "passed on" or "passed away" is the proper way to say it.) Mother and I went to the funeral in Leiden, and I met all sorts of van Gogh relatives I didn't even know existed.

Father didn't come with us because we're selling Villa Vincent and buying a summer home in Laren, and he had a lot of business to attend to. Also he's not feeling too well a lot of the time. Poor Aunt Wilhelmina! During the funeral, she couldn't stop crying. Mother says Wilhelmina is going to be "lost" without Grandmother.

If you invited me to visit you in Bussum one of these weekends, I'm sure Mother would let me come. Have you smoked a cigar yet? Or drunk any beer? All the boys in our school have. I didn't particularly like it, but at seventeen it's the thing to do. Don't forget to ask if it's all right for me to visit you. And don't forget I'm using my initials. Though to old friends like you, I guess I'll always be— VINNIE

— · — · —

JOHANNA GOSSCHALK-BONGER
Jan Luykenstraat 44, Amsterdam

8 December 1907

Dear Letti,

Andries came home for St. Nicholas, couldn't get over how his nephew had grown. Vinnie will enter the University at Delft in January, along with six of his classmates. Is Hans still planning to study with Jan Veth? Or will he try for the Art Academy?

I thank heaven I have Johan to keep me from being overprotective. Last summer, when we were spending weeks at a time in Laren. I worried about leaving Vinnie alone in Amsterdam. (His technical school is year-round, not like an academic school.) "He's just six months away from being on his own

242

in Delft," Johan pointed out. "If he gets tired of eating out, he can go to the Bongers'. If he gets sick, he can call Dr. Jacobs. If he needs to talk something over with us, there's always the telephone." I had felt so torn between my son and my husband. How foolish of me! A lazy, relaxing summer in Laren was just what Johan needed. He looks and feels so much better now.

Remember taking me to the Laren country fair when I first moved to Bussum? We thought then that it was an enchanting place. I never dreamed I might someday be living here. As soon as Johan is completely well, we want to invite you all for a weekend at "Summerplace."

Perhaps this coming summer? Love, *Jo-Jo*

— · — · —

THE PERSONAL DIARY OF JOHANNA GOSSCHALK-BONGER

30 April 1908 [The next spring]

"Summerplace," Laren: This place is so beautiful it's hard to stay away. I had planted a bed of tulip and iris last fall, and couldn't resist coming up this week to see if they'd bloomed. (They had!) This year I want to put in a small kitchen garden so I can have some really fresh vegetables right outside my back door. No more marketing—just pick and cook!

10 May

Johan informs me there's a review he agreed to write for the *Amsterdammer* that will take him into the city next week. I made him promise this will be the last one until fall. We don't need the money, and he has been looking tired of late. I have threatened to tie him to the wicker rocking chair on the porch if he doesn't learn how to relax. That man is impossible!

30 June

Wilhelmina has been visiting us for the past week. It's been almost a year, but she's still lost without Mother van Gogh. I'm taking advantage of her being here to go off for a day to see how Vinnie is doing in Delft. He writes, and he phones, but I've got to see for myself. (Heaven help the young man with a worrier for a mother!)

3 July

Oh my God, I've been worrying about the wrong person. Vinnie is just fine. *But I found blood on Johan's pillow this morning!* Wilhelmina says he coughed all night.

4 July

Aletta Jacobs says there could be many explanations for a bloody pillow—a nosebleed, a loose tooth, ulcerated gums. She says if it is not a nightly occurrence, it's probably one of these. I feel foolish phoning her every time I'm worried.

9 August

There've been no more bloody pillows, thank heavens! I really do have to stop being such a worrier. Johan has been napping in the hammock almost every morning, and spending the afternoons painting. That spectacular appetite of his has returned. Once again my husband is a joy to cook for.

31 August

We'll be closing our Laren "Summerplace" and returning to the city in time for my birthday. This summer's rest has done Johan a world of good.

— · — · —

SUMMERPLACE
Rosenlaantz 12, Laren

25 September 1908
Jan Veth—

Pay no attention to my dear Jo if she tells you to cut down on my assignments when I return to work next week. Ever since the Stedelijk show (which I confess was more work than anticipated) my wife fusses over me like a mother hen. After a summer in Laren, I feel rejuvenated.

Letti and Hans are coming to town for Jo's birthday on the fourth. Let me know if you and Veronica can join us. Best, *Gosschalk*

JOHANNA GOSSCHALK-BONGER
Jan Luykenstraat 44, Amsterdam

10 October 1908
Dear Letti,

How good of you both to come to town for my birthday. I've missed you so much this past summer, wanted to come to Bussum for a visit—but didn't want to leave Johan alone. We both never quite recovered from the enormous amount of work involved in the Stedelijk retrospective. I was truly worried, and determined to see to it that Johan fully recuperated this summer.

He complained that I fussed over him like a mother hen. I saw to it that he led a lazy, quiet life, ate and napped as much as he wanted to. Well, it's paid off! You saw how tanned and healthy he looks. In August he felt strong enough to paint some landscapes. Three have been accepted for exhibition in the annual Christmas Luminist show. Perhaps we can all go to Laren for the opening. It's not too early for your son to make contacts with Holland's influential contemporary artists. Love, *Jo Jo*

—·—·—

THE PERSONAL DIARY OF JOHANNA GOSSCHALK-BONGER

12 March 1909 [The following spring]

Johan is like a child with a new toy. Yesterday he brought home a letter from Roger Fry, director of the Grafton galleries in Bloomsbury. Grafton is planning a giant Post-Impressionist exhibition next November. Among the artists to be invited are the late Gauguin and the late Cézanne along with Matisse, Vlaminck, Sérusier, Derain. "Any survey of Post-Impressionism would be incomplete without the work of Vincent van Gogh," wrote Fry. He requests approximately twenty paintings.

After dinner, there is no dissuading Johan. Right then and there we had to decide which twenty to send. Out came the inventory and sales lists. We stayed up until after midnight going over them, finally settling on twenty-two. Next Johan started worrying about the condition of the selected paintings, wanted to go up to our attic storeroom right then and check.

Tomorrow is my morning at Family Planning, but I told Johan I'd spend the entire afternoon in the attic, if necessary. Our stairs are precariously steep. Johan promised to wait until I got home.

_ . _ . _

PTT: POST, TELEGRAPH, AND TELEPHONE
TO V. W. VAN GOGH STOP DELFT TECHNICAL UNIVERSITY SCHOOL OF ENGINEERING STOP UNABLE TO REACH YOU BY PHONE STOP JOHAN FOUND COLLAPSED IN STORAGE ATTIC STOP DR. JACOBS ARRANGING FOR CONSULTATION WITH SPECIALIST STOP LETTER FOLLOWS STOP MOTHER 13 MARCH 1909

_ . _ . _

JOHANNA GOSSCHALK-BONGER
Jan Luykenstraat 44, Amsterdam

14 March 1909
Dear Vinnie,

He *promised* me. The night before, we had decided on twenty-two paintings to send to a large exhibition in England. Your father promised he wouldn't go up to the attic storage rooms alone, promised he'd wait until I came home after my morning at Aletta Jacobs' clinic. He made it to the attic without falling down the stairs, but the effort was too much for him. I found him collapsed just inside the door. I've never been more terrified! Fortunately this week Andries was in Amsterdam, not Paris. Father sent him over to help me get Gosschalk downstairs and in bed. He was burning with fever.

Dr. Jacobs tells me we're very fortunate. An English specialist, Dr. H. Hyslop Thomson, is in Amsterdam for a conference. He's in Holland to lecture, not to see patients, but agreed to see Johan as a favor to Aletta.

Later: Vinnie dear— My worst nightmares have just come true! Enclosed is Dr. Thomson's report. Can you come home? *Mother*

To: Aletta Jacobs, M.D. Re: JOHAN COHEN GOSSCHALK

Patient is a white male in his late forties. Wife informed us he had lost weight this past year, and that premature gray hair was a family trait. Pulse weak, temperature dangerously elevated. Examination by stethoscope revealed a respiratory murmur. Firm percussion revealed a suspicious pulmonary resonance. Took sample of sputum to check for tuberculin bacilli. Fairly certain the microscope will reveal the presence of more than a few. Tentative diagnosis: pulmonary tuberculosis. *H. Hyslop Thomson*

— · — · —

JOHANNA GOSSCHALK-BONGER
Jan Luykenstraat 44, Amsterdam

27 March 1909

Dear Andries,

Just returned from seeing Vinnie off at the station. I don't know what I would have done without your help those first two days, or without Vinnie these past two weeks. At first, Johan was so weak that Vinnie had to carry him up and down the stairs like you did. Now he has regained enough strength so that he can manage the stairs with the help of Anna and me. (Anna has been coming over daily.) But Aletta is cautioning us not to think in terms of a quick recovery.

Aletta says we're fortunate that Dr. Thomson happened to be in Amsterdam when Johan collapsed. His book *Consumption in General Practice* is considered a classic reference. Dr. Thomson urged Johan to enter a sanatorium, either his own in Liverpool or one in Switzerland. When Johan learned I would not be allowed to accompany him, he refused to even consider it.

We finally compromised. Under Aletta's guidance, I am rearranging our lives. We're keeping the town house, but no more Amsterdam for Johan. (You can use it whenever you're in the city, as will Vinnie.) Even as I write, "Summerplace" is being winterized. Aletta offered to get a male nurse so I could spend a day in Laren, but I couldn't bear to leave Johan now, even for a day. Made all the arrangements by phone—including a monthly delivery of anthracite, winter *and* summer. "Summerplace" will now be our year-round home.

Dr. Thomson knows a specialist who practices in Laren and is transferring Johan's case to him. It's ironic! My stubborn husband, who managed to elude the medical profession until his total collapse, now has *three* physicians—Dr. Thomson in Liverpool, Dr. Jacobs in Amsterdam, Dr. Schuyler in Laren. Will be moving next month. *Jo*

— · — · —

THE PERSONAL DIARY OF JOHANNA GOSSCHALK-BONGER

12 April 1909

Can you believe it—Johan is insisting that, before moving to Laren, we check on the condition of the paintings to be shipped to the Post-Impressionist exhibition. So Anna and I took the list and spent an hour in the attic storeroom. We threatened to lock our patient in his bedroom, unless he agreed to nap during our absence. (I personally don't think he could have gotten up unaided, but with Johan one never knows.) Found one dented canvas (restretching is all it requires) and one damaged frame. Physically my husband may be an invalid, but mentally he's still the energetic manager of the Vincent van Gogh legend!

— · — · —

V. W. VAN GOGH
School of Engineering Delft Technical College

19 April

Dear Dad,

I'm glad that you'll be living year-round in Laren with its downstairs bedroom. The stairs in the Amsterdam town house are much too steep for comfort. I worried about how you would manage with me away at school. I thought I should stay home, but Mother said, "Absolutely no."

Did I ever tell you how much I wanted you to be my father? I remember writing Grandmother van Gogh that if you hadn't proposed to Mother on your own, I'd have begged you to. (I was only a little boy at the time and didn't really understand *everything* about marriage.)

Mother writes that I can stay in the town house in Amsterdam during school holidays, but I've already decided that I'll want to stay in Laren with you. I miss our "man-to-man talks." Mother is wonderful, but there is so much that women just do not understand. I know if it weren't for you, I'd have never gotten a bicycle. And I might have had to board with Grandfather when I went to a higher burgher school.

I'm doing well at Delft Tech, and have almost decided on my "specialty." I'm going to be a steel engineer. What do you think? They make good money and get to travel all over the world. You're going to be very proud of me! Please do what the doctor tells you and get well soon.

Afterthought: By now, you'd think I'd be able to write without using ruled paper. But the school insists that scientific essays must be neatly presented, and without ruled paper, my handwriting is a scrawl! Your son, VINNIE

— · — · —

J. M. SCHUYLER, M.D. D.P.H.
Kapelstraat 32, Laren: Phone 682-4

22 April 1909
Dear Mrs. Gosschalk-Bonger,

I do wish your husband had agreed to enter a sanatorium. Perhaps he would have changed his mind had we told him frankly how much he's putting you at risk. We now know that pulmonary tuberculosis, especially in its later stage, is a highly contagious disease. There is even a stage called auto-inoculation when the patient is continually reinfecting himself. It is not enough for the sickroom to be kept clean, it must be kept as sterile as possible. This means the daily washing and boiling of all towels, handkerchiefs, bedclothes, and bed linens, and the daily removal of all dust and debris from floors and walls, as well as the bathing of the patient himself.

I do not want to see you exhaust yourself with these tasks. One patient is enough for me! Your assignment will be to prepare healthy, tasteful meals for your husband and to keep his spirits up. For sickroom management and patient care, you'll need special help. I have in mind a male nurse who lives in

Laren, whom I've had occasion to use. I've never known anyone so utterly bent on destroying every germ in sight! A tall bearded man, but gentle as a lamb. You may know of him. I believe he used to have an apothecary shop in Bussum. His name is Jeremiah Wijnberg. If you like him, have him contact me for instructions. Yours, *J. M. Schuyler.*

— · — · —

The Personal Diary of Johanna Gosschalk-Bonger

5 December 1909

Our first winter spent in Laren. The pond froze solid last night. An eerie mist floats over everything, giving each house and hedge a half-life—now you see it, now you don't. "Summerplace" belies its name. It is now warm and snug. Thank heaven there are no drafts. I am not allowed any heavy drapes that cannot be laundered weekly. We're waiting for Vinnie, who's coming home for St. Nicholas. Hope he finds a rental carriage at the station. Wait till Mr. Wijnberg sees the "baby" he once cared for. It's hard to believe that "Little Vinnie" will be twenty next month.

24 January 1910

We had a quiet family St. Nicholas celebration, just the three of us. Now it is one week before Vinnie's birthday. I had almost forgotten, and was certain Johan had—he'd not been feeling well, running a fever, sleeping poorly. But today he asked me to phone the *Amsterdammer* and check on the Remington writing machine he ordered a month ago. It's to be transshipped to Delft—a birthday gift! Vinnie will be delighted, but I think I shall miss those handwritten letters on ruled paper.

10 February

A letter from van Rappard asking for permission to publish Vincent's letters to him. Why not? Bernard has already published his collection. Johan chides me for putting Theo's collection aside. I cannot make him understand that *he* comes first.

10 March

A letter from Cassier containing the latest reviews and essays from Germany. Johan was particularly interested in Meier-Graefe's continued contributions to the Vincent legend.

15 September

Went to the city to check on the crating of Vincent's twenty-two paintings being sent to England. When you add the shipping costs to the carpenter's fee, one wonders if it's worth it. I doubt if a single painting will be sold. But I agree with Johan—Vincent's reputation does not permit his absence from such a landmark exhibition.

20 November

The first reviews from England arrived today. The exhibition at the Grafton Galleries shocked the conservative English. Vincent's twenty-two paintings were mentioned in several scathing reviews, although a few critics praised his expressive powers and emotionality.

Johan was disappointed—I was not. One does not expect much from a country where, after thirty-five years of French Impressionism, it is still dismissed as an extremist craze. When the civility of English Edwardian traditions are being challenged, how can the English be expected to embrace an art that mocks the past and glorifies the future?

10 June 1911 [The following summer]

Yesterday, Mr. Wijnberg removed the storm windows from Johan's screened sleeping porch, and we can now breakfast there within sight and smell of my bulb garden. (How did I ever let Piet omit hyacinths from the garden at Villa Helma?)

Again Johan is suggesting I hire a gardener. He can't understand I love kneeling and digging in the earth. It's a new experience for this city girl. I've got to have something to do—and I've never been one for needlepoint, lacemaking or embroidery.

30 August

Where did the summer go? Once again Johan looks tanned and healthy, has started talking about joining me on one of my weekly excursions to Amsterdam. Mr. Wijnberg asks, "Would Mr. Gosschalk enjoy walking around the city in leg irons?" (I'm just discovering Wijnberg's sardonic black humor!)

10 September

The months float by. Everything is effortless, thanks to the unobtrusive efficiency of Mr. Wijnberg. Our life has taken on a dreamlike quality. Over breakfast we discuss the news and reviews in our just-delivered *Amster-dammer* or *Chronicle*. After breakfast we take a stroll around the gardens. After lunch and a nap, Johan sketches while I work in the kitchen garden and flower beds. I'm afraid I don't wear gloves.

We're together the whole day long, and I love it! Curiously, we do a lot of touching. Not too much hand-holding (Mr. Wijnberg has cautioned against it) but Johan likes to run his hand through my hair, to caress the nape of my neck, my arms, my cheeks. I feel constantly loved, without his ever once kissing me. Yesterday he asked if he could unbutton my bodice. I said "no." (I was afraid I couldn't control myself.)

4 October

The miracles of mail order! I had not expected Johan to remember my birthday. He had written for de Sinkel's catalogue, and presented me with presents all day long—among them gardening gloves and an amethyst ring. (As though we were courting!)

7 December

I've never seen Vinnie so frightened. I had been writing how well Johan was. On St. Nicholas Eve, Vinnie arrived laden with presents, and was able to see his father for only a few minutes. An early winter storm had caught us by surprise, wind-driven sleet and rain. Johan's temperature rose with the wind, and when no amount of Mr. Wijnberg's cold sponging or compresses could control it, he told me to phone Dr. Schuyler. Niemeyer's pill (a mixture of quinine, digitalis, and opium) brought the fever down. Mr. Wijnberg insisted Vinnie wear a mask when he went to say goodbye.

10 March 1912 [The next spring]
How I hate winter! Johan has never fully recovered from his St. Nicholas Eve attack. The bulbs are beginning to look like green exclamation points, but he is still too weak to leave his bed. Next July, after the sun has worked its magic and Johan is tanned and energetic, I'll see that Vinnie visits for a few days, so he will not think of his father as an invalid.

—·—·—

SUMMERPLACE
Rosenlaantz 12, Laren

18 May: Sunrise
Beloved—
I feel I will be leaving you before this day ends. I am now so weak I can barely hold this pen. Every breath is an agony. I no longer fear each breath may be my last—I pray it will. But it's all right. I have known more happiness during the eleven years of our marriage than most men know in fifty.

Before I go, I need two promises from you—the first, that you will continue your work on Vincent's letters once my leaving frees you. It saddens me to realize that you put the letters aside to care for me. This is something you must now do for Vincent, for Theo, and also, I suspect, for yourself.

The second promise—that you will not observe the mourning dress conventions for me, as you did for Theo. That you will not spend the next two and a half years in First Mourning, Second Mourning, Ordinary and Half Mourning. Dearest Jo, I think of you as a bouquet of spring flowers. No black, please—not even embellished with jet spangles.

Too exhausted to continue—
and I haven't told you how much I loved you . . .

18 May 1912

I knew something was wrong when Mr. Wijnberg brought me a cup of coffee while I was still in bed. When I asked, he gave me the letter—let it speak for itself.

Why this sense of shock? You'd think I hadn't expected it for years. For a minute I sat there paralyzed, then said I wanted to see him. "Not yet. He's at the funeral parlor." Wijnberg handed me the phone. "You'll want to phone Vinnie." I spent the morning phoning—my son, my family, Johan's father, Letti, Jan Veth, Andries.

Later I smelled smoke—went outside. Johan's empty bedroom and adjoining screened porch reeked of carbolic. In the far end of the yard, Mr. Wijnberg was burning all the bedding (even the mattress), the linens, clothing, curtains—everything he used to sterilize every morning. I recalled reading about an Indian custom—a wife is expected to throw herself on her husband's funeral pyre. I watched the flames leap higher, heard them crackle, and desperately wished I was in Calcutta.

9

"—perhaps then we can all rest in peace."

19 May 1912: Laren

Today I took the morning express to Amsterdam to make arrangements for the funeral. When Mr. Wijnberg asked me where I wanted Johan "laid to rest," I realized that during the last years of Johan's illness, I had never considered the possibility of his leaving me—as though it couldn't happen as long as I refused to make any plans.

At first I was in a panic, but then I recalled Zorgvlied, a nonsectarian cemetery overlooking the Amstel. I had never seen it (it's at the southern edge of the city), but several years ago Johan had mentioned the view after attending the funeral of a colleague. It was a long tram ride from Central Station and a fifteen-minute ride by rental cab after that. But the view of the river was worth it! I had arrived a little late for my appointment. Several people were in the waiting room. I gave my name to the receptionist, I heard him tell someone, "The widow is here." Puzzled, I looked around. Where? And suddenly realized they were referring to me. Widow? I'm the *wife.*

21 May: Amsterdam

I hadn't expected any of Johan's colleagues to attend the funeral—it's been several years since he has been active in the art community, but surprisingly, a number of them came to pay their respects. I invited Wilhelmina to stay with me in Amsterdam tonight. I worry about her. Ever since Mother van Gogh died, she has become so withdrawn—rarely speaks.

30 May: Laren

I'm glad I kept the town house. I simply cannot remain here in Laren. Anna and Letti have come to help me pack—there isn't much. My few clothes and Johan's artwork and papers. He kept a scrapbook of articles and reviews he'd written. I was amazed to discover how many there were, and how many he modestly permitted to be published unsigned. There's also a portfolio with close to a hundred carbons of letters—both business and personal. And a note from Johan to me, written last May: "Jo—look through these *carefully.*" (I'll do that next week in Amsterdam.)

If only it had not been necessary to burn all the furnishings! If only Mr. Wijnberg had been able to leave everything as it was, I could still sit and read in the rocker beside Johan's bed, have breakfast on the screened porch overlooking the bulb garden, relive those last lovely times. Now only empty rooms smelling of carbolic.

5 June 1912: Amsterdam

Tonight I have been going over Johan's correspondence portfolio—have just come across two letters that seem incredible. Both are dated September 1905. One from Henrietta to me, and another from Johan to Andries explaining he'd intercepted the first letter, did *not* intend to show it to me, and would keep it with his private papers. And there's a third letter, to me from Johan—this one *dated just a month ago!*

— . — . —

HENRIETTA BONGER-HANSEL
Paulus Potterstraat 65, Amsterdam

5 September 1905
Dear Johanna,

I am absolutely furious with Andries. He faithfully promised me he would go through the papers in his study. He started to—then suddenly left for "business" in Paris, leaving a mess behind! He hasn't cleaned out his desk since our marriage. (I'm certain some of the papers predate it.) Here I am, waiting to finish Fall Cleaning with only ten days left before the reception I'm giving after the opening of the opera. I simply decided to take matters into my own hands, finish the job myself.

I've sorted through everything, found one paper from The Utrecht Medical Institute that appears to belong to you, at least it appears to involve Theo. He did spend his last days in The Institute, didn't he? I'm not going to wait to ask Andries what he wants done with it. (He neglected to tell me when he expects to return.) His desk is now tidy with everything neatly organized. My first idea was to throw this paper out. But if he felt it was important enough to save all these years, it seemed wisest to send it to you and let you dispose of it as you wish. *Henrietta*

—·—·—

SUMMERPLACE
Rosenlaantz 12, Laren

8 May 1912
Dearest Jo—

The last thing I wanted was for you to find out this way. My darling, I wanted to be with you, to comfort you, to help you understand. If you are reading this now, you know I can't be with you. Remember when we sat looking up at the barred windows of The Asylum for the Deranged in Paris—how I held you, murmuring, "It's over, all over. Long ago and far away." Now it is truly over—there are no more secrets. You always suspected I knew more about Andries' reasons for leaving Henrietta than you did. That marriage (what there was of it) dissolved when Dries learned what Henrietta had done. The Utrecht paper she found among his private papers (a carbon of an interview Andries had with Dr. Moll) was labeled CONFIDENTIAL. Sending it to you, even twenty-two years later, was despicable. When it fell into my hands, I decided it should be intercepted. At the time, I thought the truth would be too much for you to bear. Now I hope the truth can set you free.

In your heart of hearts you have always known that Theo did not die of "congenital disease, chronic ill health, overwork, and grief." But you must realize that Theo did love you dearly—as do I. Always, *Johan*

—·—·—

THE PERSONAL DIARY OF JOHANNA GOSSCHALK-BONGER

5 June: Amsterdam

Dear Johan— How like you to reach out from the grave to try to comfort me. You're sure that Theo loved me dearly? Why, then, did he try to kill me? Was his reason even then being destroyed by syphilis? *Or was it something I*

259

had done wrong? There! I've said it, put into words the question that's haunted me all these years.

15 June

Today a letter from Andries, saying that Anna is worried about me, reports I am becoming a recluse. Perhaps I am. Nothing much seems to interest me anymore. I take long walks in the Vondelpark . . . sometimes take the tram to the cemetery, sit with Johan a while, then walk along the riverbank. Vinnie will be graduating the end of this summer—I hope he won't want to move in with me. (What a terrible thing for a mother to say.) But right now I need to be alone.

20 June

Mr. Wijnberg was in the city today, stopped by to bring me news of Laren. Then became very angry. "It's been a month. When do you intend to start working on Vincent's letters? Your husband's last request, and you *ignore* it?" The words tumbled out of that long black beard. No angry Jehovah could have been more vehement. There was no refusing him. "Tonight," I told him. "I promise, I'll start tonight!"

Evening

I finally found the very first letters Vincent wrote to Theo. At that time Vincent had been been working at Goupil's art gallery in The Hague for almost three years, while Theo was about to start his career as an art dealer in the Brussels branch. (Uncle Cent, a Goupil's partner, had arranged for both brothers' employment.) *I'm so happy that we shall both be working for the same firm,* Vincent writes Theo. At nineteen he is very much the big brother, advising fifteen-year-old Theo how to get along. *The beginning will perhaps be difficult, but keep your spirits up and it will all come out all right.* How different from the last years, when their roles were reversed and Theo became the wise adviser—*I do not advise lowering your prices, as you insist,* Theo wrote his brother. *Trust me, there is no need to sell yourself cheap.*

25 July

I never dreamed Vincent's letters would prove to be such a time- *and* soul-consuming task. One of the very first ones disturbed me—it was almost a love letter, referring in veiled terms to an experience the teenage brothers shared while taking a walk in the country.

From the beginning, the special bond between brothers is something Vincent mentions often. From Dordrecht he writes: *It is well known that the love between brothers is a strong support throughout life. Let us seek that support. To cement the bond between us, let us not have any secrets, but always be true and outspoken toward each other, just as we are now.*

After Theo visits him in The Hague. Vincent's farewell letter reads like a love letter! *Still quite under the spell of your visit. I should have liked to see you off at the station, but you had already given me so much of your time, I thought it would be indiscreet to ask to see you again this morning.* Vincent continues: *I am so thankful you have been here. Through what you showed me, a new horizon has been opened to me in painting.* I am just beginning to understand the beautiful relationship between the two brothers. But can't help wondering, how would a wife fit in?

7 August

I was surprised to rediscover Vincent's attitude toward the money Theo sent him. Once Vincent gave up his brief career as a lay preacher and determined to become an artist, Theo supported him—at first anonymously through their father. When he discovers the source of his support, Vincent accepts Theo's financial assistance as his due, constantly complaining it is not enough. And, of course, it can never be enough, because he often uses the money to help the unfortunate.

10 August

Today I went over the correspondence concerning one of Vincent's models who became his mistress, a pregnant prostitute he wanted to save from "a life of sin." She moved in with Vincent, along with her first child and her mother. Vincent writes Theo, demanding more money, saying his expenses have increased, and now he doesn't have enough to cover his household as well as art supplies.

5 September

So many times, Vincent taunts Theo, almost dares him to desert him—a less patient man would have done just that. And after one quarrel over money needed to support his mistress, Vincent writes: *If you can give me nothing more than financial help, you may keep that too! Perhaps I had better find my own outlet for my work, in short, become my own dealer.* Become his own dealer? Vincent had yet to sell anything!

19 September

There was a period when Vincent quarreled with his brother almost constantly—so many times that Vincent's vituperation must have seemed almost unbearable. After Theo chided him for quarreling with their aging father, Vincent writes: *I think it noble of you that you take Father's part, so I shall try to find a way not to "bother" you or Father any longer, and am now proposing to put a stop to our arrangement about money, in order not to "bother" you anymore.*

Theo simply does not respond, continues to send money as usual. And a few months later, when Vincent was convinced that Theo was not trying hard enough to sell his sketches, he writes: *I believe it is in our mutual interest that we separate. My intentions are irrevocable.* Again, Theo ignored it.

15 October

I'm discovering how much Theo influenced the artistic development of his brother. For the first few years Vincent drew from morning till night, sent a constant flow of sketches to his brother for comment. At Theo's urging, he tried watercolor, then oil. His first paintings were powerful, but in the European brown soup tradition—a good example, *The Potato Eaters*.

After Theo introduced him to the Impressionists' work in Paris, Vincent wrote to Wilhelmina: *Theo has opened up a whole new world of art to me! Right now I am concentrating on flower studies, trying to learn how to intensify and heighten colors, to leave behind my addiction to gray.*

25 November 1912

I'm almost finished reading through the letters, trying to understand this remarkable brother whom Theo loved so dearly. There is a pattern, a horrifying correlation to Vincent's episodes of illness that seems to be emerging—a pattern so unbelievable, I keep checking and rechecking the dates, hoping I've made a mistake. But there's no doubt about it.

Vincent's first attack occurred after Theo had written telling him of our plans to be married. (How clearly I remember our change of plans that Christmas . . . how Father almost called off our engagement because Theo rushed to Arles to be by Vincent's side.) Other attacks followed—one after our wedding day, one after Theo wrote that we were expecting a baby, and another shortly after the birth of our son.

The day Vincent shot himself was the day that Theo planned to join me in Leiden for what my husband kept referring to as a "second honeymoon."

What does it all mean? We had assured Vincent that Theo's continued support would in no way be diminished by our marriage. I remember the first letter I wrote Vincent, telling him I knew how much he meant to Theo, assuring him I knew that nothing could break that brotherly bond, begging him to to find a place in his heart for me as his little sister.

Poor Theo! Had you discovered that pattern before you left for another world? All these years I've been asking myself if it was something I did, or left undone. I now realize that nothing I could have said or done would have made any difference.

30 March 1913

I'm beginning to understand some things that seemed incomprehensible at the time. When Theo attacked the baby and me in Paris. I kept telling myself, *This wild-eyed stranger is not my husband.* The fear, the terror, the heartbreak of that moment was something that I tried to forget, and until now refused to examine. I was sure that if I really looked at the "why" of it, I would discover it was my fault.

What had I done wrong? Vincent's letters have finally given me the answer—*nothing, except to exist.* I keep finding mean little phrases tucked away here and there. The first time I came across one, I said to myself, Vincent couldn't really mean that the way it sounds! That was the letter written from the hospital in St.-Rémy with the remark: *I am so glad that if there are sometimes cockroaches in the food here, you have your wife and child at home.* And from Auvers: *Now that you are married we can no longer afford to live for great ideas, but must be satisfied only with small ones.* Over and over again, a sentence here, a phrase there. Finally I'm beginning to understand.

Vincent summed it up in an earlier letter to his brother during one of their quarrels about his prostitute-mistress: *A wife you cannot give me, a child you cannot give me—only money. Well, if that is all, you can keep it!*

Poor tormented Vincent could not bear the thought of sharing Theo's love. The happier I made Theo, the more he hated me. What was it he said to Theo when he saw him after he'd shot himself? *Please, no tears: I did it for the good of everyone.* Really? I think he did it to bind Theo to him forever. I recall the letter Theo wrote me. *For the first time in years we have talked intimately as brothers should. Vincent told me he feels so alone. I promised to never leave his side.* Now I know what I must do—

— · — · —

The Personal Diary of Johanna Gosschalk-Bonger

2 July 1913
Dear Vincent—

You've won. When the train for France departs tomorrow, Theo will be on it. You won twenty-three years ago when Theo wept uncontrollably as he buried you on that hilltop in Auvers. You've been calling him to you ever since. I've suspected it for a long time—finally realized I had to find enough money to arrange to send Theo from Utrecht to join you.

I can't accompany him—the winds of war that are beginning to blow through Europe make an international journey unwise. Dr. Gachet's son says he will meet the train, see to everything. Theo will be buried next to you on that windswept hilltop overlooking the wheat fields you painted.

I've arranged for a single blanket of ivy to cover the double grave. I wonder—will there still be crows wheeling through the blue July sky? *Johanna*

7 July 1913
Dear Vincent—

Fourteen months ago I buried Johan under a linden tree in the nonsectarian cemetery overlooking the Amstel. Today I did what I always knew I would do—purchased the plot next to his for myself, when my time comes. In the end, Theo and I will each be where we really want to be. No more torment—perhaps then we can all rest in peace. *Johanna*

EPILOGUE

"Johanna's diary is not available for research."

For the rest of her life, Johanna continues with her two missions—Vincent's art and Holland's feminists. In the end, both succeed. But it takes a long, long time.

1914 The first two volumes of *The Letters of Vincent van Gogh to His Brother* are published in the Netherlands. The third volume (in French) is published in 1915.

1918 Although Dutch women still cannot vote, this year the first woman delegate, a Socialist, is elected to the Lower House.

1922 Dutch women win "active" voting rights—the right to vote as well as hold office. Some argue "Passive" votes are so successful that the right to vote seems unnecessary.

1925 Johanna had been translating Vincent's letters for an English edition. When she dies on September 2, at the age of sixty-three, she had reached letter 526. She is buried next to her second husband, Johan Cohen Gosschalk, in the cemetery overlooking the Amstel.

1927 The three-volume English edition of *The Letters of Vincent van Gogh to His Brother* is published simultaneously in New York and London. It is prefaced by a Memoir for Johanna, written by her son, V. W. van Gogh, now a successful steel engineer. He quotes from a diary which he says she kept since she was seventeen.

1957 In the Netherlands, the age of marriage without parental consent is reduced from thirty to twenty-one, and a Dutch woman is now allowed, by law, to have a bank account of her own. Few married Dutch women choose to work outside their home.

1973 V. W. van Gogh sells the collection of 200 paintings and 550 drawings by Vincent to the government for less than its appraised worth. The government agrees to build a special Vincent van Gogh museum, one block south of the Rijksmuseum, for their continual exhibition. The board of directors is headed by a member of the van Gogh family, initially Johanna's son, and after his death in 1978, her grandson, Johan.

1990 During an inventory sponsored by the archival service of the city of Utrecht, the record of Theo van Gogh's last days in the city's Medical Institute for the Insane is discovered. The record seems to have been "misfiled" almost a century ago.

1992 Johanna's diary is kept on a locked shelf in the museum library. To date, all requests for it, both by biographers and by art historians, are met with this response from the van Gogh family: *The diary is not available for research.*

AUTHOR'S CONFESSION

With the exception of the Epilogue, all of which is true, the novel you have just read is "faction." I have never seen Johanna's diary. None of the diary entries attributed to Johanna exist, except in my imagination. Johanna did keep a diary, but as of this writing the van Gogh family has not made it "available for research." The letters and documents in the novel are products of my imagination, although wherever feasible, they are based on fact. All we know for certain about Johanna is limited to the nine-page Memoir written by her son after she died, and published as a preface to the English edition of the The Letters of Vincent van Gogh to His Brother.

On the other hand, for Vincent, Theo, and the Impressionists, I found a wealth of information available in well-researched biographies. All of the described exhibits of Vincent van Gogh's work, both group and solo, are based on fact, as are all references to the art and artists of the period. Unfortunately, lack of verifiable documentation resulted in the fictionalizing of many characters who left scant historical evidence behind—among them Johanna's entire family, the Bongers of Amsterdam; the Cohen Gosschalk family of Zwolle; the Vondel-Dirks family of Bussum. My apologies to their grandchildren.

What is "faction"? As an example, let me separate fact from fiction in the two letters in the Prologue. Both are fictionalized letters based on fact. In the imaginary letter to Johanna from her publisher, the name of the publishing house and all the details of publication are accurate. Johanna did indeed write an extensive biographical Memoir to preface the Letters of Vincent van Gogh in which she was most discreet, using the acceptable euphemisms of that period. Vincent did not commit suicide—"he found the rest he longed for." Theo did not die—"he followed his brother six months later." Johanna's reply to her publisher is also "faction." The reply is imaginary; however, the details of Vincent's suicide are accurate, as are the details of Theo's resultant mental breakdown and his attempt to kill his wife and child. And the discovery in November 1990 of Theo van Gogh's "lost" patient records reveals that, in deference to the family, The Utrecht Medical Institute for the Insane did indeed attempt to obscure the cause of death.

There is a saying: "I cannot hear a word you say, your actions speak too loud." The facts are: In 1913 Johanna did rebury Theo next to his brother, Vincent, and did arrange to have herself laid to rest next to her second husband, Johan Cohen Gosschalk.

Claire Cooperstein